Murders
Among
Dead
Trees

The Collection
Robert Chazz Chute

LICENSE NOTES

Murders Among Dead Trees
Robert Chazz Chute
Published by Ex Parte Press
Copyright 2012 Robert Chazz Chute
ISBN 978-1-927607-01-5
First Edition: December 2012
Print Edition: January 2015
Cover design by Kit Foster of
KitFosterDesign.com

Acknowledgements
Thanks to Brian Wright for suggesting I publish a
new edition combining two shorter ebooks. The

short stories from *The Dangerous Kind & Other Stories* and *Sex, Death & Mind Control* would have come out short if published in paper individually. Now combined with new stories, sneak peeks and commentary, I'm very happy with the outcome.

Finally, as always, my thanks to J, C and C. They know the struggle and have sacrificed much.

PREFACE

You'll find most of the murders in these pages are metaphorical. Those are the most interesting kinds of death: the death of delusion, memory and self. But it's not all serious and dire. There are jokes, too. Everyone is a puzzle to me, but I like psychological puzzles. I write stories about broken people trying to heal or escape. Amid these tiny tragedies, you'll find surprises and sometimes, redemption. From the thrillers in my *Hit Man Series* to the short stories, it's not Good versus Evil, but Bad versus Evil that interests me.

Reading suspense reminds me of the old joke about television: it allows you to have people in your living room you would never allow in your living room. Fiction is where strangers meet at a safe distance. Let's watch, you and I, from the safety of this grove of dead trees.

You should know, I do listen to readers. My favorite three-star review ever was of this very book you hold. The reviewer gave me the idea for a title for one of my crime novels: *Intense Violence, Bizarre Themes*. She liked the writing very much but...well,

not everything is for everyone. I hope you enjoy this ride on my crazy train.
   ~ RCC
   December 2012

TABLE OF CONTENTS

END OF THE LINE

This story won third place in the Toronto Star's annual short story writing contest. I was already doing a lot of speechwriting and non-fiction features for magazines at the time, but this win was a big step in increasing my confidence in my ability to write fiction. ~ Chazz

"You must listen very carefully," she said.

"Uh-huh," I said as I flipped through her file. Every call from a collection agent is meant to accomplish two things: squeeze blood from coconuts and gather more information to squeeze more blood from coconuts. The rule is we can't call more than once a week and we stick to that rule as long as we're getting somewhere. We rotate agents so the deadbeats have to tell their sad stories to a new caller every time. Talking about outstanding debt over and over compounds the target's humiliation. I wanted to be an actor but I've been paying my bills by talking to people who don't pay their bills. My horror, shock and surprise at their failure to pay sounds equally fresh with each call so I guess I act for a living after all.

"You are not listening," Dr. Papua said.

I tuned in. "Oh? Have you said anything that changes the fact that you owe $382.51?" Never say "about $380" or "about $400." Always be specific about their debt. It squeezes.

"I do not owe it. I told your colleagues to send me a copy of the original receipt. All you sent me was a letter saying I owed the money but no proof, not even what the purchase was supposed to be. I could make a lot of money, too, if I just sent out random bills."

"It was a Taunton's account."

"Those stores have been out of business for years and you have no actual record. All you have is my name and the time to harass me."

"You need to at least send us a goodwill payment to keep this from going to court and so I can help you protect your credit rating." Always say "you need to" not "I need you to." Everyone is terrified of being sued and paying a lawyer, especially for such a relatively small debt. A lawyer would charge her more per hour than it costs to pay me to go away. "We need to clear this up today." Always say "today" not "soon." "Soon" means never. "Today" means now.

"This fictional debt is almost ten years old. The statute of limitations on debt in Ontario is six years. You have no case."

I let my heavy practiced sigh drop on her and gave her a moment of silence. Lay a pregnant pause on most people and they'll rush to fill the empty space. The longer they stay on the line, the closer you are to getting the money. She didn't take the bait though. "Even if you don't have a legal obligation to pay your debt, you do have a moral obligation," I say finally.

I heard—or felt—something change then. I don't remember there being static on the line but she suddenly came through so clearly I fought the stupid urge to glance over my shoulder. It was as if she was standing over me.

"A *moral* obligation?" she said. "You have made a tactical error."

I smiled. In a moment she would be screaming into the phone and telling me she'd get me fired. The screamers were the reason we didn't use headsets. It's quicker to hold a phone receiver away from your ear than to snatch off a headset. She would hang up and stew for a week and one of us would call her again. Soon she'd send us the money. In a moment I would be skipping on to my next call and the next and the next.

But she didn't scream and my smile dropped away. "Now you need to listen to me very carefully. Listen to me as if your life depends on everything I say." Her tone was cool and I noticed for the first time that her accent sounded vaguely European, but not Zsa Zsa identifiable. She pronounced words in a way that said she formed each one with great care, as if each had to be dealt out letter by letter, syllable by syllable in a Morse Code of spoken language. "Are you ready?"

I held the receiver away from my ear. I thought she was going to blow a whistle into the phone or something. An old collection agent told me the worst is getting hit through the phone with one of those air horns fans use at football games. It damages your hearing, it's so bad. Then I realized she really was waiting for me to tell her I was ready.

"What?"

"No matter what happens in the next few minutes, you will not hang up."

"I'm not going anywhere."

"You are correct. You are not going anywhere in life, either." She spoke slowly and clearly as if I was a dull child. "No matter what I say, you will not let go of the phone." She hit the word "not" hard, the sharp blade of a shovel striking bone.

My hand tightened around the receiver. I shoved the handset to the side of my head, squashing my ear. I took a sharp breath in but she headed me off. "You will not interrupt me and you will not yell or ask anyone for help. Do you understand?"

"Sure," I tried to sound casual but didn't make it. "Where is this going? This doesn't help you solve your problem."

"Your feet and legs can't move."

I almost laughed at her but all I had was a gasp. Somebody tells you your legs don't work and without even thinking about it you move your legs to show them they are ridiculous. My feet were cemented to the floor. I couldn't even wiggle my legs the least bit sideways.

My head suddenly felt hot. I could hear the buzz of the other call center workers but I couldn't see anyone without shoving my chair way back. I craned for a glimpse of my shift supervisor stalking by. No one.

"You will not try to get anyone's attention or

assistance, Mr. Gayed." Had I told her my last name? No, I never tell the deadbeats my real last name. She was worming into my brain. "You will answer my questions truthfully and without obfuscation. For your benefit you will comply."

"Yes," I said. What did she mean, for my benefit?

"You don't care for people very much, do you?" she said.

"No." I said, a little surprised.

"That is unfortunate. There is an axiom. If everyone you meet is an idiot, it is you!" Her laughter was glass breaking.

"I don't have to take this," I said.

"Yes, you do. You want to hang up, I forbid it. You want to move your legs but the nerves and muscles aren't speaking with each other right now. You want to call out, but I forbid it."

All she said was true. I was surrounded by people making their calls but there was no one to rip the thin gray wire out of the wall and free me. "You bitch, you — !"

"I do not approve of name-calling, Mr. Gayed."

"Why not just 'forbid' me? You're deeply into that. I notice you never use contractions. Does that make you feel like you're a higher class of deadbeat?"

"Mr. Gayed. You sound articulate and functionally intelligent. I have already paralyzed your feet and legs. I wonder why you think it would be difficult for me to shut down your diaphragm?" My jaw moved more but no sound came out. My hand cramped around the receiver.

She made a *tsk* sound of impatience. "Stop breathing."

With my free hand I grabbed at my throat.

5

Useless. I looked down and saw that my torso was not rising and falling. The realization seemed to ignite fire in my lungs. I looked at my desk clock and watched the second hand sweep around half the face. I had not taken a deep breath before my breathing stopped and the air hunger was beyond a burning need. Need is not a big enough word. Black spots appeared at the edge of my vision and grew larger. Would the paramedics be able to move me when they arrived? Would firefighters have to saw me off at the ankles? Would they take my body to the morgue and leave my feet in my shoes forever glued to the Berber carpet? I pitched forward from the waist and my head slammed into the desk.

"Start breathing," she said.

My first gasp was a great heave and it was several minutes before my breathing slowed. The bridge of my nose was bloody. It stung like bees. The air tasted cold and sweet. I decided not to call Dr. Papua any more names.

"Please let me hang up. I won't bother you again."

"I am fascinated with the workings of the body. When I studied anatomy, I was awed by its complexity. I thought its design was proof that there is a god."

"*Please* don't do anything."

"Then I studied pathology. When you see all that can go wrong with this incredible organic machine, it makes one think there must surely be a devil. Do you know what the Circle of Willis is?"

"No."

"It is a little circle of blood vessels at the top of your brain. It is a very common site for strokes...your heart is starting to pound much faster now."

I could feel the gallop in my chest instantly and I breathed harder.

"The hand that is not holding the phone to your ear is numb."

It was. "I'm just doing my job. Look, I'm sorry!"

"Your job compounds misery. You harass people. How many files do you have on your desk which are dead cases like mine?"

"I-I'm sorry...what do you mean by dead cases?"

"Those which are more than six years old, of course."

"I have all the old Taunton's files."

"Ah, yes, of course. You are the 'go-to guy' of the office, are you not?" She used the expression as if the words had a strange taste.

"Yes." The numb feeling crept up my forearm. I gave it a tentative whack on the edge of the desk. It felt like my arm was asleep, only the near border of emptiness crawled toward my shoulder.

"A stroke can be terribly disabling and disfiguring. It can twist one side of your face or just kill you." I wet my pants then, not in a spasmodic squirt I could try to hold back but a long hot coursing stream down my immobile legs. "If you were to live but could not take care of yourself, who would help you?"

The numbness was still spreading and tears began to slide down my cheeks. "My mother would help."

There was a long terrible pause. The minute hand swept around twice before she spoke again. I couldn't hear her breath or any ambient sounds. It was as if her end of the line was in some underground space lined with cotton. I couldn't feel the right side of my face. "Hello?"

"Are you a disappointment to your mother?"

7

"Of course I am, Dr. Papua. No kid wants to grow up to be a bill collector. No parent dreams that."

"So, you are disappointed in yourself, as well?"

"You know you are a sadist, right?"

Her laughter trilled again and a chill went through me that started with the cooling urine down my legs and crawled with spidery feet up my spine. Spine-tingling is not an empty cliché. It's real. I know that now.

"You dare to offend me. You still have some dignity. You may be redeemable."

A little flame of hope sparked that she would finally let me go. Dr. Papua was quick to douse my little fire. "I let your predecessors live. That strategy does not seem to be enough to stop these calls from your firm. You know I can do more than simply stop your heart. I could instruct you to put a baby in an oven and broil it for your dinner if I was so inclined. If you fail me, you fail yourself. The world is full of phones."

"Y-yes." I would have grimaced but my face wasn't under my control anymore. Were straining blood vessels in my brain about to burst? Had they already? She talked and all I could do was make urgent agreeing sounds from deep in my throat. When she was done she told me to close my eyes and count backwards from ten. I did so, though from ten to five I couldn't speak and the numbers were only in my head like the opening of an eight millimetre film counting down. At one, the line went dead. No click. No dial tone.

I lurched backwards and yanked the phone away from my burning ear. A long vowel sound burst from me as I shot out of the chair. People surrounded me, asking questions and telling me to sit down but it was all a meaningless buzz. I swept up the files and hugged them as I strode to the door.

Engells, my supervisor, appeared in front of me. At first he was perplexed and then he tried to hold me back and grab the files. I pushed him away. He leapt at me and I pushed him down. I had to get out. As the door closed behind me, I glanced back to see Engells still on the floor staring after me with bug eyes.

I burned Dr. Papua's file in a steel drum behind my apartment building. Then I burned the rest of the files. I watched the paper curl in the heat and turn to ashes. My cell phone went in next. I stood back from the drum and watched. I don't know for how long. When the cell phone battery exploded with a tinny bang. I woke to the night and the cold that was gathering its strength around me.

"It's time to come in out of the dark," I said aloud to no one.

I climbed the stairs to my apartment, feeling lighter with each step. Tomorrow I would begin again. I'd get my acting career going, this time for sure.

After I ripped it off the kitchen wall, I shattered the phone on the floor. I kept kicking until all the phone's components skittered across the linoleum in small jagged pieces. I put on clean pants, sat on the couch and listened to my heartbeat. The pounding in my temples finally began to slow. A hot tear slipped down my cheek. I was so grateful for my breath, as if I had finally surfaced after being underwater a long time.

I am still grateful. Dr. Circe Papua, wherever you

are, thank you.

THE FORTUNE TELLER

Sometimes the muse strikes on demand. I came up with this story in a few minutes at a writing craft workshop with Brian Henry. I first met Brian in my days working at Harlequin when, for $50 a manuscript, I evaluated slush pile submissions. I remembered everything about him from 20 years past and he didn't remember a thing about me. Despite that, I remain convinced he's a nice guy...or I'm not nice enough. ~ Chazz

Paul pulled back the tent flap for Sarah and they stepped into the gloom. He couldn't see the edges of the room, just an old woman sitting in a circle of white light at its center.   He guessed the old woman's business must have slowed since this afternoon's rain. The old tent, off the broadway of the more lucrative games and rides, seemed a forgotten, minor attraction from an age before television, back when carnivals were popular. He cursed himself for taking Sarah here. First dates were hard enough without increasing the level of difficulty by going to a third-rate fair.

"Not too late to go on the roller coaster one more time," he said. "And I'd like to take another shot at winning you a bear. Those carny games are rigged but, toward the end, I was getting the hang of that rifle."

Sarah shook her head. "My feet hurt," she said. Let's sit a minute and I'll get my palm read. C'mon, it'll be fun." He noticed that, as she moved, her helmet of blonde hair didn't move, as if she had stepped off a magazine cover. That magazine would be called "Unattainable."

The fortune teller looked up at them sourly. She smiled but the gesture looked like it caused her pain, the muscles required for the job were weak and their work didn't travel to her eyes. She was very fat, dressed in a garish muumuu no doubt intended (and failing) to conceal her colossal dimensions. She sat on a worn lawn chair that looked inadequate to its task. A paperback romance looked tiny in her lap and a large expended bag of potato chips littered the floor at her feet.

It seemed cold and unnaturally quiet in the tent and it was so dark he couldn't see the walls. It was as if the carnival had dropped far away. The combination of sudden silence and darkness made him feel off balance. He closed his eyes. If he hadn't known better, he could have been fooled into thinking they were underwater in an abandoned stadium.

"Sit. Sit." The fat woman gestured for Sarah to take the chair opposite her. From the back, Paul could see it was just another old lawn chair someone had draped with a red velvet blanket.

"I'd like to get my palm read." Sarah extended one beautifully manicured hand and gave the old crone a bright smile. Paul thought it was the kind of smile that says, "I'd be glad to accept whatever you give me. With this smile, you'll want to give me everything."

Her father was a dentist. "Nice caps, huh?" she had said, within a minute of their first meeting that morning.

"Huh," was all Paul answered. He made sure he didn't smile too much after that, not so much that his own teeth showed. Sarah's sorority-girl good looks filled him with new need and just as much self-consciousness about his broken teeth. One ragged, snaggletooth poked out at an embarrassing angle from his bottom row of yellow teeth. He'd never had the money to fix it correctly and had gotten through the hell of high school with the cruel nickname of Fang.

The old woman eyed Sarah's hand for a moment and waved it away. "No palm reading," she said. "I do *deep* reading. Are you sure you want to know your future?"

Sarah looked taken aback and quickly withdrew her hand but stayed seated and gave a prim nod.

"Hey," Paul said, "just do your thing and we'll get you back to your reading."

The fortune teller's eyes narrowed and she threw her book aside, into the darkness. "Ten dollars."

Paul pulled out a ragged bill. The old woman snatched it away and tucked it into the depths of her brassiere. Watching the bill disappear made him feel queasy.

"Close your eyes, young lady," the old woman commanded. "Let your defences fall away so I may read you properly." As she spoke, she never took her eyes off Paul. Her sneer slowly transformed into a smile.

A moment passed.

"You have just met," she said.

Sarah gasped. "You're right!" She turned back to look at Paul, favoring him with another of her perfect white smiles.

"Of course. This is what I do. Now *sh*! You must know something very, very important. I am serious about this. I must warn you. This man is not good for you."

"What — ?" Sarah said.

"You heard me. No good. He has little money and if you stay with him it will only lead to sorrow."

Sarah opened her eyes and stared at the fortune teller for a moment more, as if the old woman communicated something else unspoken that Paul could not see or hear.

"He is a jealous man. If you stay with him, you and your lover will die young and violently. This man is dangerous. Too, too jealous. This man cannot stand other men looking at you, and of course, wherever you go, men look at you. Run away before it's too late and never return a phone call from this man."

"Sarah! Don't listen to her. This is crazy! I know what she's doing. It's called a cold read. She didn't see a ring on your finger and made some easy assumptions. I pissed her off so she's decided to screw me over...screw *us* over. Please!"

Sarah stood up, her gaze shifting from the fortune

teller to Paul's face.

"What is this? What? For $20 you kick me in the nuts and for $50 bucks we get the good fortune?"

Sarah started for the door. He stepped in her way but she brushed past him and kept moving. "This is too much. Th-this is f-freaking me out. I gotta go." She paused at the door. "I'm sorry, Paul."

Her face was fear. In a glance, he knew he'd lost her forever.

Paul turned on the fortune teller. "You...cow!"

"I've heard that before," she said.

He stood still and they were once more plunged into that eerie, cold silence. She studied him.

Paul reached into his jeans pocket and pulled out another ten dollar bill.

The fortune teller took a deep breath and let it out slow. When she spoke again her tone was even. "You will kill me someday. Soon, I think."

"Will I get away with it?"

Her voice broke as she said, "Yes."

CLEAN UP

This is another story I came up with while attending a Brian Henry writing workshop. At this same workshop I met a fellow writer, Mark Young, who became a friend, a valuable beta team member and the first guest on the All That Chazz podcast. I make new friends about as easily as Samoa launches rockets, so writing workshops can provide unexpected benefits. ~ Chazz

I twist and pull the orange dish towel, wringing it ragged. The fat man in the wrinkled suit sits in Dad's chair at the kitchen table, gazing at the family album.

"I shouldn't have gone away," he says, over and over, but I think he's talking to himself. Every time he turns a page he sighs again and mutters. "I'm so sorry."

I peer at the pictures from my seat across from him. I'm upside down. When I was a baby my hair was so blond it was white. There I am, a little boy with a stick. A thin young man with an air rifle. Then a big man kneeling beside a dead deer, cradling my rifle.

My faces are different, but the look is the same. And we had so many dogs. They either run away, pass away or go away. My hair is heading back to white now, like my father.

"Why come back now?" I ask.

His mouth gets small, the lips flat. The whites of his eyes are a map of broken blood vessels. He tells me he didn't see my father's obituary until a couple of days ago. "I jumped on a flight as soon as I could get away," David says.

David. I'd never heard the man's name even mentioned, but he's my uncle. Well. Half-uncle.

I'd always thought my grandparents were inseparable, bound together in sepia-toned photographs with dark thumbprints along yellowed edges of old photo albums. I don't have any pictures of one of them alone. They always sit or stand side by side, stiff and posing for the camera, frozen together under greasy streaks on thin glass.

Family and photographs: Tricks is all.

I'd never thought of Grampa as a young man catting around. It never occurred to me he could have a bastard son or that Dad had a half-brother. My father never told me. I'd sat by his deathbed, hour after hour, watching. As his days shrank, he shrank, but he'd had strength left at the end. He'd gotten away, after all.

"I lived in this house for the first nine years of my life," David says. He looks around, takes in the old pot belly stove, the faded fridge magnets shaped like roosters and chickens, the scuffed fake-brick floor tiles. He squints at a high shelf. The green paint on my John Deere model tractor is chipped.

I can't read people's faces, but I guess that he's figured out there's no inheritance to be had here.

"It's hardly changed," he says finally. "Somehow it all seems smaller. But I guess that's what people always say."

"Is it?" Things people say puzzle me — maybe it's simply that he's taller and fatter.

He doesn't take my question seriously. "Your grandmother was always good to me. Treated me like family. I'm sure she was disappointed in your grandfather, but she never took it out on me."

I nod and say nothing. In David's eyes I see my father's eyes as he died. There are always secrets too dangerous to share. I understand that. But Dad somehow kept his half-brother from me.

That won't do.

David squirms in Dad's chair, burdened with my heavy stare, my silence like sandpaper. "You hear all those clichés about evil stepmothers. Your grandmother disproved that rule."

He smiles at me the same way I smile at everyone.

I nod. I twist the dishtowel, like that solves all my problems.

David's talking and talking, making me tired. Something about his house in Connecticut. His hands are thick and red, knuckly and scarred. He's used to outdoor work. Even though he's old and overweight, David could still be dangerous.

If Dad could keep family from me, it wouldn't do to underestimate another man's power just because he's old. Repeating mistakes is a weak person's luxury.

David says my grandfather's mistress is still alive. The whore must be unreasonably old. To me, David looks gray, almost dead, though he volunteers that he's "only seventy years young."

The dishtowel is well made.

"I always thought I'd get back together with your dad. You know. Visit. Be friendly." He raises his eyebrows at me.

I think I've missed a signal but I don't understand body language. Why can't people ever just say what they mean?

"I sent Christmas cards every year but never got one back," he says.

My face must have done things.

"I'm sorry if you feel this hurts your grandfather's reputation." Eyes wide, he says it quick, like he's rushing to slap cool balm on a hot water scald. "I'm not out to bring pain to your family."

I don't care about that. I was little when Grampa died. I was stuck in a hospital around the time Grandma died so I missed that funeral, too. I wanted to go, but Dad said I was too young to see a dead body.

"You're not embarrassing any family anymore," I say. "It's just me now."

It was the Christmas cards that got to me. That hurt like cigarette burns in hidden places. David shouldn't have told me about the Christmas cards. His fault.

Every December, Dad had a fresh reminder, a new opportunity to tell me the truth and give me an uncle. My father probably torched each card in the wood stove after I went to bed or maybe slipped them into the chipper at the mill.

I liked Christmas: Cold air sucked through a scarf; colored lights under thick snow; the smell of the pine

I chopped down myself; the escape from school. Each Christmas memory was a betrayal now. Dad got away with lying to me and there was nothing I could do about that now, short of digging him up for a stern talking to.

David finally puts the photo album on the table. He ignores the steaming cup of black coffee I'd set beside him. "So...what do you do, Billy?"

"William."

He clears his throat.

The kitchen clock ticks off the seconds.

"What do you do, William?"

I knock the hot coffee into his lap. I stand and slip behind him. That sound must be what people call a strangled cry. I brace my knee against the back of his chair as I twist and pull.

I show him what I do.

I treat him like family.

A GIFT FOR CURSES

This story is partially true. It was inspired by my first, and last, foray in Yorkdale Mall in Toronto on a very busy Boxing Day. I tell these stories because it's an outlet for a lovely little revenge fantasy. If I didn't have this outlet, I'm afraid of what I might do. ~ Chazz

I met Jack and Diane for 15 to 20 seconds on December 26, 1987. Jack and Diane grew up in Toronto in a tough area of low-rent housing off what's called the Jane-Finch Corridor. Both kids had working-class parents who didn't do much wrong beyond inattentive parenting, but they should have cared more about the practice of good manners with dangerous strangers.

Diane started out as a sweet girl who went boy-crazy when puberty struck. She "blossomed too young" her teachers said — the females said this with chagrin while the males said so with a shy smile which betrayed their titillation. "Blossoming young" really meant that she grew a startling pair of knockers the summer she turned thirteen. A smarter girl might have seen this early development as a curse. Thus fortified, by her mid-teens the sweet child had turned demanding and vain.

Jack was always just ahead of being put in a Special Ed. class, which meant that he spent all his time either tolerated or ignored at the bottom of regular classes. He got into fights defending his little sister from bullies. To defend himself from older kids, he was soon hanging out with the biggest and dumbest kids around his age. Jack was nine when he had his first serious talk with a police officer after he was caught shoplifting a bag of chips from the convenience store next to his apartment building. The owner banned him from the store forever. Jack had to walk six blocks to the next convenience store, so he was determined to steal more than one bag of chips to make the trip worthwhile.

After school one day, Jack and two buddies beat a little terrier till it couldn't walk because it nipped at Jack's leg. Jack and his friends were trying unsuccessfully to break into the dog's owner's home at the time. The criminals-in-training were caught by a neighbor. The judge let them off with a warning. I don't give warnings.

Since their cars sat unguarded and vulnerable just outside in the parking lot, Jack's teachers were nervous about disciplining him in class. Diane was the girl in the rear of the class who never raised her hand. She was bored and put a lot of energy into looking bored at all times. A year or two after graduation her teachers could recall her face, but none could remember her name.

Jack and Diane shared some classes in junior high off and on and had teased each other in a clumsy dance of flirtation, pulling and pushing without touching, weak magnetic poles working against eventuality. They got together as a couple in their last year of high school. It was October, the first dance of the year. He wore his older brother's blue suit. It fit like a garbage bag. She wore a pink dress that was no defence against cold winds seething early.

They didn't know how many possibilities were still open to them. Every day, with every single, tiny choice, possibilities narrow until we reach the end of our lives when there are no choices left. We measure our time by the arbitrary divisions of sixty seconds in a minute, sixty minutes in an hour. We should measure our time by how many choices we have left. Jack and Diane thought they had time and the world was their buffet. They were sure everything would work out for them. It is a mystery to me why people think that.

Jack asked Diane to dance. She ignored his bad teeth. They danced to a Pet Shop Boys tune and broke apart awkwardly, not having anything to say to each other. They were about to drift back to their different groups of friends when the next song came on. It was *Jack and Diane* by John Cougar Mellencamp.

The song was from the summer of 1982. It was now 1986. Funny how roads turn. If that song hadn't played just then, they would not have been together as a couple when they met me. Fate moved a hand and the song played. They laughed about the coincidence and danced to it slowly. She sang the lyrics to him, her eyes suddenly bright. He held her tighter so she sang the rest of the song with her head on his shoulder, her warm breath in his ear. The biological imperative asserted itself and various hormones poured into their bloodstreams. Pheromones emanated and they saw each other in a new way. Chemistry pushed and they fell into each other. The next song was slow and by the end of that, they were an item. Choices had narrowed again. Events funnelled them toward me.

Diane was Jack's second girlfriend. He was still in love with another girl named Cassie, but Cassie had moved away with her family at the end of the summer and Diane was here. Diane was willing to pass the lunch hours kissing, groping, and wrestling with clothes behind the stage in the school's gym. Jack was Diane's fifth boyfriend in three years, though all her boyfriends were pretty much interchangeable. Three of them were named Mike.

That fall, Jack got a part-time job putting furniture and stereos together for floor displays in a department store. Christmas was over and they wouldn't need him back until New Year's Day. Every penny he made went toward paying for gas and dating Diane.

On Boxing Day, Jack picked her up in his mom's car and drove her to Yorkdale Mall. She wasn't happy with many of the Christmas gifts she had received that year and was hoping to return a couple of books. She had no use for books. Jack hated Christmas because his parents' fights were always worse around holidays. He didn't want to go to the mall, either, but if he could make her happy, maybe Diane would be "nice." That's what he called it. Jack thought things would even out.

I went to Yorkdale on Boxing Day with my future wife. She was reluctant because she knew what the crowds would be like. I usually avoid crowds. I *should* avoid crowds, but I wanted to get out. Her house was beginning to feel like jail and shopping for bargains on Boxing Day seemed like something ordinary people do. I want to be like ordinary people. The mall's wide corridors were full of them. Everyone took baby steps forward and most everyone seemed to be looking but not buying much. Diane and Jack were baby stepping directly behind us.

"I hate being behind slow people!" Diane wailed. I looked back and shrugged at them. No one was traveling fast because we were in a slow current in a sea of humanity. It's a law of physics applied to malls: You can't go faster than the people ahead of you. Jack caught my look of irritation at his girlfriend. "Go to hell!" he said. I gave him a thousand watt smile and said brightly, "Merry Christmas!" so Jack felt the urge to repeat himself, with even more venom this time. The current shifted at that moment and we came apart as the crowd moved forward.

He cursed me in his way and without another thought I cursed him in mine. I can't tell you exactly what happened next. I won't tell you much about myself. I don't want to be tracked. I will say that my job is not to do what I did to Jack and Diane. I'm actually a healer. I use my gift to help sick people most of the time. I'm not a bad person, though in the ways that matter, I'm not really a person at all, strictly speaking. I don't believe in bad. There is cause and effect. That's all there is.

There is an power in each of us, a remembering of the place we all come from. This place holds dark power and I reach into it deeper than you can. I eat starlight and feel the crackle of vibrancy that hatred can bring if focused just so. A *muddying* of auric fields is involved. In another age, what I do would be called rewriting Akashic Records or casting the evil eye. Unfamiliar with those concepts? Good. You and the world are better off.

What I did was basically an intervention in their energetic fields, like dipping your hands into warm water to stir the current counterclockwise. I reached into their etheric energy, looking backward to see where the energy had gone. That's how I know all I've told you so far. In an instant I peered forward to see where the energy could be directed. A true curse is quantum physics, but applied to your world in ways your science doesn't yet understand. When that knowledge is understood widely, that will be the end of everything.

I cursed them and moved away, the damage done in a moment. For the sake of the continuation of the species, I'll say no more than that. This energy has nearly wiped out the world's population at least once before. The agent of the curse last time was the bubonic plague.

An avalanche starts with a subtle shift you can't see before it builds to deadly momentum. Fate is patient because it is an amoral witness. It's all about the physics of the dance to gods and things like me.

Diane dumped Jack the night before Valentine's Day, 1988. She did so at about the exact moment he saw her climbing out of the back of another guy's van in the school parking lot at lunchtime. Humiliated, Jack took a swing at the guy, a rugby player on the school's team. Jack thought himself a tough guy, but that perception was based on beating up kids a year or two younger than he with the help of his friends. The rugby player was Jack's height, but forty pounds heavier, much of it muscle. Jack bounced up from the pavement with a bloody nose. Each time he was knocked down, Jack came back from the ground a bit slower. His punches became more wild and desperate. Finally, Jack went down, went limp, stayed down.

Jack and Diane spoke to each other only once after that in the hallway outside of the Home Economics classroom. Two weeks remained till their graduation from high school. Jack smiled and asked if he could sign her yearbook. The caption under her class picture listed no clubs. It read only that Diane was voted "most likely to appear in films." This was a cruel joke among the kids who edited the yearbook. The English teacher, their yearbook advisor, insisted they change it to "films" from "porno."

Jack grabbed her yearbook and therein wrote the word "bitch" in a large looping red scrawl across her face. Jack handed back the yearbook with a look that conveyed an unearthly contentment. Diane's mouth dropped open when she saw what Jack had written across her picture, her perfect face forever marred. She slapped Jack across his left cheek so hard she left the outline of her hand burned in red. Their paths have never since crossed (unless you count this confession worming its way into your brain.)

Throughout her life, Diane's yearbook was stowed in a box or on a bookshelf. The two insults, both crude and secret, were kept static and pristine. Meanwhile, my intervention was gathering steam, whittling away at her cells. The subtle shift of the avalanche gathered weight and potential energy.

They both turned 36 this year. Diane had a succession of boyfriends and then two husbands, not any of them much good. The second husband is staying with her, hoping against the lessons of experience that things will get better. It's the second marriage for both of them and they are staying together because they both suspect they can't do any better. They're right.

The couple has one child together and each have a child from a previous marriage. Child Protective Services counsellors knows this family well and the kids don't know whether to pray that their parents will get along or just get the screaming over with and break up. For the record, I had nothing to do with this part of the disaster which is Diane's life. That's all her. Her energy told me she would make plenty of disastrous choices without my mucking about. True, I could have helped her with that, but inducing illness is my peculiar specialty.

Diane still dresses like she's twenty and her blind sense of fashion leads her to wear belly tops long past the time she should. She also thinks that using the whole can of extra hold hairspray is a look that will return any moment now. She's still demanding and vain, but as each year passes, she's got less with which to trade. She looks much older than she is and all the cigarettes and tanning are making the clock spin even faster. She coughs up black stuff into the toilet each morning. She should see someone about that but she will wait for a long time because, for some reason, she thinks nothing really bad should ever happen to her.

A double radical mastectomy will save Diane's life for awhile. She won't be sure if it's part of a blessing or a curse when her husband finally leaves. Her kids will grow up and move away, except for the youngest, who will live less than a mile away but will never call or visit. Diane will become lonely, fading to invisible in the slipstream of other people's lives. She will be a pale cloud in peripheral vision. She has had more focus than she deserves, so she will draw no more.

When Diane's long list of choices reaches bottom, she'll be 68 years old. It will be cool rainy May, late in the afternoon when the low-slanted light in her gray hospital room will suggest to her that she will live for one more day. She'll be wrong about that. Her last wish will be that the doctors and nurses would just let her go and stop beating on her once-fabulous chest. No choice then, of course. Just a rising up as I finally release her from my physics lesson.

Her children will gather. They won't say so, but they'll be relieved. They won't be relieved because she will be at rest after a long battle with lung cancer. Remember what Jack scrawled in red ink in her yearbook so long ago? He was right about that. On the day of the funeral, Diane's youngest daughter, the smartest one, will leave a bouquet of flowers. Not for nothing, they will be Impatiens.

And Jack? Jack has worked as a roofer, pumped gas and took some training in auto bodywork. What he really wanted to do was race stock cars. He didn't know how to get into that so he raced his third-hand Toyota for a while until he put it into the ditch one rainy night after drinking too much. He rolled it, but got out of the accident without a scratch. He stumbled up the embankment and back onto the road, cursing his luck. It was the first passing car that shattered his jaw, his pelvis and his right leg. Since the accident — he was just 23 then — Jack often speaks of himself in the third-person. He calls himself "The Gimp."

Jack has drifted from job to job and place to place, driven by his needs and the discovery by a series of employers that he's a petty thief. He falls in and out of favor with a series of drinking buddies, driven together and apart by Jack's urge to fight when drunk. He's lame and still just 141 pounds, so the fights rarely end well for him. Marijuana helped with his aching leg each morning. Then it sccmcd stronger drugs were necessary to make it to Happy Hour. After several years of experience, Jack finally noticed that no one looked very happy around Happy Hour.

Six years ago, when Jack turned 30, the people in his family who were still talking to him held an intervention. His little sister, Tracy, stuck by him and defended him from the family as he had once defended her from school bullies. She spoke of Jack's potential. She believed. She pushed the idea so hard the family believed. Even Jack almost believed it. Tracy paid for Jack to go to rehab and Jack tried to turn his life around. He thought he could become a youth pastor to counsel kids. It sounded like easy work so he grabbed at the idea. Jack got things together. Part of the dance is that things come together and apart.

One year into Jack's hard-won sobriety, a friend

from rehab showed up to celebrate his chemical-free anniversary. They'll start the evening talking about the healing power of Jesus working in Jack's life. The assertion feels comforting at first. Then needing Jesus to tell him what to do makes him feel weak. Jack blew his life apart. He and his friend share a vial of crystal meth around dawn.

Jack will be suffocated slowly by crystal, his small life force guttering in a high wind of pain and hunger and panic that will hold him too tight to draw a deep breath. He will be so weak and close to death so often that he will be blind to what's going on around him. He'll be so muddled, images from that time are blurred even to me.

One morning Jack will wake up in jail with no memory of how he got there. I helped the life force muster just then to let Jack have his head. When he is released he'll go to a halfway house and then a homeless shelter. My hook is in him deep. I'll let my fish have some line before I beach him. The fun is in the play.

Jack will try to get his life back together again. It will be Tracy who gets him turned around to the life of a citizen. He'll find the determination to stop his old habits when she stops sending money or answering his pleading phone calls. By losing his only ally, Jack will succeed for a time. People who have hope fall farthest and hardest.

He's never been much of a reader but that will change. He'll go to the library often and not just because it's warm and safe. Jack will grow a new addiction. He will read more and more. He'll like fiction, especially Stephen King. He will resolve to read all of the author's work. When he reads *Carrie*

and *The Stand* and *Misery*, he'll begin to see he's
been running through dark narrow tunnels with his
head down. Books will be escape hatches. The books
he hasn't read yet are waiting for him to disappear
into them.

He should hurry, maybe take a speed reading
course. Jack will wake one morning on a December
26 around 11 in the morning — an anniversary of our
encounter in a mall so long ago. The room will spin.
Every time he opens his eyes, the room will spin so
badly he'll want to throw up. It will be Meniere's
Disease, a rare inner ear disorder. He'll take drugs
that won't work. He'll have several operations which
won't work. He'll live a long time, but it'll seem much
longer. Just before he dies, a memory will come to
him. He'll remember me. He'll know he was a fool
who became a puppet and a slave. He'll try to tell
people about me, but by then, no one will listen to
the shrinking, bedridden, crazy man.

I'm telling you all this because I took my kids to a
festival in the park last Friday night. My wife had
gone to a movie with her sister and I felt too restless
to stay inside with the kids and watch television.
Despite the thunderstorm that had swept through in
the late afternoon, the park was very crowded along
the paths. I pushed the double stroller ahead of me
and tried to block out the chatter of the crowd's
noise. I averted my eyes from their pretty, fragile,
tempting auras.

My nine-month-old twins, a boy and a girl, silently
watched the masses moving before them like a tall,
colorful curtain blown by lazy but ceaseless breezes.
They see what I see, but they won't learn how to use
their gift until their late teens. The people crowded

around small booths buying trinkets from smiling vendors are still safe from my children for years.

It was comfortably cool. The air was cleansed from the hard rain. I planned no work for the weekend. I had no plans at all.

Stephanie, a wide middle-aged woman with dead cow eyes, lumbered behind me. She said to her companion, "Move around on the grass, Trish! These people are too slow!"

I'm sorry, Stephanie. It's a reflex.

CUTHIAN'S WAKE

From Sex, Death & Mind Control, this story was written shortly after my mother's death. The jokes and macho control fantasies are mine. In the end, this is a tribute to my parents' romance. She was terrified of dying in a hospital. He was utterly devoted to her and saw her through to her death at home. ~ Chazz

The night before I got the phone call, I was in a girl's apartment listening to her life story. The rule is, if you can listen long enough, or look like you're listening intensely enough, you're in. This time though, my patience wasn't paying off. It was past one and she yawned. In another minute or two she was going to say she had an early morning or that I should get going since the subways would shut down in an hour. Toronto's late November wind was whipping up outside. I'd be walking in another minute. It was time for one last pitch — The Pitch.

"I'm feeling really close to you," I begin, like I always begin.

"Yeah?"

Shut up and listen, I thought, *you'll throw off my rhythm.* "I'd like to share something with you."

"Yeah?"

She looks at her fingernails, evaluating whether to paint on another layer of polish, maybe. I've got to work fast, but I keep my tone smooth. "I've never told anyone this before and I want to get it all out. It's...heavy." She nods her blonde head like a teacher giving a student a moment more after the bell has rung before dismissing the class.

"My mom was studying to become a librarian in London when she met my father. He was a barrister," — always say "barrister." It impresses North American girls much more than "lawyer."

We're sitting on her living room floor and she fidgets, shifting her weight off her knees. She puts her head on her arm like a pillow as she leans on the seat of her sofa. I'm losing.

"Anyway, my parents were married a long time. She quit her studies to follow my father back to Ireland." I subtly jig my Irish deep into greener territory. Toronto girls love the accent. By the end of the story, I'll really pour it on so thick it'll be cartoony. Fancy tricks with vowels is what they expect instead of the clipped words and flat tones of a true Irish accent. I blame those stupid leprechaun cereal commercials.

"Me mother had me brother and me Da worked and worked," I say. Mother and brother comes out *mudder* and *brudder*, just for her.

"Mother took care of us and that was her whole life

until later, when we were in our teens. She ghosted a couple cookbooks by a famous English actor. She had won a few writing awards when she was young but didn't pursue it again until we were pretty much raised. Dad was away a lot working, but we had Mum and a house full of books. Our bookshelves reached from the floor to the ceiling and the books were two rows deep."

"Which actor did she write books for?" (They always ask.)

"I'd tell you if I knew, but she kept that secret her whole life. She'd only say that the contract stated that if she told me, she'd have to murder me with a wooden spoon." Mystery and a dash of humor. That hook has a shiny lure.

"My father worked for the Irish government. He was always fuzzy about what he did for them." More mystery. Tell a girl your father's a spy and she'll giggle and kick you out. Let her figure it out for herself and you're closer to your destination.

"Where was this?" she asks. I tell her Dublin. Sometimes I say Belfast. They're the only two Irish cities anyone in North America seems to know.

I pause here, like I'm gathering my thoughts for the final push to unburden myself. I believe in method acting, so I method act and picture myself on the toilet squeezing out huge bran muffins. "I...ah... maybe I should just go." It's not even a gamble. I'm a human being in pain.

"No, go on," she says. She's not yawning now. She looks alert.

"A couple years ago, Mum started getting sick. The doctors did some tests but messed up the diagnosis or screwed up some lab work or something." The tragedy is in the details.

"She was dying, but the worst thing was that first she was slowly going blind. Reading and writing were her life and when that began slipping away from her, she wasn't Mum anymore. She got depressed. Trying to read the newspaper gave her headaches. Large print books were okay for a short while, but in a couple of months she couldn't read at all."

I look up from the floor and fall into her eyes. Whether her gaze is voyeurism or compassion, she's taken the bait and the hook is in deep.

"My father owned a sailboat called The Cuthian. We only took it out a few times a year, always on a weekend. It was my favorite thing about my childhood, but now..."

"Yes?" She gives me a small, encouraging smile and moves a little closer, leaning in. Time to reel her in all the way.

"My father took Mum on a...last...trip in the Cuthian. They closed up the house, left the keys with my brother and sailed off at dawn one day. My brother said she looked happier that day than she had in weeks. She said they were going to count sunsets together."

"Where'd they go?"

"Into the sunset, I guess. I think they decided to do it when she couldn't see the pretty colors anymore. Mum said they were going to count sunsets. It was kind of a grim countdown."

"What are you saying?"

I can almost taste her lips now. Her eyes are a bright blue you never see anywhere but in a young girl's eyes. I love dating girls. I'm going to get so depressed when I get so old I have to start dating women. I gaze into those eyes and I love what they see.

"Some fishermen found the boat abandoned."

"Oh?"

"Empty and drifting. There was a half-empty bottle of champagne rolling around the deck and two broken glasses by the rail. The last entry in the Cuthian's log had just one line in my father's handwriting."

I drag it out and she's just about to burst but out of respect she swallows it down and waits, vibrating a little. Her blue eyes are wide but those pupils are tiny dots.

"The last entry just said, 'Warm breezes but no sunset tonight.'"

"What are you telling me?"

"Well, you see," I say slowly, putting on the Irish even more, "my parents' insurance wouldn't have paid out for a double suicide."

She swallows hard and her eyes are wet. This may be the saddest thing she has ever heard. "Um. So...?" She swallows with a click.

"So they went sailing," I say. I do things with my face that I think will approximate regret, then a resolution to be brave that falls just short of succeeding.

"Wow," she says.

"Uh-huh," I say. "I think my Da loved my mother more than I ever suspected. I think the two of them had a rich inner life they never let me or my brother see. They must have had such a..."

"Passion?" she said.

I look her in the eyes. "Passion. Yes. You're right.

38

Deep and surprising and fresh right till the black curtain came down." Nobody talks like this unless it's rehearsed — which it has been, many delicious times — and it doesn't matter at all. I'm a tragic figure yearning for the mythic love my erstwhile parents had.

I pull her into the boat. And yes, she shudders and flops like a fish when I land her.

* * *

My cell rings harshly while soft light arrives slowly to illuminate an unfamiliar bedroom. It's my brother on the phone. I'm up, and following my trail of clothes back to the living room. Her roommate is up early for work and freezes, her coffee cup halfway to her mouth as I pull on my underwear. I ignore her stare and clap my cell shut. "Can you give me a ride to the airport, please?"

She of the bright blue eyes emerges from her room wearing just a T-shirt. She looks thoroughly tousled. Rightly so. "What's going on?"

"Uh...I've got to go!" I yank on my jeans and start lacing up my sneakers as fast as I can. I don't know where my socks are.

This is the first I've met the roommate and the sight of me without pants seems to have amused her. "Your date wants a ride."

"I gave you a ride," Blue Eyes says. Her red lipstick is still smeared, like she's a kid who got into Mommy's make-up.

"I don't have time for this. I've got to *go*! Uh! I'll have to go by my place before I go to the airport!"

"What's the big emergency?"

"My mum died last night."

She is not sympathetic. She throws things at me — shoes, a plate, the roommate's coffee cup and, oddly, a couple of dishtowels. I run down the long hallway to the elevator and push and push and push the down button. She's screaming curses. I look back down the hallway. I do not know what to say. I have no script for this.

She stops and runs back into her apartment. It's quiet for a moment and just when I let my shoulders loosen a little, she emerges from her apartment door with a floor lamp in her hands.

Uh-oh.

The person coming at me is no longer a girl so easily deceived. She's now a woman on a rampage. I suspect that, as well as our first date went, there will not be a second. She's grown up a lot in the last few minutes. I'm really just a tall boy.

The elevator doors slowly part and I push and push and push the button to close the goddamn doors. A flood of salty curses washes over me and she's coming fast, running now as she senses I'm about to escape. After a few decades of her advancing footfalls, the lazy doors close.

It's early morning in Toronto, so naturally the elevator stops at the very next floor down and Blue Eyes is still kicking the elevator doors and cursing. The hollow of the elevator shaft above us gives each insult a black weight, like thunder directly overhead. A middle-aged woman in a smart pinstripe business suit steps on the elevator. She listens to the storm rage above us and rolls her eyes.

I look away and wonder if we could all be

obliterated by a happy asteroid strike, please. The elevator floor's carpet smells of mildew and chemicals meant to kill mildew. The woman is wearing dirty and scuffed sneakers for her morning commute. When I look up, she looks back at me. Her nose and the corners of her eyes crinkle as if I'm a new and particularly nasty species of swine she has never encountered.

In fairness to me, I'm sure she has met my kind. We're everywhere. The woman's mouth is hanging open as we continue to descend toward the ground floor. The storm recedes but doesn't seem to have less power. Blue Eyes has quite a temper.

I meet my new companion's gaze with a blank look that I hope conveys, "Who? Me?" I smile and shrug. "Somebody ran out of decaf, huh?" I stand there for an Ice Age before the doors slide open and she steams out.

I'm in the street trying to get a taxi to stop when I realize my shirttails are still flapping outside the waist of my jeans and my fly is south of where it ought to be. That's the moment I realize that, all at once, I've lost my socks, my mother and my magic story.

And this is what forever feels like. The feeling of loss is a vast cold bottomless sea.

I get on a plane. The blackness reaches deeper and deeper. I fly across the Atlantic. I am ice.

The loss does not begin to drain away until I arrive at Shannon Airport. Only then does my ocean refill with ugly dread. I get on a bus for Galway. From there, I get on another bus which will finally takes me home to my tiny village of Cuthian.

My father sits by my mother's body. His one good

suit used to be for both weddings and wakes, but the last wedding he attended was my older brother's, years ago. On the phone just last week my parents gently chided me, saying I'd better hurry up and marry that special girl. My father observed that the only use he'll have left for his suit is his funeral.

"Oh, Da! Don't talk like that! I'm settling down soon," I said. "Soon enough."

Her casket stays open. I glimpse her face but the cherub is gone. The corpse's sunken cheeks make her face horse-long. I cannot look so I watch my father watch her. He says she's beautiful but she seems to me merely a bad copy, an approximation made from afar. Ma without animation and laughter is just a familiar stranger. Wherever she is, she is not here.

I made bread with her, kneading the dough, squishing it cool and soft and buttery between chubby fingers and floured palms. We made biscuits, too, each one made perfect, cut with the mold of the mouth of a water glass. Push, twist left, right, lift away, and plop the biscuit dough on a cookie sheet. The kitchen was always warm from the oven. I refilled the firebox and kept it hot. Yeasty smells and pine mixed with vanilla always call me back home. It was safe there. Nothing was asked of me that I could not do.

Da holds her hand a long time. "Her hand is warming under my touch." He smiles at me, lost in memory, lost in history, lost to history. I shudder at this abandon, his quick nullification. He loved her more than he loves himself. I'm astonished. I can't imagine daring it.

SIDEWALKERS

This was originally called The Storyteller. Not much of a title, but in any case, I think the story works out as an exploration of our true motivations, even when we think we're doing good. ~ Chazz

Oz hums some nameless tune stuck in his head. I suspect he's trying to get rid of it by letting it worm into my brain but I'm preoccupied with yesterday's maggots. I balance my journal on one knee. Oz steers for potholes. I ignore him and my loopy writing gets jagged, slashing with each bounce of the van's worn suspension.

About the maggots: A wild one went lame and I offered to look at his leg. He rolled down his sock and maggots slithered out. Why do ugly scenes make you look closer instead of wisely avoiding the baggage of heavy memory? I looked. White maggots boiled through blue flesh. I didn't know what diabetes could do. We dropped the guy at St. Mike's and I threw up behind an ambulance.

43

"I can't believe you, girl!" Oz said. "We're bus drivers and babysitters, not doctors."

"I was worried about the guy."

"Curious, more like it."

"You wouldn't look at the poor guy's leg?"

"I don't even sit on a public toilet. Hell, even at home I hover."

"Thanks for the second great visual of the day."

That was yesterday. So far, today is gloriously maggot-free.

I flip back a few pages, find a sentence I like and read to Oz. "They are nomadic exiles in a concrete hellscape."

He looks at me like I'm one of them. "They're low-functioning people with crashed operating systems."

"Thud."

"You've been riding this bus for like a week."

"Six months."

"Jean, being perpetually uncomfortable isn't cool. It's camping that never ends. Resist romanticizing." He stabs at the radio and cranks the volume.

I turn back to the first page. We net a lot of kids. The first one I pulled in was a ten-year-old girl. She'd made it all the way to Toronto from Saskatoon. I started keeping a journal after I forgot her story. The first line reads, "She had so many lice, it looked like her scalp was moving."

All my tragic fascinations were cute little kids once. They each have a turning point, the moment things really went sour. It's so easy to fall and what tripped you can only be seen clearly when you look back.

Vanilla citizens move with purpose, chugging between debt-slave labor, lattes, and retail assaults.

Oz still thinks I'm his idiot apprentice, so I'm pleased when I spot the next stray before he does. Sitting motionless on broken steps, she's the one with nowhere to go, wearing too many clothes for a warm September afternoon. It's easier to wear too much than to carry too much. Homeless people are closetless people.

"Client!"

Oz glances away from the traffic to scan the sidewalk.

"Right side. Library steps. Lone female." Our job talk is telegraphic, like we're on safari spotting game.

Oz hits the four-way flashers half a block down. Even though Oz is flamboyantly gay, women sometimes get squirrelly if he goes in alone. I leave him to his thermos of coffee. When I look back, he's adjusting the van's big mirror on my side so he can make sure I'm safe while I corral her.

I'm dressed down, slinging my heavy Mary Poppins bag. The only sign I'm official is the identification badge clipped to the strap. We're supposed to flash our IDs but sidewalkers already have a problem with authority. Oz insists I keep the Agent of the State thing low key. His mantra is "They're your crazy Aunt Sadie. Be friendly, not scary, helpful but wary."

I march up. She sits, the eye of a consumer hurricane. Black smudges her temples but it's dirt, not bruises. She's got a round face that could be pretty if she smiled. Bad news: It's ugly to be pretty out here. Good news: She's in her mid-30s, so she's too old for johns on The Stroll. Her eyes are cry-your-eyes-out red. That means either she's smoked lots of weed or she's not numb yet. Cherries accept help more easily because there's no street mom or pimp. Yet.

"I'm Jean Driscoll," I say. Her furtive glances don't meet my eyes. I take it slow. Anxious is okay, better than the thousand-yard stare. The crazy gaze means sexual assault, depression, addiction and concussions.

"My friends call me Jean. You can call me Jean." Yes, it's obvious and manipulative and it usually works. Except this time it doesn't. She gives me a dismissive flick of her head. Maybe that means she's prone to aggression or less desperate than she looks. Maybe she's just smarter than most clients.

I take a breath and take her in. She's sweating through a watch cap and three layers of clothes. It was cold enough last night that she needed at least that much. Citizens in captivity sleep in warm beds. Walls keep the world out. When your bed is a sewer grate, you don't care about what percolates through your skin with the steam.

I move a little closer. Cops stand over the homeless, so we crouch. Our eyes meet at the same level. "Are you feeling okay?"

"Jean?" she says.

"Jean." I turn on The Smile. C'mere, timid deer.

"Blue Jean. Are you blue, Jean?"

"I'm okay. How about you?"

"I'm blue, Jean,"

Is that code for *I'm off my meds*? She smiles a little. Her teeth look good so she's definitely fresh to the street scene. There is still light in her eyes.

I dig into my bag. In the van we carry sandwiches in a cooler called the bait box. We give the bait out freely without asking for information. "Would you like one?" I hold it out like I'm reaching through the bars of a cage. Hunger is a pinched look. She plucks it out of my palm. I help myself, too. It's my third stale ham and cheese today.

I have a clipboard in my bag, but that's for later. The blankets and sleeping bags are in the van, but for those we need information. Some accountant cooks the data into a pie graph to justify city funding and I get to keep wrangling.

She pumps the sandwich down like I'll snatch it back. They all eat like that. I wrap up the other triangle of my sandwich and put it on the step between us and give her an encouraging nod. She snaps it up.

Reading people is much more challenging than reading books. Stories are wrapped up with neat red ribbon. The magic trick to working the street is to do what no one really does — look and listen. For instance, she chews with a click that's probably nothing but might mean an ex broke her jaw once upon a time.

While she eats, she people watches and I do her math. I can see the citizen she was — no visible wounds, piercings or tattoos. The young runaways look haunted and worn. The pros too old to work get harsh and serrated. Sixty-six percent have addictions and sixty-six percent have mental disorders, though it's not necessarily the same sixty-six percent. Her cheeks are clear of tell-a-rotten tale meth scabs that make 20-somethings look like 50-somethings who won't be 60-somethings.

I sit beside her and wait, but not too close. Oz says he keeps smoking just so he can't smell the clients. I've got other reasons. Masks and gloves are ready in my bag if she starts coughing. Before I went on safari, I was a social worker in the shelters. That's where I picked up TB. It was a resistant form, so I ended up taking the tuberculosis drugs for a year with a public health nurse checking on me daily to make sure I was a good girl.

After that, my boss said I was an antisocial social worker and sent me out with Oz to breathe the fresh air mixed liberally with car exhaust. Most homeless tread water or drown. If I catch them fresh, they might swim. Theoretically, I'm useful again.

The throng streams by, eyes straight, salmon with cell phones. To the casual observer we could be friends sharing lunch, but never be casual. Oz Rule. She's got a lumpy hockey bag at her feet. I see no weapons but I watch her hands.

Lots of street people carry something to ward off monsters. Last week three college boys rolled a man of no fixed address by University Stadium. They gave him quite a beating but the cops caught them because the guy, a sometime client I know named Sam NoLastName, successfully knifed one in the spleen. They were freshman business majors on an Orientation Week adventure. They're oriented now, I guess.

She tears at the sandwich cellophane with filthy paws. Fingernails tell stories. Long ragged nails tug at scabs. Fingernails bitten short say anxiety. Yellow fingernails mean nicotine. White spots on the fingernails mean zinc deficiency and not enough nutrition generally. Upside down spoon nails mean lung disease. Her claws are caked in black and her hands and forearms seem to be striped with smudged, sooty camouflage.

"I told you my name. What's yours?" You always give first so you're owed a take. Always get a name first — real name, street name — doesn't matter. Oz Rule. Names make us real, he says.

"May...may not. Are you going to convert me to Allah or Jesus or L. Ron?"

"No, I work for the city."

"Taxes, then?"

"Nope. Just here to help."

"I doubt it's really 'just', but my name is May."

"Pleased to meet you, May."

"Uh-huh."

Another silence stretches out so long I wonder if I'm giving her line too much play. Then she says, "Look at them. They have no idea." A few clothes horses click by in spike heels, eyes fixed on the horizon, always knowing what comes next. The future is iPhone-scheduled.

I study her profile. She feels my stare and whips her neck to look at me full on. Her thin pale lips are a hard line. Her eyes harbour secrets. Her gaze strips me of mine.

"You have no idea, either. I see things the way they really are, Jean."

"How's that?"

She bends forward and reaches into the hockey bag. It's full of paper. I peer closer and see art tablets and napkins and newspapers. Every sheet is covered with drawings in charcoal. "You need to know everything." She hands me a tablet.

Her drawings capture people. Some of the sketches are very detailed. Others are minimalist swoops of a sure hand exposing the bare bones of a scene. Some are crude doodles. She doesn't seem to have one style but as I flip through the pages I see a unifying theme: Each drawing is an ending.

A man at a desk looks like he's trying to phone for help but he's clawing at his throat. The bridge of his nose bleeds.

In a corner of the same page, a few deft lines suggest the shape of a baby in an incubator. Empty eyes stare up to forever.

Flip.

A withered old woman trapped in a hospital bed goggles horrified as a little old man brings her tea. His expression is serene. Only she sees the centipedes that crawl over his shirt and face and into the cup and saucer he holds out to her.

Flip.

A cartoon of a flying iron would look amusing except that it's flying into the face of a sleeping woman.

Flip.

Surrounded by books, the naked old man is dead in a chair. Beside him stands his starving, salivating dog, eyeing a limp arm with longing.

There are hundreds more grim drawings. My hand shakes as I return her pad.

"Three months ago I was a children's librarian," May says. "One morning, the kids walked in and I'd covered every wall with the truth."

I imagine young mothers rushing to cover their children's faces with hot palms, wrenching their heads away from the crazy librarian's mural of horrors.

"It's not my fault. There's a voice behind my eyes. It tells me who to kill next."

I swallow hard. "Kill?"

"Of *course*. I do it with the *drawings*. I don't kill them all. Some I just torture and break."

Is that pride or resignation?

"It's God's fault, you know. It was bored so It created us. That's why you're so godlike, Jean Blue Jean, God's Drama Queen. It wants to hear everybody's awful story, too. Stories need conflict. We're it. God's a kid with a magnifying glass and an ant farm." She taps her tablet. "I'm the magnifying glass."

We're not supposed to play into their delusions, but she's sucked me in. "So God and the Devil are the same thing?"

"Adorable, Jean Blue Jean! You're simply divine!"

"But..." I struggle. "Things aren't that bad. Miracles happen every day." The way it comes out, even I don't believe it.

"Try babbling those platitudes at the pediatric burn unit." Her laughter is a grinding cackle. She struggles up under the weight of her load of paper. I watch her sway away.

I wait for better answers than what keeps coming up. She's got books of awful drawings. I've use a journal to keep the horrors fresh. Shame burns. Now I'm the one staring at the ground.

"Whatever she said, I'll remind you that seventy-five percent of homeless women are crazy." Oz crouches in front of me, his eyes level with mine. His smile looks sincere. "She was crazy, but not all she said was untrue. She basically called me a ghoul."

"Don't let her stick her finger up your nose."

"Oz. Am I a good person?"

He looks like he's doing long division in his head.

"I suck. The Great and Powerful Oz has spoken without even speaking. Should I pay no attention to the little man who's out of the closet but behind the curtain?"

He straightens and takes a long drag on his cigarette. I'm suddenly smaller, like I'm one of them. He lets out a slow plume of smoke. "There are a million stories in the naked city. Only one of them is about you."

"I'm a voyeur."

"I know." He shrugs.

I don't like him at all.

"You've got a white knight complex, sure."

"You don't?"

"Nah. It's a job. Maybe I was like that at first, but sainthood gets beaten out of you."

"You — "

"You talk about them like they're animals, Jean. *You* call each shift a safari. *You* call the sandwich cooler the bait box. You think it's clever, but no one wants to ride with you."

I start to cry and he looks away.

"You're doing the job. If you think it matters why, then don't get back in the van. Or take the subway home. It's a block over. If it's actions that matter, get in the van. There's a few thousand people headed for the shelters tonight and it'll be dark soon."

He steams off. He doesn't look back. Should I get up before Oz pulls away? I'm frozen and I've only got seconds to decide.

He doesn't wait. I'm just about to rise and run after him when I notice May left a napkin behind. It's a deft picture of Oz in the van's driver's seat hanging upside down by his seatbelt. He's alive, but broken.

I dig a blue pen out of my Mary Poppins bag. I sketch in a wound in his neck. It doesn't take long at all and I can draw much better than I ever remember doing. I add a fall of blood from his throat so it looks like the edge of the seatbelt opened him. The whimsy tugs the corners of my mouth up as I make his facial features more surprised.

Down the street by the bridge, a crash and the sound wrenching of metal rises and shrieks.

I don't think that voice in my head belongs to God.

THE EXPRESS

After my story, *End of the Line*, got so much
publicity from *The Toronto Star*, I received a
snarly note from a hypnotist complaining
that hypnotism couldn't make anyone do
something they didn't want to do. I explained
that *End of the Line* isn't about hypnotism.
It's magic. His note annoyed me enough that
I decided to write *The Express* to give him
something to really complain about.
However, I think I got around his objection
with some elegance.   And yes, Paul is the
same character from *The Fortune Teller*, this
time in a battle of wills with a different
iteration of Dr. Circe Papua. I love to play
with Circe, so think of this as a rematch in
another dimension.
    ~ Chazz

He arrived late and shiny with sweat, breathing as
if the air was too thick and had to be pushed in and
out with effort. I apologized about the elevator. He
filled the doorway so completely that the waiting

room darkened. He looked down at me and seemed to be waiting for me to invite him in. I thought of the rule for vampires, about needing a specific invitation before they're allowed to come in and kill you. That made a kind of sense later.

"Paul?"

He lifted his chin at me in a way which was more of a go-ahead motion than an acknowledgement of my question. I gave him the intake forms and he grunted. When I gave him the pen, he held it like a hammer. His hands were red and rough with long, filthy nails. I thought of claws on something that pawed through dirt to catch its food.

I don't know if it was that or the smell that came off him that was setting off alarms. A clammy odor of sweat hung about him. He wore a dress shirt, but jeans instead of a suit. His pants cuffs were rolled up, not hemmed. My clients are usually in power suits or power pantsuits. I was already thinking he wouldn't be a good fit for my practice and this would probably be a one-off looky-lou session. We'd barely met and I was already preparing the brush off. I'd do the "Sorry, so busy, let me refer you to a colleague I hate who specializes in your particular hang-up," whatever kink, phobia or antisocial deviation it turned out to be.

I retreated to my office to give him time to fill out the form, refilled the carafe with fresh decaf and set it on the small table by my chair. He obviously wasn't a talker. I'd have to do all the heavy lifting for the first twenty minutes of the session to draw him out. If that didn't work, the rest of our fifty-five minutes would be spent in a staring contest with me counting the little diamond patterns in the wallpaper behind his head while I waited for him to break.

There was something else about this man that stuck with me. His eyes had the empty look of the homeless people you try to avoid as you drop change in their palms. The surprising thing was the other smell he gave off. I smelled wood, cedar maybe. All my patients are a bunch of neurotics and stockbrokers who work within walking distance of my office. They tell their secretaries they're taking a long lunch and come here instead. A couple are in the building and occasionally I run into them in the elevator — when it's working — and they pretend I'm a stranger instead of someone who knows things about them they don't want their spouses to know.

I wondered who referred the guy. One of my regulars freaked out that he couldn't afford the kitchen reno his wife insists they need. I guessed this guy was their carpenter, or probably a carpenter's assistant. He might be good with his hands — with his communication skills he had better be — but he didn't look bright enough to handle measurements.

I had just opened my day planner to see who was scheduled that afternoon when I heard the floorboards creak by the office door. I don't know how long he had been standing there. "Uh...done already, Paul?"

"Done."

"Well, you're quick."

"Done."

He smirked as he handed me the intake forms. They were blank. This was new to me and I didn't know quite what to say. I tried to keep my face blank as well. When dealing with passive aggression, it's essential to strike a tone that's neutral but firm. I

56

was still wondering how to match up the neutral words with the firm tone when he took over.

"Let's talk first."

"Usually it works the other way around. I get your information and — "

"Usually. Not today. People come in here and they spill their guts to you and they don't know anything about you. That's not right. I've got to know who I'm talking to," he said. He sat down heavily in the recliner opposite me, apparently waiting for me to audition. We'd begun a dance but were listening to two different pieces of music.

"Therapists don't talk about themselves because the session is supposed to be about you."

He looked around my office. "Cozy spot you've got here. I thought there'd be a couch."

"That's a Freudian thing. If I can't meet your expectations, I'd be glad to refer you to a Freudian psychiatrist."

"Well, listen to you. You're anxious to get rid of me, aren't you?"

I held the intake form out to him. "I need this to be filled out before we can begin anything."

"Slow down, doctor," he said. "You're used to people doing what you tell them to do. You're sounding defensive."

I had underestimated him because of his appearance. I tried to appear unfazed. "Well, you got me there," I said with a big smile smeared across my face. "I *am* used to people listening to me. I'm accustomed to new patients filling out the forms I require."

"You're not used to trying out."

"I reject the premise. You made the appointment.

You must have been referred by someone. Who sent you to me?"

He ignored my question with a dismissive wave. "What are your professional qualifications?"

"I've been a psychiatrist for almost ten years." He stared at me with hard eyes. I picked a spot on the wallpaper just behind his head and plunged on. "I graduated magna cum laude. I interned in one of the best hospitals in the country."

"Specialty?"

"I've done extensive work with hypnotherapy and PTSD and contributed to a textbook on the subject. PTSD is — "

"Post Traumatic Stress Disorder."

"Right," I said. I snuck a look away from the spot of wallpaper. He was still glaring, so back to the wallpaper.

"So you're considered an expert on PTSD?"

"Yes, though I've moved away from that and don't deal with it much anymore."

"Why is that?"

I debated then about how much of myself I wanted to reveal. The short answer was nothing, but I had dealt with aggressive people and usually if you gave them a little that made you more human, they'd relax and let the walls come down. "I did a lot of it after 9/11 and burned out on the subject."

"So you don't work with people with those sorts of problems anymore?"

"Is that why you've come to see me, Paul? Have you gone through a bad time you want to put behind you?"

For the first time I thought I saw a hint of a smile

at the corner of his mouth. "I'm going through something I don't want to deal with."

I gave him space and silence, hoping to draw him out or reel him in. Instead he said, "So you aren't dealing with PTSD anymore as an expert?" He said "expert" like it meant something else, something with a lot of legs that crawls away fast when you turn on the light.

"Uh, just one thing. I'm testifying — " Then I knew who he must be. My head was suddenly hot and I couldn't get my breath.

"Testifying," he said.

"If I say anything more about myself I might have to blush." My laugh sounded false.

"Uh-huh," he said.

"Your turn, Mr. Paul...?"

"You aren't that good an actress, Dr. Padua. You know who I am."

"I suspect I do," I replied, trying to keep my tone even. "What I don't know is why you're here. From what I hear, you do need a psychiatrist, but since I'm counselling your victim. it's not appropriate for you to be here." I looked right into his eyes then, determined not to look away. I was suddenly sure that if I looked away, what happened to Susan might happen to me.

"Well, smell you, all grown up and staring me down." He smiled, but there wasn't anything amused or kind or good to be found there.

I had never seen a cruel smile till that moment. That's when I knew I had to get back in the saddle. So far I was the cow not the cowgirl. If I didn't want to end up like Susan, I had to take control. I brought my left index finger and my left thumb together and forced myself to breathe deeper and slower. I let myself close my eyes. It was dangerous to take my eyes off him, but I needed to focus. The meditation method was a long-practiced cue and my heart rate began to come down almost immediately.

His face was an inch from mine when I opened my eyes. I felt his hot breath on my nose. His face was some angry contortion of a human face. He might have been looking down my blouse in the few moments my eyes were closed. He might have been thinking about biting off my nose. He'd done that before. An old Intro Psych axiom burbled up: The best predictor of future behavior is past behavior.

But now I wasn't worried about those possibilities. He saw it in my eyes and pulled back. I wasn't the tiny woman about to be tortured anymore. I was something new he hadn't encountered. "Sit down, Paul," I said.

"Hell, no — "

"Sit, Paul. It's only a fifty-minute hour and you are wasting time."

At that, he did laugh. "You are — "

"You came for a reason, but not the reason you think. You came to me for help and I am going to give it to you. We are only going to meet this once so let me tell you what you really want. You're going to feel much better when we are done, I promise you."

He sat.

"Good. You're already making progress."

"I hear you selling but that doesn't mean I'm buying."

"You didn't sit to listen because you're curious, though that is part of it. You sat down because what you really want is peace. You want someone to hear you."

"What makes you say that?" he said. It was a challenge, but I'm through the door and into dialogue. He's mine. He just doesn't know it.

"I know you want peace and you want to be heard because that is all anyone wants. Everyone who comes to see me has a handful of issues they deal with but underneath that is all they really want."

"And you tell them that and mama makes it all better?"

More mocking, but still my breath is deep and my heart rate is steady and slow. "No, they tell me their stories and they tell me about their feelings and I let them talk and talk and talk until they figure it all out for themselves."

"Quite a job you got going on here for a hundred bucks an hour. You just sit there while the suckers do all the work."

"You are jealous because you did not think to become a shrink. Here is the deal, Paul. I am going to give you the peace you are looking for. Then you will leave. Then we are done."

"You just told me you're a fake. What makes you think you can do anything for me? Why should I trust a thing you say?"

"I am a fraud, Paul, but I am not a fake. I know things."

"Sure, sure," he said. "Now shut up and I'll tell you —"

"You came here to intimidate me. You think I can get Susan not to testify against you. She has been hiding since you posted bail and she does not have any family. You saw my name on the court documents when you talked to your lawyer, somewhere with the victim impact statement, I suppose."

"Okay, okay," Paul replied. "That doesn't tell me you've got anything I want besides your cooperation. I want to find Susan. I have to talk to her before this thing gets out of hand."

"What you really mean is before you go to jail."

His face boiled red and I thought he was going to launch out of his chair and fall on me with his yellow teeth and ragged claws.

"Paul. You had a good question. Let me answer it." His muscles were still tensed but he hesitated. I had to be very careful and very good now. "Your mother was critical and distant and you hate being ignored. Your father is dead, absent from your childhood or an apathetic wimp your mother controlled. You want to be in control. You deserve to be in control. The world does not allow you to be in control. The world wants to control you."

He looked at me and for the first time looked down at the rug. He sat back a little in his chair. Direct hit.

"So you are stressed," I said. "We are all under stress but you never learned how to handle it. Instead of handling it correctly, you smoke and drink too much. You wanted to feel you were in control so you tried to mellow out before you came up here with a cigarette. Your nerves are jangling right now and you would love a cigarette. I can smell the nicotine coming out of your pores with the sweat. You eat a lot of sugar to make yourself feel good and it works for a few minutes and then you feel like crap so you have more sugar and feeling like crap all the time feels normal now. You sleep badly and you are underemployed. You are a hamster who can't get off a wheel. You came here to scare me, maybe even hurt me. You will not."

He laughed. "Why the hell not?"

"Because you are not an animal. You are a person who needs help and compassion and understanding. You will not hurt me because you know I am right about all these things. If you were going to hurt me, you would have done it by now. You have lost momentum. You had to get your nerve up and now all the steam is gone and you are cooling off."

"I could hurt you, make you tell me — "

"And have more charges against you? I think you are smarter than that. You are here because you want to stay out of jail. If I am assaulted or dead, how long will it be before the police knock on your door?"

There was a long silence. I waited for it. And waited.

"So...what are you selling me?"

"A way out of this. Free."

"How?"

"It starts with slowing your breath. We have to convince your nervous system you are not running from a bear all the time."

We had twenty minutes before my next session. It was just enough time. I showed him the finger cue and as he brought his thumb and forefinger together I knew for certain I had him. In another three minutes his neck muscles relaxed and his head came forward to his chest. I watched the pulse in his neck slow to seventy, then sixty. I talked him down, his nervous system slowed and his mind opened up. Any stage hypnotist can make susceptible people jump around and pretend they are chickens. The posthypnotic suggestion I had in mind was much easier than that.

The police showed up at my door eventually, of course. Once they figured out who the guy in the elevator shaft was, someone made the connection to me. The detective was a tall, handsome man who accepted my offer of tea and wriggled his bulk into my office chair to get comfortable before he took out his notebook.

I told him what Paul had done to Susan. I told him I thought Paul was going to hurt me and kill his ex-wife. I told him I didn't feel bad at all when I heard the scream fade all the way down the 12-storey shaft. I smiled then. I couldn't help myself.

His brow furrowed and he studied my face. "Didja push him?"

"Not exactly."

"What does that mean?"

"I told him to sit and I gave him a suggestion."

"Doctor, my understanding of hypnosis is you can't get someone to do something they wouldn't do anyway."

"It's a simple trick of the mind, Detective," I said. "I just told him to take the elevator to his new life and that's what he thought he was doing, at least until he started falling. I suppose he had a moment to think about it. The maintenance people left that yellow warning tape up to tell people to take the stairs while they went for parts."

"I find your tone disturbing, doctor."

"I don't know why. It was self-defense. Under similar circumstances, *you'd* have shot him."

"Maybe."

"You wouldn't say maybe if you saw Susan.

Despite our medical advances, prosthetic noses look awfully fake. A clown nose would be more aesthetically pleasing."

The detective stood and gave me a hard look. "I read the report on his ex-wife before I came over here. The guy was an animal who needed to be put down. However, the time you saved the court and the money you saved the taxpayers will have to go to your court case now." He fished out handcuffs. "I'm sorry. I really don't want to do this but — "

"Do you mean that?"

"What?"

"Do you mean you really *want* to let me go?"

He didn't hesitate. "Of course, but — "

"Then please *do* sit down, Detective. I want to show you a neat trick."

THE CLAWED BATHTUB

Several people refuse to speak to me because of this story. I don't mean to make anyone nervous. It's fiction and I'm a sweet guy.
Cross my heart and hope they die. ~ Chazz

His wet clothes plaster his body, dark against his cold, pale skin. His red plaid shirt and soaked jeans give you a better grip when you pull him out of the big bathtub. He seems heavier than he really is, as if he's a baby who, even in sleep, resists you. Though the water washes it away, the man's mouth still tastes of peanut butter.

When your cheeks blow out but no air goes in, you realize you are rushing and sloppy. The smell makes you nauseous but you pinch his nose and wrench his head back to open his airway.

You take a breath and put your mouth on his and blow. Even as you force oxygen into his lungs, you strain your peripheral vision to see if his chest rises with your effort. It does, but slower than seems right.

66

Seven breaths later, maybe ten, you're cursing yourself because you thought you were in better shape than this. You thought it would be like blowing up a balloon but instead you're inflating a water bottle like the strongman in an old-time circus sideshow.

You blow twice more and you know by the pulse in your ear you're going to have to slow down. Panic kills. Work instead. They taught you no battle plan survives engagement with the enemy. You give him five more steady breaths. How much of your air is worming its way up into his brain? How much is enough?

You pause for a moment to check for a pulse at his wrist. They taught you not to use your thumb so you don't mistake your pulse for that of the drowning victim. That sounded silly then, but now, with your own heart cranking hard, you understand.

Sweat and salt run into your eyes and you've lost track of how long you've been trying to save him. Your legs tingle a warning so you shift your weight for relief, praying your legs do not fall asleep. Your heels are jammed against the bathroom wall. As you bend to give him another few breaths, you feel the bristles of your brush cut against the tub.

The hard tile makes your kneecaps ache. There's no bathmat to put under your knees. Who doesn't own a bathmat? Oh, yeah. Mr. Peanut Butter Sandwiches. The knee pain is your own fault. You should have thrown down a towel first. It's a small detail, but you need endurance to make him live again.

Tick! Tick! Tick!

Time is life, a small thing that slips and scurries

out of your grasp. You can't keep flogging him back to life much longer. Sweat runs down your spine like ants. It is so hot in this small room. You could get up and open the bathroom door or smash the small frosted window to let in fresh air, but you do not dare break your rhythm.

His lips are blue. The rest of him looks washed out, as if the water has diluted him. You almost raise your head to check the bottom of the tub. Are bright Crayola colors even now draining away to some far off place? Is whatever makes up his essence circling the drain?

You pass another few breaths into his lungs and rest your head on his chest to listen. Time stretches out. Have you finally lost him?

You can't accept that. You soldier on.

You're surprised by a sickening couple of snaps and a sinking, boggy feeling as something gives way in his chest. Just as they taught, you ignore the broken ribs and keep the steady compressions, reminding his heart it should wake up and get on with it. Beating. At least with the ribs broken at the sternum, you don't have to work so hard to compress his heart.

Please...oh...please.

Your movements are smooth and unhurried as you rock forward and back, the weight of your torso pushing down through straight arms. You are a steel clock. This is easier than trying to push air into his dying lungs — especially since the ribs snapped — but the respite is too brief.

Your breaths are gasps.

You don't have the wind to do the count aloud so you run the numbers silently. For a moment, the

weakness is waved away and all you hear, feel, see
and do is the count.

You keep alternating between pushing his chest to
the count and squeezing air from your lungs to his.

How long is too long to bother anymore? You can't
feel your legs and that lightheaded feeling says you
better just breathe for yourself. The exhaustion
comes back in full and you're losing count again.

Is this it? Heavy disappointment and failure begin
to replace that full, stopped-up feeling of frustration.
You rest your head on his chest again.

And wait.

Please.

Oh.

Please.

Wait.

And give up.

* * *

Almost.

There it is. Yes! His heart is starting up again,
though there is a long pause between the lub and the
dub. That stillness must be the sound of reluctance.
That's the fourth time his heart has stopped in the
last fifty minutes. It took much longer to get it
started again this time. It came back easier the first
couple times. Next time will be the last. That's
almost okay. You're so tired from the grinding effort
of keeping him alive.

You put your ear by his mouth to listen for him
moving air on his own. You watch for the rise and
fall of his chest and, seeing none, give him another

quick breath. This time the water in his stomach does rise up and somehow you feel the lurch shuddering up through his body in a wave. You get out of the way as he spews bathwater.

You carefully turn him on his side so he doesn't choke and the water keeps coming in a gush. The spasms bend his body back and forth in a rigid, grotesque dance. Interesting.

Your shoulders relax and a smile slowly crawls across your mouth. "Finally," you say aloud. The sound of your voice in the small room startles you. It's the first word you've said since entering the bathroom. He's still sputtering and disoriented. You spit into the bathtub and hope you can find some mouthwash in the medicine cabinet.

Still on your knees, you press into his back, rolling him farther on his side to give him time to swim back up from wherever he was. His lungs must be burning. You give him a little recovery time. He gasps and sputters. Through your kneecaps and hands you feel his tortured struggle to push out water and bring in air.

He's a fish yanked out of the murk, flopping on a dock.

Triumph pulls and stretches you out, making you feel physically, spiritually bigger. Elation bubbles up through your cells. You want to laugh and sing. There's a soaring feeling in your chest, like your heart is expanding and wants to pull you up and off your feet.

He comes back to life.

You could fly.

You look around the bathroom. A couple of ragged-edged towels hang on the back of the bathroom door. They were probably once pure white, but with repeated washings they have faded and pilled. Though the tile is yellow old, the bathroom is very clean, even in the corners. On a rack along the wall behind you hang blue towels embroidered with the word "Guests." They look like they have never touched wet skin.

Behind sickly sweet peanut butter, sweat and the sour stomach acids in his long greasy hair, another smell is lurking. You can't quite identify its component parts, though you guess there might be lavender, bleach and some kind of lemon cleaner in the mix. That unquantifiable, other smell tells you the man must live with his elderly mother. That's old lady aroma in your nostrils.

A long-unused brain cell awakens. A dormant synapse triggers. You're surprised by something you thought was lost. You see your grandmother in her house on the Big Island. You're looking up at her. She smiles as she washes your hands in a grey tin washtub. And there's that same smell. Funny to think that you would have anything remotely in common with the man on the bathroom floor.

Your pulse begins pounding again in your left ear. There are little bones in the inner ear called the hammer and anvil, but to you it really does sound like iron striking iron. Though your heart slows, this throb is steady and grows louder. It's a form of tinnitus. Most people with the disorder get a ringing, whining or whistling sound. Some people hear loud sirens day and night until it drives them to suicide.

You've heard this pounding in your ear since that bright morning when a bomb knocked you off your feet. First there was a flash of white followed immediately by blackness that enveloped the world. When you opened your eyes, the sun shone through a cloud of dust that hung still like a photograph of a windstorm in the desert. The dark figure of a medic leaned over you. His face was stretched long and urgent, shouting. You searched his face for meaning. He was not screaming in pain. He was trying to tell you that you'd be okay, you decided.

As if anyone knows anything about anyone by looking.

The ringing went away and your hearing came back, but the pulse in your left ear, iron pounding iron, remained. It's like a time bomb ticking down. Each strike of that inner clock is almost painful. Each tick gets you closer to that blackness that swallowed the world when the bomb went off. When you start thinking like this, it is time to move and get out of your head.

The man's gasping and sputtering subsides. He turns his head away to place his forehead on the cool, wet tile — as if he's trying to gather strength. They taught you that if you find yourself in a fair fight, you have not planned properly. You drive your left knee hard between his shoulder blades. He gasps in pain, but he's past surprise.

This is the last chance. "Remember anything?"

The man is quiet, afraid he will be punished for his silence but stalling for time, nonetheless.

"I asked you a question," you say. You keep your tone flat, like this isn't urgent. Like you're a machine. You could do this forever.

"I remember..." He gasps and begins to cry again.

"Yes?"

"I couldn't get away," he says weakly. His hands

are free and they flutter to the shower curtain. He pulls it toward him like a blanket.

Back in the second round of resuscitation, he pulled the curtain down into the tub with him as he flailed. He hit his head on the side of the tub as he went down. With his heart working again, the raw swelling on his forehead is powering up, leaking blood into his left eye. He blinks the blood away as priorities rearrange themselves in slow motion behind near-dead eyes.

"Did you see the tunnel? Something?" Your tone is casual and curious, not angry.

Almost imperceptibly, he shakes his head.

"I thought so."

You yank him upright. He's not up to fighting. You used thick plastic zip ties on his ankles. There's no running away. He asked what you planned, but you could tell he didn't want to know. In the first round, you knelt on his head as the old claw-foot tub slowly filled with hot water. The tub's deep and it took some time to fill. The water heater is empty now so the tap only runs cold now.

He lasted much longer than you thought he might. This sort of thing isn't covered in the regular army manual. This is from *another* army manual.

He asks you in a rasp to kill him and be done with it, once and forever. The heavier his body gets, the lighter you feel. Some unnamed energy is passing from him to you. Is this life energy you feel, or just adrenaline? Is what was his now yours or is that just the chemical echo of physical domination pulsing through your veins?

He fades away this time. You can't revive him anymore.

When you're done, you leave him face down in the bathtub. He never once asked you why. That's good. He knew what he did. Maybe you saved him after all. Maybe baptism works.

It's pretty slick in here now, what with all the playful splashing. You wipe yourself dry with the blue guest towels and leave them on the floor so the old lady won't slip on the wet tile when she comes in and discovers Junior.

This is the war at home. They say it's all for a flag and only by necessity. You know better. Soldiers kill and die for each other and for the tribe. It is as it always was.

But when the tribe is done with you, what then?

With each baptism, you are born again. You are lost and, through death and resurrection, you find yourself strong — a warrior hero once more. The difference between here and there, hero and villain, is a hundred imaginary lines dividing the earth. Maps are for smug men defining nature by creating kingdoms. You know it is nature that defines Man.

For the next one, you should try baptism by fire. Where are you going to find a couple of fire extinguishers at this time of night?

You look up. The stars look as bright and cold as ever. The sky is oblivious to your night travels, but your head is clear. There is a light feeling over your heart that could pull you up into the night. You can barely hear the pulse in your ear. You begin to sing *Amazing Grace* and the song's haunting beauty is unsoiled by the strike of iron on iron.

POETRY BREAK

***I mostly only write poetry when my
mother dies. ~ Chazz***

Last One Out
120 pounds...
The lymphoma took over her body,
110...
replacing her with each tendril of metastasis.
102...
She slipped in and out
98...
through drugs and exhaustion.
95...
She knew it was coming.
90...
Two days before dying she recited
"Under the spreading chestnut tree the village
smithy stands..."
87...
She saw the bullet coming at her in slow motion.
85...
And three seconds before her light went out,

she waved goodbye
and was gone.
At age 82 she weighed 82 pounds.
Did she really wave goodbye
or flick a switch
to welcome the darkness?

Been Away Burying Mom
It took awhile.
We dug her deep.
She's on her way! said Dad.
I was baffled.
It's a short trip.
Just six feet.

THE DANGEROUS KIND

As I wrote this novella, I combined two small towns I know to get the right sense of place. My home town in Nova Scotia pretty much emptied out of my generation because there was nothing for us there. It appears to be limping along, but given how many houses stand empty and for sale, the village is a future ghost town. I'm still making new things out of old ghosts. ~ Chazz

As long as I can remember, I wanted to get away. I grew up in a speck of a town so small men still stop and remove their baseball caps when a funeral procession drives by. Everyone knows each other. They treat that as if it's a virtue, as if proximity's friction is warmth. Dad would have helped me escape Poeticule Bay, but the edger at the mill pulled him in by his wedding ring.

My brother Jason rambled through the eulogy. "I know Dad di'nt ever have so much — most of us have nothing, so that's alright. But you can feel good

77

knowin' Darren Kind made do with as little as what God gave him. That's what a man is." He talked as if he and Dad were best buds.

We watched Dad's coffin sink into the ground beside Mom's grave. We cried. The people from town — Dad's people — watched us. As the coffin disappeared, Jason wheeled on me so fast I expected him to swing at me. Instead, he wrapped his arms around me and squeezed. I went stiff.

His Jim Beam breath mixed with maple syrup from this morning's pancakes. "Don't worry. Big brother's your new boss man." That morning's pancake charged up my tight throat but I swallowed and pushed it back down. While Jason shook hands with Dad's friends, I fled. I got behind the truck before I puked. If they'd seen, they wouldn't think worse of me, but they'd never shut up about it, either.

Dad told me once he felt like a spy at the mill. "It's loud, Joey. Boy, it's loud. Those friggin' saws just whine. I nod to the boss. I smile as I pass the other working stiffs." He cracked open another beer even though he was nodding off, too sleepy to finish his drink but driven to start another. "I cut the wood and nobody bothers me. While they're all bullshitting over their lunch, I go out in the yard and smell the cedar and pine. All those bullshitters.... They'll never know."

At the funeral they talked about Dad like best friends talk, like they really knew him. "Always a smile," somebody said. The big ear protectors Dad always wore made that smile possible. Most of the guys from the mill were neither smart nor kind. I couldn't remember any of them ever coming to the house.

The father I knew just made do at the mill Monday to Saturday noon, forty-eight weeks a year: two weeks off for fishing in July, two weeks clear for ice fishing over Christmas. His Saturday afternoon smiles were the real thing. He drank Coal Porter through the weekend and fell asleep in front of the TV. The deeper he got into the weekend, the surlier he got. By Sunday night, he'd be barking at Jason and me. I didn't get mad at Dad like Jason did. I knew Dad wasn't really mad at us. He was mad at Monday morning.

Last New Year's Eve, I told him we should move to the city. I was thinking New York, of course, but any city would do. "I've got the house and your mother's grave to tend," he said. "And Jason will do better here than with people from away." Jason worked as an electrician's assistant but told everyone he was an apprentice.

We watched the ball drop in Times Square. "Jesus, look at all those people. Imagine being in the middle of all that, huh?" he said.

"We don't have to imagine, Dad," I said.

He shrugged. "I can see it from right here and not freeze." He saw my expression. "Imagination is a curse for a fella like me, Joey." He looked at the beer in his fist and added, just above a whisper, "But you'll get there someday."

In my dream city, no one knows my name. If they ask, I tell them my name is Joe and it sticks. In real life, people nod and a minute later, they call me Joey again. It is as if I died at age eight and will never get older. The roots are too tight in Poeticule Bay. They will not let anything new grow. If you know somebody since they were in diapers, you own them. I still have another two years of school. Poeticule Bay does not have a bookstore. The drugstore has a dusty paperback rack. Summer people buy picture books full of shots of lighthouses and lobster traps at the B&B. A library bus wanders our way a couple of times a month. I dream of working in a Starbucks in a bookstore. My life will start, I'm sure, when I head down the highway. When I finally escape from here, I'm never coming back.

"We could at least visit New York. It's like, eight hours!"

"Let's not and say we did." Dad took a swig and eased his recliner back. The greatest city on earth waited less than a day's drive away. Dad never saw it.

Dougie Mac, Dad's boss, told us a settlement was coming. "The insurance company's stalling. You boys sit tight. The mill will do right by you."

Jason had big plans for the money. "We could fix this place up. There'd be enough for a new porch out back and a hot tub. This place could be party central."

"And I could clean it!" I say. My teeth hurt from the gritting.

"Got any girls in your class who wouldn't mind a little weed and a naked whirl?" he asked. He didn't look at me when he said it, trying and failing to sound casual and only half-joking.

Hanging out at home with Jason was no fun so I escaped to school. Everybody looked at me with sad eyes and even a couple of guys I thought were assholes patted me on the back and said they were sorry. Everybody got quiet, like having me around made them picture my father getting pulled into the whirling blades. People always say they are sorry when someone dies which, of course, doesn't make sense. They didn't kill him. Staying at the mill even though he hated it killed him. For that, I will always blame him a little. Someday I'll be around strangers who don't know what happened and they'll ask about my father. "Suicide," I'll tell them. And maybe it's true. I knew about the blankness behind his smiles.

Every day after school I headed straight home, washed the dishes, made my bed and Jason's, too. Jason didn't like my cooking — I only know how to do spaghetti, hot dogs and stuff that comes in cans — so after a couple of days we switched to TV dinners. He held the remote in his big fist and even took it with him to the bathroom so I couldn't change the channel from ESPN. He didn't have to do that. After he took it into the bathroom with him once, I wouldn't touch it.

I didn't ask how much insurance money I'd be due. Dad started at the mill before I was born so the named beneficiaries were my mother and Jason. Mom's dead. Dad did not have anything besides the insurance money, the house and half the truck. Dad left no will, so Jason would control the money the same way he held onto the remote.

A couple of weeks after the funeral, Jason lost his job. First, he said, "Laid off" and blamed Obama's economy. Eventually he admitted the electrician, Ian Drury, fired him.

"Imagine that," Jason said. "Firing me with Dad not cold in the ground yet? Should be a statute of moratorium of firin' a guy who's just buried his dad."

I heard what really happened through Big June Iverson from homeroom as she entertained a circle of my classmates over lunch break. Her father works at the mill and she spread the story, mimicking Dougie Mac's lisp dead on and everything. June said Dougie Mac caught Jason drunk, burning hot rubber circles into the mill's parking lot with Drury's company van. He ran out yelling, "Jason, stop! You're going to make those tires as bald as me! Stop! Stop!"

Even I laughed, along with everyone else, as June jumped up and down (her huge breasts thumping up and down, too) as she waved her stovepipe fatty-floppy arms in the air and shouted, "*Thtop! Thtop!*" My brother peeled out, fishtailed out the front gate and almost lost it to the ditch in the turn down the hill. Dougie called Drury and said he'd call the police ("the *poleethe*", June said) if he ever saw Jason drunk driving again in the mill's lot.

Jason was home all the time after that.

By noon each day, Jason washed his worries away. He chugged the first couple of bottles of Porter to rush to the buzz before slowing down for the hard drinking. "I know what I'm doing behind the wheel. The boss man worries too much about how I drive. That's what he's like."

Jason's best friends since high school, Dick Glass and Rich Robishaw, were a couple of oddjobbers who hung out at the fire hall. "Those boys got a little too much of what the cat licks his ass with," Dad used to say. "The way they go on, their tongues must hinge in the middle."

Dick and Rich told another version of the story which, they thought, cast my brother in better light. The new story was that Jason had marked up the mill parking lot out of grief, pumped the finger at

Dougie on the way out and almost rammed into a family van from out of town as he sped through the gate. Jason laughed it all off and his buddies treated him like a hero.

Big June's version hadn't included anything about almost killing out-of-towners and she made it sound like Jason peeled out in a panic instead of defiance. Her version was probably closer to the truth and better told, what with Dougie Mac's lisping and all. The bit about Jason giving Dougie Mac the finger had the ring of truth to it, though. Whatever happened, there was no end to the speculation and embellishment all over town.

Not long after that, Jason looked in the fridge and counted beers — six left. He drained the last of the coffee into his mug and waggled the pot at me.

"I'll make more in a minute."

"It's always in a minute with you." He gave me his most tragic, mocking sigh. "I talked to Dougie Mac again about the insurance money. It's all wait, wait, wait with him, too. And the unemployment check isn't much more than beer money, you know."

"Less beer equals more money," I suggested.

Jason glowered at me. I stared at my cereal.

"You don't think Dougie could get our check for himself somehow, do you?" he asked. "Like maybe he's blowing us off while he's planning a trip to Disney or something? It's been months since Dad died. If he's stalling us while he's plannin' something for my money, I'll kill him."

I noticed he said 'my' money instead of 'ours', but let it pass. Instead, I told him we were getting down to the bottom of the freezer on food. "We'll be down to ice chips soon."

Jason nodded and paced as he sipped the black coffee. He was excited, which made me nervous. "We're goin' huntin'," he said finally.

My head came up. "For Dougie?"

"No, numbnuts. He says the insurance money is all about red tape and channels and shit. Fine. He wants time to make our payday happen? That's fine, too. We'll give him some time, but in the meantime, we gotta eat. Deer meat will fill that freezer. A man doesn't need a grocery store."

"We really don't have enough from the dole to get some groceries?"

"Don't call it the dole." His eyes were glassy. I knew not to push back when he was like this. Jason had a special knack for twisting my arm up behind my back until I thought my shoulder would pop out of its socket.

"Deer meat!" he bellowed. "The woods are full of groceries. That's the way it's supposed to be."

My brother hadn't tried the pop socket trick since the funeral so I went along with his hunting idea. I didn't have a plan then. I had a lot of time to think about what I did before I did it, true. But I wouldn't exactly call it premeditated, either. My crime is one of opportunity, so don't go thinking you're better than me. Don't jump to that too fast.

Jason pulled Dad's old iron sight hunting rifle from the footlocker by the furnace. Using something that belonged to my father seemed wrong even though he wasn't around to ask permission.

Jason had tagged along when Dad hunted sometimes but I had refused. Some particularly hot summers, when the water dried up in the backwoods, the deer would come closer to

84

civilization to drink from the stream behind our house. They traveled in little families and, in the field behind us, the tall grass would be matted down where they slept at night. In our backyard the deer stretched their necks to eat from the apple tree. I saw my father shoot a deer out back once. I was on the back step, still as a stone, watching four deer pick apples with their teeth. Dad shot a doe from the upstairs bathroom window. When it was gutted, dressed and decapitated, the doe's eyes still looked just the same as when she was alive. They were black and wet, looking at me. I wanted nothing to do with killing a deer.

Instead of saying no to Jason, I told him about my earliest memory: a white goat with little curled horns hangs upside down. Its tongue hangs out, eyes like marbles. I felt the animal's fur beneath my fingers. My hand came away wet. Then I saw the red slash of gore at the goat's throat and the blood clinging to my hand. It wouldn't shake off. I cried. Men laughed behind me. No. I think they *cackled*.

Jason told me I was remembering a fragment of a day at our grandfather's farm. It must have happened just before Mom's first heart attack because she was still strong enough to carry me. I could also remember my mother's fat, bosomy softness against my cheek as she scooped me up into her arms.

I watched Jason's fat greasy fingers fumble to load the rifle with old brass shells. The dead goat is an anchor for my memory, but Mom was there, too. In bad moments, I often reach for that feeling of being carried.

Jason's rictus grin split his face as he hoisted the

rifle. "Dad said, 'God took Mom. The bank took the farm. Then granddad took himself away. Did it with this .30-30. Get your school backpack. Leave the house unlocked. We'll only be a few hours."

I asked Jason if he cleaned the barrel. He shrugged and said he could still smell gun oil so it was probably fine. He slung the rifle into the crook of his elbow and walked off toward the woods. I carried the pack, heavy with Jason's beer. He didn't have a hunting license. "Shouldn't need one when you can get to the woods from your own back step," he said.

"Even the weather's all fucked up," Jason said. "When Dad was a kid, there was always at least a little snow on the ground by November first for the opening of deer season. We'll have to look for tracks in the dirt instead of snow."

It was as if we had slipped winter's notice and fall had decided to hold on until the seasons found their proper order. The Indian summer had stretched out so long this year that there were plenty of leaves still clinging to the trees even now. Last week's Halloween was the warmest I had ever known in Poeticule Bay: a few local kids had found our door, but they all wore their masks on top of their heads, their little faces shiny with sweat.

The weather had only begun to shift this morning. For the first time that autumn, I could see my breath hang in the air when I exhaled. I pretended to smoke, but quickly grew bored of it. I was too old for pretending. Some of the guys and a bunch more girls in my class already smoked real cigarettes. They all would have laughed had they spotted me trailing after my brother, miming drags on a cigarette and blowing plumes of steam.

The chill cut at my lungs and I hoped the sun would warm us and make the slow uphill climb more pleasant. The forest went quiet as we stepped into the tree line. A minute later, a squirrel rattled an alarm and skittered away as we pushed through a weave of dogwood. The glass bottles clinked as I walked. We hiked to the old logging road where trees close in to bow and touch overhead. Grass filled the middle of the logging road so high, and the ruts cut so deep, the trail looked less like a road and more like two narrow paths running parallel by coincidence. Jason put a finger to his lips. Staying quiet was all Jason knew about hunting. I tried to tread carefully so the bottles wouldn't knock against each other. When I began to fall behind, my brother looked back, mouthing curses.

As the rising sun burned off the gray cloud cover, trees cast another forest of tangled shadows on the ground, adding another thickness and plane to the landscape. The pack straps pulled at my shoulders. Despite the sun and the cold air's green taste, my footsteps became heavier as we pushed on and up. The sweat trapped under the backpack sucked my shirt to my skin. My breathing became heavier. We walked another half hour past where I thought I was too tired to trudge up the slope. Salt sweat burned my eyes before I ramped up the courage to complain. "We're going too far, Jason."

"Wuss." He pointed ahead with the rifle barrel. "I was thinking we'd go there." The clear cut loomed above us, a ragged oval where trees used to be.

Out west, they would call Hanley's Mountain a big hill, but this was Maine. Here, every wide spot in the road has a name and we call every ground down hunk of Appalachia a mountain. Sometimes ill-mannered tourists point this out. "They used to be taller than the Rockies," we say. New Englanders — Mainiacs, I call them — are obsessed with what was. The future is for everyone else, people from Away.

Poeticule Bay locals complained about the clear cut, of course —"The Scar" some call it, or just "eyesore." It stood directly behind the town, a mark in the side of Hanley's Mountain. The storeowners even worried the summer people would bypass the town. They would take one look and motor on in their houseboats and yachts, pushing south to Boston or north to Halifax or Mahone Bay or Lunenburg.

"Even if you get a deer up at the Scar, how you going to get it back down?"

Jason shrugged. "It's downhill. No biggie," he said. His eyes were glassy so I didn't argue.

By noon, the trail angled up so sharply I had to lean forward under my burden, the weight on my toes. "Enough," I said. "We've gone way too far." I let the pack slip from my shoulders and sat on a small boulder to the side of the trail. I pulled out a Coke and a ham sandwich.

Jason watched me for a moment, deciding whether this act of insubordination was worth a thumping. I didn't dare look in his eyes. I've heard that about animals, too, how if you look them in the eyes it's a challenge and they'll attack. I kept eating, but braced my leg muscles, ready to throw myself into the brambles if he took a swing at me. Jason walked over and stood too close to me, pausing long enough to make me feel the fear. With less than a foot between us, there was no way I could dodge a blow.

"You want something?" I asked. "You're not my type."

He laughed at that and reached past me into the pack. He yanked out a bottle of beer. I watched his hands. "I'll help you lighten your load, little brother."

He wiped dribbles of beer from his chin with the back of his hand. "I could get used to this unemployment thing," he said. "We could really make the insurance money last, you know? You think walking around up here with a pack is work? Try digging around somebody's attic for a wire and a junction box covered in itchy pink insulation. Man, you don't know what work is."

A chickadee sang its sweet persistent song, oblivious.

Jason fished out a couple Mars bars he'd hidden in a side pocket. He offered me neither and ate both at once, mouth open as he smacked and sucked down the chocolate. Watching him eat, I knew why Jason's love life was a series of first dates. Some women don't mind a man with a temper, but who could sit across from that noisy mess at a dinner table and keep an appetite?

"What's on your mind, sunshine?"

I said nothing.

"You scared I'm gonna hit you?"

"Some."

"That don't need to happen no more," he said. "Brothers can be hard on each other, but I'm the new boss man now. Doin' it right."

"Hard *on each other*, yeah?" I said. "I don't remember me being hard on you. The beat-down train only ever runs in one direction as I recall.

When do I get to be hard on you?"

Jason sighed and lowered himself stiffly until he was cross-legged in the soft, tall grass in the middle of the logging road. He cradled the rifle like mothers hold babies. "Check the safety. Pull the bolt." He relished the rifle shell's sunlit gleam before slamming the action back. Clack-clack! "I love that sound. It just sounds...right." He opened the breech and slammed it shut again.

He belched and let sour air hiss out between crooked teeth. "Ate too fast," he said, grimacing and patting his stomach. Instead of opening his next beer, he held the sweating glass to his forehead. "Got to slow down. That chilli you made last night isn't sitting right."

"Complain to the guy who put the chilli in the can, not to the guy who put it in the pot for you."

"Fair enough." My brother frowned as he surveyed the woods. "According to Dad, if you shoot a deer in the heart, it'll jump straight up in the air before it falls down dead."

"Yeah? You believe that?"

"'Course."

"Uh-huh."

Jason belched loudly and gave me a tight smile. "Dad told me he got buck fever once. He was hunting deer with Granddad. They're at the edge of this field and out from the woods come five deer. This would have been Dad's first kill. Granddad hands him his rifle with a scope on it so he lies down, lines up his shot. There's a big twelve-point buck out front. Dad follows this buck through his scope an' he starts to sweat bullets instead of firin' 'em. Then he starts to feel it."

"It?"

"Buck fever starts with a little shake in the hand. The shakes snaked up his arm until he's shakin' like a seizure."

"He get the deer?"

Jason shook his head. "Fired five shots and none of the deer even felt the wind of a bullet. Not even close, even by accident. Dad said he had to work up to it. The next year he shot a couple partridges and that next winter he bagged a couple rabbits. The next time he had a deer in his sights, he knew not to think about it too long. He said he felt a little shake in his trigger finger and before it could get worse, he pulled it quick. Bang! Bagged his first doe. After that, the killin' came easy."

Jason opened his beer, took a swig and squinted at me as if guessing my weight. "Dad said when you got a problem, it's better not to think too long. That's your problem, Joey. You think about things too much. You got a problem? Just rip that Band-Aid right off. Stop tryin' to worry it off. And do something about your acne. It's makin' me sick."

Jason bobbed his head and raised his beer high in a toast, our meeting adjourned. Before he could bring the bottle to his lips he grimaced again, one hand to his stomach. "*Hoo*. Goddamn chilli."

I watched his face. Beer kills too slow, I thought.

Norman Rose — "Chief" to everybody in Poeticule Bay — was both police and fire chief. At that moment, he must have been looking at his watch, sausage fingers hovering above a button. I never actually saw it, but I always pictured a big red button, like the president must use to launch nuclear missiles. The fire hall's siren rose up in one long wail as it did every weekday. I called that daily rising and falling blast the audible comma; all of Poeticule Bay paused at noon. That siren was my secret reminder that I was supposed to live somewhere too big to need to test the siren; New York fire stations don't need to test their sirens. Their sirens go off all the time and nobody needs a reminder that the day is half-done and things are changing. New Yorkers are busy living and changing all the time. Bayers don't change. They're allergic to change.

Though I had no money to go anywhere, some of my classmates would escape to universities and bigger towns. Most would join the family business and fish or farm. A few of the most desperate would go into the military. I didn't want to join the Perma-war, though. The TV said the army was fighting for freedom. From where I stood, America must be losing. Freedom is only among strangers. There is no freedom where there is no anonymity. Growing up in a small town didn't teach me much, but I got that lesson.

Here, I would always be Darren Kind's son or Jason's little brother. They didn't know what was going on behind my father's eyes — or mine, either — but they all thought they did. Small town people act as if they own you by the power of two accidents: birth and geography. Unhappy accidents, like a drunken brother or a father chewed up by saw blades or a town so small it strangles? That shit can define you forever.

These were my thoughts as the siren rose and died. Then the sight of the buck erased my thoughts. It stepped out of the woods, large and quite close, but its hooves made no sound I could hear. My mouth dropped open. I should have shouted, not to draw Jason's attention to the deer, but to scare it off.

* * *

The .30-30 boomed. The sound rolled up the mountainside to fill the blue sky. The shell's force staggered the deer left and its front legs buckled. Then it regained its height and bounded off into the woods, its rump a white flag. I froze but Jason tore after it. He crashed through the brush yelling for me to follow. He disappeared from my view, yelled something incoherent — all vowels. It was enough to give me a bearing.

The stag took the path of least resistance down the mountain. I followed Jason's yells. The sprint through the undergrowth soon winded him and I caught up, one strap over my shoulder, the other dragging. He grabbed at his side again and grimaced, chest heaving. "Got a stitch," he wheezed. "Where were you?"

"You got the gun, so behind you."

The moss was soft and springy, like walking on the carpet in the office at the funeral home. If I were dying, I would lie down where the moss is soft and deep and go to sleep. It buoyed me for a few minutes until the green cushion gave way to loose shale and, more cautious, I started walking sideways down the slope to avoid twisting an ankle.

The blood trail led us through dense branches that scratched and pulled at us. Jason swung the rifle muzzle in front of him in a wild arc back and forth. When he pushed the branches away, they sprang back, whipping my face. The deer, disoriented from blood loss and panicked with pain, moved in loose circles.

"Didja see?" Jason yelled. "I shot him just about as fast as I saw him! I wish Dad had been here to see that! We got to finish him quick though. First thing Dad taught me 'bout hunting. Never leave an animal wounded. We're gonna do this goddamn right."

"Yes, I wish Dad were here, too."

Though we were headed downhill, Jason wheezed and complained his stomach and chest hurt. I ignored him and pointed him down the grade, scanning the trees. We lost the trail once. Jason told me to walk in a wider circle and, after ten minutes, I found blood again.

"There!" Jason screamed. He raised the rifle and got off another shot. Missed. My ears rang. I glimpsed the buck leaping in a high arc just before the forest swallowed it again.

The air among the trees cooled our sweat-slick necks. Jason's hair stood out in wet spikes. His face was a sheen. Trickles of sweat joined forces to hang in drips from his nose and chin.

"I just wanted to eat 'em before," Jason said. "Now? Now I really want to kill him."

We walked in another circle. We weren't halfway down the mountain but the terrain levelled out here. The deer's trail now described a jagged tangent. Just ahead, the staggering deer crashed through water and broke branches. Jason's war cry turned into a ragged curse as he stepped forward. Soft black mud sucked his left boot down. He held the rifle high over his head, unsure how deep his weight would take him into the water. The new logging road stretching above us toward the Scar must have diverted a creek to create a swamp in the hollow head of this small plateau.

Jason reached for my shoulder to steady himself and almost pulled me into the cold water. A spasm contorted his lower lip. "Good Christ, that hurts! This is the worst goddamn heartburn I've ever had."

I wasn't sure if he was telling me or talking himself through it. I pulled away to stay on dry land as Jason slogged forward through water past his knees. He cursed the cold as it invaded his boots. After a few steps, he found his footing on a rising bar of sand. I heard a flutter of branches and leaves as he disappeared from my view. He let out a whoop and I knew he'd found the buck. I braced for another burst of gunfire but instead I heard a heavy thud followed by my brother's surprised cry. After a moment of silence, a volley of shots.

"Joey!" he yelled. "C'mon! What you waitin' for?"

I left my pack at the foot of a pine. I couldn't avoid the water soaking me to my knees so I opted for speed. I waded through as quickly as I could and peered through the thicket, parting the way with my hands and body, choosing each step carefully to avoid more watery sinkholes. The deer's head was a mess of blood and gore. I glanced and looked away. I refused to look at it directly and focused my eyes on the body instead. The deer was well-muscled and the short smooth fur was a perfect light brown.

Only when I noticed Jason's hunting knife, unbloodied beside the deer's neck did I look up at him. A deep gash marked Jason's forehead above his left eyebrow. Blood ran down his face so thick he couldn't see from that eye. He ignored his head wound, however, and grabbed at his chest and tore his shirt open. Though the skin was unbroken, a semi-circular bruise above his left nipple, was already turning purple and black. Hoof print.

"I thought it was down and done. I was just going to walk up and slash its throat. The goddamn thing kicked out at me. I should've just stepped back and blasted it. Stupid! Stupid!" He stomped his feet. "I came up on it too quick. It was bleeding to death but it wasn't dead enough." Jason's breath came in little gasps. "I was feeling shitty, but he really did a job on me. Real fighter. Good thing I unloaded on him." Jason smiled despite his pain. "*Told* you I could do it! We've got venison for the winter!"

My brother's triumph would have been better spent on Dad if his ghost was watching. I felt much worse for the deer than I did for my brother.

It was a heavy nine-point buck. Jason sent me back to the pack with the rifle. My brother's sweat had wet and warmed the stock. I felt queasy. I tried to wipe a few droplets of his blood from the gun barrel but instead of wiping it off, it just smeared and dirtied my jacket sleeve. Jason tried to haul the deer on his own by the antlers. The water, the slippery ground and the animal's weight colluded to bring him down. Jason's fierce lips stretched wide over bared teeth as he fell. He would have cursed more but his breath became more ragged. It was as if Jason's lung's had shrunk. I wrapped my hands around the antlers, too, and pulled as hard as I could.

By the time we got the deer to dry land, we were both sucking wind hard. We managed to move the deer another few feet, though its hind quarters still dragged in the water. Our footing was sure again, but the dead weight was too much. Jason told me to stop and when I looked up, his eyes showed something new. I had seen his pain, but now there was fear, too. We'd made it as far as the pack and the gun under the pine tree. We could go no farther.

Jason sank to his knees and clutched his chest. "Dear, Jesus! That — !" He paused and, cheeks bulging, almost threw up but swallowed his gorge.

I watched as he fought the urge to vomit, his bare torso convulsing in waves.

He flopped over slowly, his head beside the deer's limp neck. "Oh, Jesus fuck! I got pain!" He gasped and then added, "Down both arms!" He took another minute before he could speak again. "Pressure," he gasped. He pointed to his chest. Then he did puke. Bright green and black. He continued until there was nothing left. I turned him on his side so he wouldn't die choking like a druggie rock star.

When there was nothing left to vomit, I watched the spasms through his guts pull him forward and back. My brother, the dying puppet.

When he got his breath back he said, "I'm sorry, Joey. I shouldn't have gone up to the deer like that. If Dad were here — "

"If Dad were here, he'd tell you to shut up," I said.

He tried to get up but only made it to his knees. Jason swayed and fell on his back. He pointed to the center of his chest again with one hand and clutched under his rib cage with the other.

I knew what his frantic miming meant: I look like my father and Jason has our mother's nose. Watching him point to his chest, I was sure my brother had inherited Mom's trick heart, too. Or maybe the kick to his head was enough for a concussion and blood was sloshing into his brain. Either way, he wasn't going to make it down the mountain. I didn't know how I felt about that.

Jason told me to tear his shirt into strips. I helped him back into his jacket and tied the makeshift bandage around his head. I don't know if it did much good since it soaked red almost immediately.

He winced again, tried to throw up but could only give a hoarse retching sound that must have torn his throat raw. The puddle of green vomit made me nauseous. I looked away and took shallow breaths through my mouth to avoid the acidic stink. When Jason could talk again he told me to run to town. I did not move or say anything. "Joey, go get help," he said again. One hand remained a frozen claw at his chest. His other hand pointed me downhill, toward Poeticule Bay.

Before I left, I snatched up the gun. I looked back and forth from the deer's caved-in head to my helpless brother. The rifle felt heavier than it should. My arms trembled and my palms were slick with sweat. I knew if I held the rifle any longer, I would begin to shake. I gritted my teeth and abandoned the gun beside him. I left him the box of shells. Truth? I hoped the pain might inspire him.

"Leave the pack, too," he whispered. "Just run." The spasms worked up and down his body again. The splotch at his forehead spread out through the fabric of the bandage, reminding me of a poinsettia blossom.

As he began to shiver, he looked less human. It was as if I was numb and standing outside my body. I watched myself study his torture and memorize his pain. No, not numb. There was a trickle of something new. Jason's torment felt good. His pain was like air scrubbed fresh by a summer downpour. His fear made me feel taller. The out-of-body experience was so strong that, when I shook myself awake, I scanned the woods expecting to glimpse myself. I really thought I might look around and see me, or a ghost of me, watching a new and improved and different me standing beside my brother.

Of course, it was a mind trick born of shock, but I must have been rising out of the shock quickly. When I looked around a second time, it was to make sure we were alone.

I walked in the direction of the trail, but perhaps just fifty feet away, soft moss among the trees spread out, a silent invitation. I could see where the foliage thinned ahead. The oak and birch branches spread farther apart by the logging road. The afternoon sun brightened the sky. The forest shadows were short stabs of darkened quiet. I didn't have a watch, but it couldn't even have been two yet. I was tired. The moss was a mattress.

I sat with my back to Jason. I couldn't see him but I could hear him. He thought he was dying alone, cursing and crying and grunting. My father once told me that when you are in the woods, find a spot and sit still so the forest can forget you. "First things go all quiet, like the woods are listening for you. Then everything wakes up around you. Pay attention and the wind will whisper things. You'll swear it says something if you listen long enough."

I waited. At first, all I heard was Jason struggling. Then birds sang to each other, first one or two at a time. More birds joined in and they sang louder and more often, confident in their safety. I listened to Jason cry, but I was thinking about the deer. After a while, I closed my eyes and pictured Times Square on New Year's Eve. I would lose myself amid the city noise, drown in it. I would have Dad's insurance money and I would not be owned anymore. With a smile on my lips, I fell into a doze.

* * *

When my head bobbed forward, I rubbed my eyes. The daylight had dulled and Jason was quiet. I didn't move until sure of my reward. The only breath I could hear was my own and the shallow sigh of the cold wind breathing on the nape of my neck. The wind said nothing to me. I took the silence for a message: God is not watching. Nature does not care. I stretched out stiff legs and crept toward the trail. I did not want to disturb the birdsong.

The Scar was up to my left. I turned right toward town. I felt fresh, calm, and rested. My legs and feet were still wet but I was weightless. I memorized this feeling so I could revisit it. "Today everything changes," I said. "New start. The slave is free."

The gray-lit sky told me it must be at least late afternoon. My empty belly growled. Dusk in Maine comes quickly in November. Poeticule Bay residents would already be looking for the last lobster boat's return in dimming light. Everyone in fish and lobster-trap towns are oriented to the Atlantic. Their heads swivel not to the sunset behind Mount Hanley. Instead they'd naturally be looking to the heave and roil of the waves to glimpse boats and seals. Everyone's back would be turned to me as I trudged into town. I waited for the burn of guilt in my head and panic to sweep over me but it didn't come.

At the bottom of the mountain, I came out of the trees and took the new logging road. Wide and flattened with slow, easy curves, it accommodated the 18-wheelers the forest feeds. I walked past the spot where Jason and I pushed through the woods that morning. I saw no evidence of our trail. The tall grass had recovered from our passing. Such easy erasure seemed a good sign.

My mother died of a heart attack on a sunny afternoon just like this had been. I did not know the word "incongruous" then. Before she died, I thought it should rain when someone loses their life. Dad died out of sight of the sky, surrounded by the smell of sawdust and the roar of the machine that chewed, swallowed, and spit him out.

Now Jason was dead beside the beautiful deer he killed on another bright day. I searched for the opposite of incongruous. "Right," I said aloud. "The word is *right*."

Once I reached a scattering of houses at Poeticule's edge, I sprinted. It would do me no good to be seen strolling. I flagged down a car halfway into town.

* * *

The fire hall siren wailed and this time, it kept going. The volunteer firefighters gathered first. Within a short time, the telephone tree brought most of the able-bodied town residents into the search. Chief Rose's Jeep smelled of cheap cologne losing the battle to fat man sweat. He asked me questions between heavy breaths. Why had I not stopped at the first house to use a phone?

I shrugged and looked down. "Panic." That, I was sure, would get me through: I was lost... I got confused.... Please save my brother.... Repeat.

Night was closing in before we got to the bottom of the trail. Dick and Rich flanked me while Chief Rose puffed behind us. I worried that the Chief was going to have a heart attack, too. I suggested he spread his forces into the woods.

"On *both* sides of the trail, Joey? You aren't even sure which side of the trail you were at?" His eyebrows met in the middle.

"I got turned around in the woods. Every tree looks like every other tree. Even if I had a cell phone up here, all I could say was I'm in some trees and there's a rock and there's the sky."

Chief's laugh was gruff but he clapped me on the shoulder. "Don't worry. We'll find your brother." He turned to tell the searchers to spread out. "No more than five feet between you, slow 'n steady!"

The small army swept the forest floor, their string of white and yellow lights bobbing. I was sure we weren't even a quarter of the way to Jason and his deer. I felt queasy at the prospect of finding him. Dick, Rich and I took turns shouting so we wouldn't go hoarse. They both said not to worry. They were never this nice when Jason was around.

"A head wound can bleed a lot, but that's only because it's a head wound," Dick said. That satisfied him that Jason would be okay. Rich said Jason's chances of having a heart attack were near impossible. When I reminded him our mother died young of a bad heart, he went quiet for a long time.

The searchers were methodical and the thick terrain made for slow progress. It was close to eleven before some people headed home. They promised to come back and look again at dawn. There were murmurs Chief Rose should call in a helicopter with an infrared camera. I wondered how long it takes a body to cool. I did not want animals to get at the corpse. However, now that my brother was an it, I didn't want to see the body, either. When I thought we were getting close to the body, I shouted to Chief Rose. "He couldn't be this far up!"

Rose consulted his map. He said we should go back but send the searchers deeper into woods on either side of the trail. A single groan rose up among the searchers but hissing whispers silenced the complainer. The reaching trees and thorny brush scratched and marked the would-be rescuers and the temperature had plummeted since the sun went down.

I wondered if I should just rent the house out at first or sell it outright? Would selling it too quickly look suspicious? The eulogy would be brief. I would be a tragic figure for the third time. I'd say, "My brother died on the last day of Indian summer." Then I'd hop into the truck and head south. My future was always waiting to the south and the I-95 would be my time machine, helping me escape to a new beginning.

I told Rich and Dick I was hungry and thirsty. Someone from the bottom of the trail brought up wrapped sandwiches and coffee from the Poeticule

B&B and the Bay Diner, but when it arrived I found I couldn't eat. My nerves killed my appetite. Everyone else was shivering from the cold, but for me, it was the excitement. I had finally achieved escape velocity and my father's insurance money was my rocket fuel.

We turned back. It was over. Someone else could find the body tomorrow.

Then two shots boomed behind us. There was a brief delay and then a third shot. Intent on being the first to get to my brother, everyone ran. Community and concern brought them out into the cold night, but competition for bragging rights and heroism were on the line now.

"Up to the left!" Rich yelled. "We're coming, buddy!"

"Jason?"

"Jason!"

A would-be rescuer to our left let out a startled cry and we heard a splash. Another searcher fell into the water trying to pull out the first. We crashed through the bushes. One spot at the base of a pine brightened to white as more people with flashlights bore their way into the circle. My brother, the new boss man, lay in the center, draped over the dead deer.

I dragged my feet but Dick and Rich were irresistible forces pushing me forward. The circle broke open to let me in and I saw Jason, a shivering ghost awash in bright white light as the flashlight beams played over him. The rifle I'd left my brother lay across his chest. Dick and Rich whipped off their jackets as if they were two people sharing one brain. Dick took the gun. Jason whispered to them. They shook their heads in unison. Jason said something else I couldn't hear. They nodded and Rich shouted for a doctor. When they stood up, they were frowning at me.

John MacGillivray and his wife Susan, the fire department's EMTs, pushed through with their equipment. Susan MacGillivray peppered Jason with questions. He spoke in a raspy voice. Jason must have been shouting a long time.

"Pain down both arms," Susan said to her husband, eyebrows raised.

"It's not so bad now," Jason said. "Not near so bad. I was dying."

"Not hardly." John MacGillivray fit a blood pressure cuff on Jason's arm and called for the crowd to be quiet as he plugged his stethoscope into his ears.

"And where was the pain?" Chief Rose asked, leaning in. Jason pointed to his chest and his gut. John MacGillivray, annoyed at the Chief's interruption, asked him to get someone to bring up thermal blankets. The Chief retreated to bark into his walkie-talkie.

I couldn't look at my brother. I watched the fat silhouettes and long shadows cavorting among the trees instead. I listened. I waited for the accusations to fly at me with claws.

Susan stood to deliver her rapid-fire assessment. "You'll need some stitches in that forehead and we'll get you X-rayed. You'll sleep in Orono hospital tonight. The docs will make the diagnosis, but my money's on gall stones."

"My heart?"

MacGillivray shook his head and shrugged. "Lots of people think a gall bladder attack is a heart attack. You're too young. If your heart was the bug, it would be just your left arm that pained you. Your BP's okay. We'll check it out at Emerge, but what you describe? I wouldn't worry so much. And cut back on fatty foods."

"Where's Joey?" Jason asked. I thought he was staring in my direction, but the ring of white light had blinded him to my face. "Where's my brother? Is he okay?"

Rich and Dick pushed me forward. "Joey," Jason smiled at me. "I thought you were dead. I must have passed out or fallen asleep or something," he said. "I lost all track of time. I thought you must have hit your head on a rock running for help."

Chief Rose bulled his way back in. "How long were you up here, Jason?"

Jason took a long time to answer. "How long since you left, Joey?"

I shrugged. "No watch." I pulled my sleeve back to show everyone.

"Must have been no more than an hour before dark, you think?" Jason said, squinting at me.

Volunteers arrived with a stretcher and blankets. Two burly volunteer firefighters I recognized from the gas station lifted Jason gently and tucked the blankets around him as if he was a little boy. Many hands strapped him in.

"Joey! Joey! C'mere!"

MacGillivray waved me in. "Make it quick, kid." To Chief Rose he said, "Let's get out of these woods. If not for the deer under him, hypothermia would have done him in before dawn. Another couple of hours... well, it's a good thing he had the gun to signal us or we might have missed him."

Jason freed one arm, reached behind my neck and

pulled me down, my ear an inch from his teeth. "We'll hunt again," he said. "Soon as I'm out, you and me, we'll be out here again."

I pulled back. In the swaying lights, I saw his glassy eyes and his grin. I imagine I had that same grin on my face as I sat nearby in the moss.

"As long as there are so many of you guys up here," Jason shouted to the crowd, "bring my buck down for me, will ya?" A shrill laugh rose up from the crowd. Someone clapped and the rest joined in. They applauded my brother. The crazy drunk driver was now a hero to everyone. They congratulated themselves. As they carried the brave son away, he pumped a fist and gave his rescuers the thumbs-up to prompt another cheer.

Dick appeared beside me carrying Dad's rifle. Rich pulled on my backpack and gripped my left arm at the elbow. "Time to go."

Chief puffed up. "Good looking buck. You boys have a permit, I suppose?"

"Jason's the hunter," I said.

"In all the near-tragedy, Jason prolly lost it," Rich said.

"Yeah-huh," Chief Rose said. "Save me the tongue and the liver, will you? I don't think we need be askin' too many questions. Young Kind has been through enough without me pilin' on, I imagine."

The Chief pulled his glasses down his nose and looked at me. I felt like I was strapped to a board. He spoke loud enough for everyone to hear him doing his job. "You come up here again, you bring a compass and learn to use it, okay? I do not know how you got so lost, boy. The mountain's that way." He pointed. "The whole Atlantic Ocean's that way.

The woods are thick and you musta been in shock, but you missed an *ocean*, son." When he laughed, his belly shook. Some of the local hyenas joined in.

The searchers shambled downhill in a ragged parade. The town had another story to chew. Stories are never swallowed and done with. For Poeticule people —Jason's people, now — stories never lose their flavor. Small town stories are Poeticule Bay's gum and glue.

Where the old trail met the new logging road, Dick and Rich pushed me into their pickup truck. Rich drove, I sat bitch and Dick cradled the rifle in the suicide seat. "The hospital is quite a ways," I said. "Can we swing by my house first so I can pick up a few things?"

Dick checked the safety and pulled the bolt back and forth. "What do you mean, *your* house, Joey?"

"Jason might be in hospital a few days. Concussion maybe, or a gallstone operation, if the paramedics are right. I don't know."

"You hope," Rich said. He lay on his horn and maneuvered the truck through a gaggle of cars. Everyone jockeyed to pull away from the road's soft shoulder and head for home, but Rich bullied his way into a narrow gap and shot through.

At the tee junction, the back tires spit gravel and we slid onto the macadam. We followed the ambulance west, our backs toward Poeticule Bay. The ambulance plowed ahead of us, dividing the night as its flashing lights — red, white, blue, red, white, blue — strobed the countryside. At the next tee junction, we stopped. The ambulance stabbed out with one siren blast and roared off north toward Orono's hospital. The ambulance's big engine growled as it took off and they hit their high beams. My brother disappeared over a hill in a corona of light.

Rich let the engine idle a moment more and then looked to Dick, who nodded. Rich swung the wheel left. We weren't following the ambulance. I was not surprised. We headed south, down the coast until another crossroad gave way to a smooth road with fresh asphalt. Xenon gaslights cast a bright yellow glow on the I-95.

Rich stood on the brakes at the bottom of the ramp. The tires squealed in protest and the truck rocked to a stop. Dick still held the rifle. He didn't want to chance being seen with it, so I followed Rich out the driver's side door. Dick shoved me out with the rifle stock's butt jabbing at my kidneys. The highway stretched south to New Hampshire, Massachusetts, Connecticut and New York. I would never see a dime of Dad's insurance money. I didn't even have a change of underwear.

"Your brother wanted us to make sure you stay until he gets out," Rich said.

"And this?"

"We're Jason's *friends*," Rich said. "We're doing what's good for him. Sometimes water is thicker than blood, I guess." He thought a moment, dug two twenties out of his pocket, threw the bills at my feet and backed away. He kept his eyes on me until he got back behind the wheel. He slammed his door and locked it. I watched them back up and begin a three-point turn. Dick rolled down his window and pointed the rifle at me. "Don't look back!"

I wondered then if they had changed their minds. Maybe Dick was working up his nerve to shoot. I felt a small circle between my shoulder blades where I was somehow sure Dick trained his aim. Without thinking, I raised my arms as if I was in an old western.

"Don't come back!" Dick screamed. The pickup's wheels squealed again as they peeled away. The back end fishtailed for a couple of seconds and then they were speeding home to Poeticule Bay.

* * *

Soon they will install the hot tub Dad's death paid for. Some of what should have been my money will pay for the marijuana Jason buys his friends to build a deck out back of the house — Jason's house now. My brother will invite Dick and Rich over to get drunk and smoke weed in that hot tub. They will invite girls. My brother will talk about his adventure in the woods. Soon the whole town will know what I did. It will come out. Anything bad always does. They will never tire of talking about me. I will be chewed up but never swallowed.

I walk up the ramp toward the circles of yellow light. I remember a hot summer day when I was little. I thought the water was too cold so I dithered at the side of the town pool. Dad pushed me in. It was warmer than I thought, and a relief to swim and play in the water.

And now here I am again, pushed.

At the side of the highway, I stick out my thumb. I have never considered hitching a ride on the I-95, especially at night. However, it is cold and cars have heaters. Besides, I am the most dangerous person out here tonight.

The first of several drivers to stop is a lonely long-haul trucker. He says he wants conversation to keep him awake but he does all the talking. It is a logging truck with a heavy load of hardwood. I imagine that, somehow, a drop of Dad's blood is traveling south with us through Bangor, Augusta, Portland and beyond.

I cannot wait to see New York City at night. This New Year's Eve, I will cheer fresh resolutions and unlikely hopes as I watch the ball drop at midnight. I will be on TV, one of the throng in Times Square. I will be safe among strangers.

I close my eyes and reach for a fragment of a memory of my mother. I feel like I am being carried.

ASIA UNBOUND

**My starlet, Asia Minor, is a prelude to
another starlet, Legs Gabrielle, from the first
story in *Self-help for Stoners*. Legs makes a
return in my hardboiled crime novel,
Hollywood Jesus. Legs has a better sense of
humor than Asia (and, as of this writing, I
haven't done any stand-up, so Legs is my
outlet.) Asia is a tormented soul but Legs
wouldn't exist without her. ~ Chazz**

He couldn't get near her at the funeral. She was at
the moving center of the universe, her own gorgeous,
ethereal gravity well. People pulled in close and
pushed in closer and he allowed the crowd's currents
to carry him to the edge of her horizon. He didn't
want to meet her again in the middle of the craven
crowd. He wanted to see her again alone so he
arrived at midnight.

The paparazzi seemed to have given up hounding
her. Maybe they knew the excitement was over for
the day or they were still filing their stories from the
circus that was the funeral. He saw her silhouette in

112

the window, sleek and tall and untouchable...or at least not touchable anymore. He had been denied her so long he felt something akin to hunger.

She watched the ocean, probably dreaming of faraway places she would soon visit again. He wondered if he would ever see any of those places.

He thought he'd be angry. Then she opened the front door and he was in love all over again. "I heard you were back in town," he said.

"As I recall, that's why I left this place. You couldn't walk outside without everyone gawking at you and talking behind your back." She looked him over. He sucked in his gut a moment too late.

"Can I come in?"

She waited a beat too long, letting him see her debate.

"I won't bite," he said.

"Unless I ask you to. I remember."

She stepped back and waved him in. After he passed her, she leaned out and looked left and right. There wasn't a soul around. The advantage of a place as small as Poeticule Bay was that strangers stood out from the crowd of locals.

He pretended to be oblivious to her apprehension. "You look great," he said.

"It's what I do for a living."

"You don't sound happy about it."

"I'm not a whiny bitch about it to anybody, but between you and me, it would be great to cut loose and have a cheeseburger sometimes."

He looked around the shabby living room. He recognized the tattered old plaid chair and three gaudy floor lamps. It was easy to peg her uncle as a bachelor who bought his furniture at garage sales.

He remembered the old green couch. Things age, he thought, even when you aren't looking.

"Sorry to hear about your Uncle Joe. He was quite the hero around here."

"He was a pig," she said. "No pun intended."

"I heard his cruiser crashed into a tree because he was in a rush to get to a fire."

"Yeah, to direct traffic around a fire. Doesn't sound very heroic."

"Well, his partner was killed in the crash, too, so don't talk that way down at the General." He meant the store. When she was 16 he bought her a popsicle just for the thrill of watching her slowly suck it. He had often replayed that memory of her melting a popsicle with her lips and tongue.

"The last time I saw you — "

"The last time you saw me I was Betty Jane Minor," she said. "Please call me Asia. Betty Jane is dead. I killed her on the boat ride away from here the day after graduation. You want a drink? Have a mojito with me."

There was a well-stocked bar in the corner of the room complete with a small fridge. He watched her as she mixed the drinks. He remembered how she always had to push her long black veil of hair out of her eyes to read and write in her notebooks at school. It was a detail he thought must have been forgotten but there it was. As he watched her, he realized her perfect hair didn't move anymore. It couldn't get in her way because, he supposed, it was now sprayed in place. He'd seen her on TV in small roles and in a couple movies that were pretty bad. He had watched her over and over again and it was all he could do not to stand up in the middle of the theatre and

114

announce to all the teenage boys drooling over her ass and cleavage, "I used to tap that!"

She held out the drink. A cluster of charms at her wrist made the glass tinkle.

"Nice bracelet." His eyes lingered over it. Diamonds beneath a variety of hanging charms.

"You want it?"

"Uh...no."

"I've got a charm on here for every country I've visited. It seemed important for awhile. Now it seems kind of pathetic, like I'm trying to hold on to something that's gone." She let cool eyes run over him and he felt smaller. "Is that why you're here, Marky?"

"It's Marcus now."

"Right. I heard! *Marcus in the Morning.*"

"Yeah. You hear the show?"

"No."

His face betrayed him, masking his disappointment too late.

"I've only been in town a day or two," she said. Her smile was kind. The silence stretched out like the room's air pressure was building up, pressing in on them and pushing them apart at the same time. He sat on the couch, hoping she'd join him. Instead she sat on the edge of the chair opposite him, ready to pop up and run in case of emergency it seemed. "Sorry I missed your show," she said. "With the funeral arrangements, things have been busy."

"No big deal. Speaking of big deals, I heard your dad is negotiating something that has to do with the Olympics so he sent you to the funeral instead. True?"

"Where'd you hear that?"

"Actually, I guess I read it online."

"Dad's not doing so well. He's got something called phantom appendage syndrome."

He gave her a blank look.

"Yeah, I know. No one's ever heard of it. Basically, he had a stroke last year and since then he thinks he's got an extra leg. I mean, he knows he doesn't actually have another leg, but he can feel it there and it gets in the way so it's hard on him to move around. Getting to the bathroom he has to scrabble sideways like some human crab. It's really kind of funny to see...the first time. Then it's a curiosity and after that it's a huge pain in the ass. Air travel is out of the question so he's taken up a hotel floor in Dubai and doesn't see anybody. He talks on the phone all day and watches CNN and the stock crawl. That's about it."

"They're talking about him like he's the new Howard Hughes."

"You ever see the Leonardo DeCaprio movie?"

"*The Aviator.*"

"Yeah. It's more interesting and fun when it's compressed into a movie that only lasts a couple hours. Marty should have gotten the Oscar for that. Instead the Academy gave him the Oscar for *The Aviator* and said it was for something else."

"Marty?"

"Scorsese."

"Right. Knew that. I just never heard anyone call him that before."

"Yeah," she said. "Listen to me. I never really thought I'd make it but I was really lucky."

Being an heiress must have sped things along, he thought.

"At first I was star struck by it all," she said, "especially when you see them all at once for the first time at the Oscars. Actors are kind of crazy. It's all the unemployment between jobs and waiting for the phone to ring and wondering if you're done and it's time to go away. The other thing that makes you crazy is all the people you're responsible for while you're between gigs."

"So you don't get star struck anymore?"

"After you get used to seeing them at all the same bars and parties, they're all just people."

"*Just*, huh?"

"Sure. Remember when I was just Betty Jane Minor, daughter of an oil rig engineer?"

"You were never *just* anything," he said, taking a long swallow. "And I'm feeling very...*rural* right now."

"Sorry." She gave him a helpless shrug.

"Don't be. I'm sorry about your dad. I always liked him."

"Thanks. He always hated you, but you know why."

"I understand better now that I'm older. When he caught us that night out in the boathouse — "

"Yeah, I know!" she said. She laughed. He didn't recognize the sound she made when she laughed. Something had changed but he couldn't say what.

Another silence filled the gap between them and he nursed his drink, making it last.

"You and I have unfinished business," she said.

He looked at her but he couldn't read her anymore. Whatever had happened to her in the fifteen years since he had seen her, he didn't like.

"I never said goodbye," she said.

He made a face and shrugged. "Oh, that's all watery shit under the bridge now."

She was about to say something more but he waved her off. "Thanks. Back home they make you grovel for the slightest infraction, and what I did to you wasn't a slight infraction."

"You left. I understand that. I'm been trying to achieve escape velocity since high school. The mistake I made was that I should have chased after you." Her jaw hardened and he hastened to add, "Hey, we were just kids. It wouldn't have worked out. I understand that now. Still, if I had come after you, you would have kicked me out eventually, but then I would have still been somewhere far away from here."

Her face softened and they shared a look that he remembered. It made him feel warm. A lock of his hair fell over one eye and he thought of the summer of 1989 when he developed a tic, flicking hair out of his eyes every few minutes. For a moment he felt much younger.

"Marky...uh, Marcus, I want to tell you something."

"I don't mind Marky when you say it."

"Okay. Marky, when I left it wasn't about you and I should have told you more at the time. Now it's all going to come out. It'll be splashed all over the papers tomorrow, so I guess this is my chance to tell someone without them reading about it first. It makes a lot of sense that you're here so I can tell you. I like the symmetry of it."

He relaxed and sat back, feeling for the first time that she wasn't going to kick him out at any moment. "Tell me."

"Today at the gravesite, I thought I was going to finally put something to rest. Not Joe. He can burn in hell. I mean, I thought I'd have closure."

"I don't know about that idea. It's been years since you left and here I am with you again and I still want to call you Betty. Asia is someone else who belongs to everyone else. Do you really believe in closure?"

"I'll never know now. Last night I wrote out pages and pages. I raged at everything I could remember about what Joe did to me. I poured out my heart about being a scared little girl. My dad was away a lot, so I was at Uncle Joe's mercy a lot. The last period of school was always the worst because I knew I'd have to go home and almost every night he'd come in to my bedroom and...what could I do?"

"I wish you had told me."

"It rarely works that way. I've talked to my therapist about it. You see pretty little girls at every school and a whole bunch of them have uncles who prove to them they're too pretty for their own good."

He shifted in his chair, opened his mouth but nothing came. Her eyes were wet. He wanted to go to her but didn't know if he should. He knew her when she was a human. How could he console a goddess? He didn't feel big enough to try.

"You saw what the paparazzi did?"

"Yes. I was at there."

"The second before I did it, I felt so powerful. It felt like such a dramatic stroke of genius. That line of hard-faced cops with their shaved heads was ahead of me, each throwing a clod of earth on the coffin, and when I took that letter out of my purse to throw in the grave I felt like I was getting the last word or something. It was supposed to be such a grand gesture. And it was supposed to be a mystery forever."

He had seen it all and it had turned his stomach. The line of photographers behind a rope were clicking away, taking picture after picture, dollar signs racked up with each click. She was impossibly chic in black, as if she had stepped airbrushed off a magazine cover. Her eyes were hidden behind huge sunglasses and for once her full lips were a thin line.

When she threw the letter into the grave, there was a gasp from the assembled that was swallowed in a whip of wind that carried the pages up, up and off to the grasping hands of the vultures behind the red velvet ropes. They scurried and leapt and grabbed up every page and ran for the woods. Some of the cops bellowed after them but did not move. She stood and wept, an ethereal creature among drooling Neanderthals. Her great rage had led her to win a moment's small satisfaction and now she stood on wobbly knees, broken and violated again. She grieved not for her pedophile uncle but for the death of the last vestige of her privacy. She wept loudly. A few photographers, not as quick as the others to grab the pages from the wind, stayed to click away, freezing her pain for the world digitally.

He hadn't gone to her then. He stood in confusion instead. She was crying again and she came to him now. She sat in his lap and buried her face in his neck and sobbed like a child.

They sat there for a long time, her cries blocking out any cogent thought. Finally all he could say was, "I'm sorry. I'm so sorry. I'm sorry." He apologized for every star struck, jealous nobody who wanted to see a goddess brought down.

When she pulled away from him, she gave him a sisterly squeeze of his shoulder. It seared him. She stood up and rearranged her black dress. There was something regal in her as she stood up. She rearranged her face to erect a shield of dignity.

"I need another drink. You want one?"

"You sit down. I'll get it." He strode to the bar. "What'll it be?"

"Screwdriver. OJ's in the fridge."

As he reached for the fridge handle, he spotted the dead mouse in the trap. "Jesus!" he said as he stepped back instinctively. "You know you've got a dead mouse here?"

From her seat she made a dismissive wave. "I know. I know. The house is infested. All the traps are full."

"All?" he said. He looked down at the mouse and saw that a line of ants had taken the little mouse's eyes and were ferrying rodent meat away as he watched. His stomach threatened to rise up in revolt against his vision.

"The house is full of traps and each one has a little mouse with a surprised look on his face. You know what I notice? With every one of them, the tail is stuck straight out. The trap snaps down on their necks and the tails go pencil-straight."

He opened the fridge door, retrieved the orange juice carton and mixed her a stiff drink. "You should really get them cleaned out. You want me to do that for you?"

"Nah," she said. "I didn't bring my assistants. I thought it would look silly to show up in Poeticule Bay again with a fucking entourage. I figured it wouldn't go over well. Back home I would have told somebody to take care of it, or they would have taken care of it and I never would have known about it. Now that I'm here I figure I'm an adult again. I should do it. I just — "

"I'll do it."

"Don't. I'll deal with it." Her tone was sharp for the first time.

He handed her the sweaty glass and instead of taking a sip she put it against her forehead. "Do you believe in reincarnation, Marky?"

"Nope."

"Me, neither, but yesterday I wasn't so sure. As long as I'm unburdening here, I'm going to confess something awful to you."

"Okay." He sat down again and looked at her long bare legs. When he looked up he felt ashamed because he saw the raw pain in her eyes again.

"I arrived day before yesterday. I'd gone straight to the funeral home first and made the arrangements. You know...all that bullshit. All I could think about was how I was going to go to this fucking funeral and some asshole was going to go on and on about what a great guy Uncle Joe was."

He took a big gulp of his drink and gave her an encouraging nod.

"You're going to think I'm a terrible person."

He wondered how she could have managed to keep her secret and keep him out.

"I am a terrible person," she said, "or at least I can be amazingly stupid."

"That just makes you human."

"Then I'm ready to stop that," she said and let out a throaty laugh. "Remember how good I was at math?"

"I always let you figure out the tip when we had clams and chips."

"You always let me pay the bill."

"No apologies. You were the local rich girl and I had nothing. You want me to cut you a check for all those clam dinners at The Skinny Dip now?"

"Nah, we'll let that go."

"Thanks, because you're still the local rich girl."

"I'm probably the richest girl on the east coast."

"Then I think I'll have another drink on you. I might even make it a double. You were about to tell me why you're such a terrible person."

She sobered. "Well, as I was saying, I was always good at math. Won first prize in a couple things. Dad thought I should go take a business degree. I was thinking astrophysics."

"I remember. Our first kiss was when you invited me up the hill to look through your telescope."

"Yeah. I'm sure astronomy was foremost in your mind."

"I was fifteen. Give me a break."

"I was fifteen, too. That's something else I have to thank you for. See, after you came into the picture, Big Joe lost interest in me."

"You think he was afraid he'd get caught?"

"No, it's sicker than that. After we started dating, I was too old for his games. I was ruined — by you, I guess."

"I'm glad. I just wish you'd told me at the time."

She shrugged and raised her empty glass, tinkled the ice, and he got up to fill it again. This time he avoided looking at the mouse.

He refilled her glass and she waited for him to sit down again. "Math always came easy and I liked that there was only one right answer. It's binary. It's right or it's wrong. Subjectivity means no one is ever simply right. Arguing some obscure point in an essay just pissed me off."

"Your history marks reflected that."

"You're getting entirely too comfortable around me awfully quickly."

"Sorry," he said.

"Really?"

"No."

She cleared her throat and warned him to be quiet with a look. "I also have a thing for symmetry. When I walked into this house after all these years...when dad was away in the oil fields or flying around the world selling stuff to the Chinese, I stayed here with Uncle Joe. This was my torture chamber."

"Sorry."

"Really?"

"You're goddamn right. I really, really wish you had told me."

"So you said. Anyway, I walked in here straight from the funeral parlor and headed straight to the toilet and what do I find but a little mouse is swimming in the fucking toilet bowl!"

"No shit?"

"No shit. Just this little mouse. Probably went in for the water and couldn't get out. And you know what? I had this fantasy that this mouse somehow was Uncle Joe's reincarnation or soul or something. I don't know. It sounds pretty stupid now that I'm saying this out loud."

"No, I can see why you'd think that. I mean, yeah, it doesn't really make sense, but I'm sure it did at the time. You'd just come from arranging your...

pedophile's funeral."

"Exactly. Thanks. I knew you'd understand."

"Just give me half what you pay your regular therapist."

She let out another throaty laugh and took another long drink from her glass. He thought she might be getting drunk but with really elegant women it was so much harder to tell. He didn't have much practice hearing the confessions of boozy starlets. When he knew Betty, she didn't drink at all. He hadn't driven a car when he knew her.

"What did you do about the mouse?"

"Hm?"

"The mouse in the toilet. Did he flush easy?"

"Well, now here's the part where you see me for what I am. I watched him swimming around and around and around, his little pink feet paddling and paddling and paddling. I watched and I smiled because I thought, wouldn't it be great symmetry if God had sent me this gift? God's given me a lot of gifts. Why not this special one, just for me? Everything I do seems to be for everybody else, so why not this for me?"

He looked in her eyes. They were wet again but her face was perfectly smooth, uncracked stone. "What did you do with the mouse?"

"I waited for him to tire out. Eventually he did, I was standing over it for an hour or so, I'm not sure. Anyway, he drowned and when he drowned I was so stupidly happy. I can't tell you."

He nodded. "I understand."

"Thanks. Even if you don't mean it. I've been a spokesperson for PETA, you know!"

He couldn't help himself. He began to giggle and

first she looked angry and then that broke and she joined him. They laughed together a long time.

When the laughter died she added, "I pissed on him at the end, just for good measure, you know. It seemed so right at the time. Then to celebrate Joe being dead I walked out here to Joe's bar and what do I find but another dead mouse. I look in every corner and there's another fucking mousetrap filled with another dead mouse. I run around the house and they're everywhere!"

"Jesus!"

"Yeah. It put things in perspective."

"So you revised your reincarnation hypothesis?"

"I guess you could say that. I ran out here, found some paper and wrote out that letter to Joe. I cried all night. Then I went to that stupid fucking funeral and threw the letter in the grave and—"

"And the wind picked it up and delivered it to the world's media."

She nodded, the tears coming in long hot lines now, burning down her face, burning away her invulnerability and divinity.

"Shit," he said.

"Tomorrow it will be everywhere. It's probably already in China and when the sun comes over each horizon my private shame won't be private anymore. It's no doubt already all over the net."

"People will understand."

"I don't want people to understand. I want them not to know!" She dug through her purse and found some tissues. She blew her nose loudly and when she looked at him, her gaze was an accusation.

"Technically, I'm media, too, but not tonight."

"What are you tonight?"

"I'm the guy who's poured you too many drinks. Tomorrow...no. In a few days this will blow over. Britney will drown her kid or Paris will blow some politician in public and it won't be long before the public will confuse heiresses and stars. They'll think your story really is about Paris Hilton."

She gave him a smile. "I'm glad you're here to pour me too many drinks. You were there for me at the beginning, so maybe you're the only guy I can trust in the world."

"We're not all so bad."

"You don't think so? Let me tell you one more story. A couple years ago I dropped out. People thought I was in rehab I disappeared so long. I got out of Hollywood and went to the one place in all of America where there's not a news rag jerkoff within a short plane flight. You know where I went?"

"Rural Texas?"

"Still too close to California."

"Where?"

"Cincinnati."

"Cincinnati?"

"I dyed my hair purple and blond, tied it in a ponytail and got some baggy Old Navy clothes. I even picked up a job working as some professor's personal assistant."

"You are shitting me."

"Nope. I'd just done my third supermodel spy movie and then my writer-director-asshole husband started banging his assistant director."

"That's so Hollywood."

"The assistant director was a guy so it was so West Hollywood."

"I have no idea what that means but I'm sure it's funny. What happened to your new life of obscurity among the mere mortals of Cincinnati?"

She drained her glass again. "God is capricious in His wrath, Marky. He sent me another dreamy asshole. I was looking for revenge so I hooked up with a guy in a bar. I called myself Suzy but he must have seen right through the disguise because...you're going to love this shit."

"What?"

"I took him home and made the one night stand mistake. I fell asleep before kicking the fucker out and he stole my brand new vacuum cleaner."

"What?"

"What. Just as I said."

"Who steals a fucking vacuum cleaner?"

"Oh, it probably ended up on E-bay. Who steals a vacuum cleaner is a guy who knows it's *my* vacuum cleaner. He knew who I was, fucked me and now he can brag about that *plus* he got a celebrity souvenir! People think it's so easy and a lot of it is. If I could eat like a normal person it might all be worth it but I can't even do that and keep my job. And I've got all these people around me. The agent, the personal assistants, make up and their fucking assistants. I quit Cincinnati and went back to Burbank as quick as I could after the whole vacuum cleaner thing.

"Of course, I still don't know who to trust. You can't trust everyone when they're all paid to be there. You should have seen them. They went into shock when I said I was flying back to Maine alone. I guess I should have kept the bodyguard so he could have thumped a few of those goddamn vultures at the funeral."

"Now I'm sorry I didn't punch out a few for you."

"Thanks, Marky. You were always my shining knight.

"You made all my nights shiny."

She gave him a big toothy grin that was so defenseless, he glimpsed who she had been when they were kids. "So I guess I'm a typical Hollyweird Celebrity. It's all about me! Me! Me!"

"Yeah. Way to hold up the brand."

"So what about you? Where are you at, Marky?"

"I got ambitious too late. Now I'm playing catch-up. I don't see how can I ever retire from a job I hate. When it comes down to it, I'm just another vulture like those twits at the cemetery."

"You're nothing like them."

He shook his head, meaning to warn her off.

"You're a journalist and a radio personality. You're a celebrity, right?"

"Betty Jane. Asia. Whatever. Coming from you, that's about the cruelest and most insensitive thing you could say."

She looked down at the filthy rug and seemed to study it for some time.

"I wanted to form a band but got a lousy technical degree instead," he said. "I fell into being a DJ and somehow ended up no farther than a mile from where I was born. Money and distance from where you're born: That's how all success is measured. There's no end in sight to me going in at five in the morning to do a morning drive show for a place so small there's no rush hour. When we were — when I was a kid, I was so sure I was better than this."

She looked at him sharply. "Tell me what you want."

"I want to live where there are palm trees and I don't have to wait forever for a vacation so I can get somewhere where there's a Starbucks. I want to live in a city big enough that I can wander around and see something different each time. I want to be able to go somewhere where I can pick up an Irish newspaper or a book that hasn't been read by someone else first."

"In other words, you still want what every kid in a small town dreams of."

"Yeah. It would be nice to go somewhere where there aren't a bunch of people who remember me in diapers. Maybe people who remember I don't want to be called Marky anymore."

She look chagrinned. "Marcus."

"Thanks. I see you and I'm really nostalgic, but the Funky Bunch obsession is way over. Even Marky Mark is Mr. Wahlberg now."

"So, why not leave?"

"I got bills like everybody else."

"No ties? I heard you married a nurse from around here."

"Cheryl. Married and divorced. Didn't last. Now it's about alimony until she remarries, hopefully to the guy she's shacked up with right now. Until then, she continues to get a free ride on the Marcus bus."

"Careful, you sound like my ex. How come it didn't work out?" she asked.

"She kept comparing herself to you."

"That's not fair."

"You're right. I'm sure that's not all of it. The point is, I can't seem to get out of here. I'll die here." He was about to take another drink but found his glass empty and realized he didn't have the energy to challenge gravity and get over to the bar for another.

"What would it take to start a new life? Where would you go exactly?"

He contemplated his empty glass for a long time, choosing his words carefully. "I don't know exactly, but that would kind of be the point. I'd like to have enough money to pay everybody off, climb in my old beater and head out. All I know is west. Then I'd see where I end up. I want to lose myself in a city and see what I end up doing there. I've got skills. I'd find something eventually. I just want some time to myself and the chance to look around. I want to —"

"Start again. You want to start again. I get that. I can feel it. I tried it in Cincinnati before the cute guy with the big cock stole my vacuum cleaner."

He winced.

"Oh, yeah, he was really cute and he was huge. I nicknamed it Moby it was so big."

His cheeks flushed red but he said nothing.

She pushed herself up out of the chair and disappeared. In a moment she returned with her purse. She pulled out a check book, all business. "How much would it take?"

"A million dollars."

"Let me rephrase, Marcus. What do you owe in debts? What does it cost to buy you out of wage slavery?"

"Serious?"

"As a disease in your lymph glands."

"Maybe...I don't know. Car payments..."

"You in an apartment?"

"Still."

"Would $100,000 do it?"

"More than enough."

She paused, as if making calculations in her head. When she wrote the check her smile broadened. He noticed it was a Mont Blanc pen.

She held out the check and he didn't hesitate a moment. He snatched it out of her hand and shoved the paper roughly into his shirt pocket. He knew he should be ashamed, but he felt nothing like shame. "Is this half what you pay your therapist?" he asked.

"Roughly, I suppose, but after all that's happened today I think I'm done with therapy. I'm tired of telling the story of my rotten childhood over and over and now that's all anyone will want to talk about. I won't need a therapist. I'll just need to escape, like you."

"Where will you go?"

"Someplace far away. I doubt I'll be coming back."

"Then we'll both finally escape. Thanks for coming back for me and getting me out."

"Don't thank me. I need to thank you. It's late."

Energized, he stood up and looked out the rear windows. Beyond that dark sea lay possibilities. Or he could drive west as far as the highway went. Then he could fly. Potential was oozing over the horizons in every direction.

She stood and spun him around, holding him by the shoulders. "You know I hated this place. Every time my father left me with Uncle Joe we did it — "

"He did it to you."

"Right. Anyway, that's what he was really all about, no matter what he looked like to the world. The uniform didn't mean anything. Every time we were alone, Joe told me how much he loved me. Every time he said, 'Wrong is a fluid concept, Betty Jane.' Blood didn't mean anything. He did it for so long I'm not even sure I remember the first time. He wore a mask for everybody. I think everybody wears a mask. Don't you think?"

He looked away and she grabbed his chin to make him look into her eyes. "This little village just about fucking killed me. I hated that everyone knew everyone and nothing ever changed. Everything was awful about this place...except you. We watched videos and later we went to the drive-in and we made out and your kisses were always sweet and you were always so gentle."

"I guess I always thought if I didn't treat you like fine china you'd break...or I'd wake up from the dream." *And I wish I'd told you how much I loved you then*, he thought.

She held him tightly and he ached. It reminded him of the truth he would never tell. It wasn't his ex-wife who compared herself to the nymph and movie star Asia Minor. It was he who made all the comparisons and had always found Cheryl wanting. Now that he felt her warmth, her breasts pressed to him. He would never — could never — be as happy as he was as a teenager. Or could he?

"You," she whispered, "were the best thing about my childhood." He turned his head to taste her full red lips again, too late. Instead, she kissed his cheek with a chaste smack that reminded him of kissing the bride at someone else's wedding. Her kiss, so warm and soft, the sort of kiss he fell into in dreams, now felt like a sharp rebuke.

They broke apart abruptly. He couldn't wait to leave. Their reunion — which he had dreamed of, anticipated so long — now embarrassed him. "I better go."

"Okay," she said. She looked away.

"I've got to be on the air in another couple hours."

"Of course. Thanks for coming to see me. I love that you came to see me."

"Yes," he said, patting his chest shirt pocket through his sports jacket. "It's been...very profitable. The circle is complete and all that." He made his way to the door awkwardly.

She laughed. "Well worth it," she said. "It's funny. I complained about how I was paying all the people around me and the first chance I get, I turn you into someone else I write a check to."

He looked ashen and grasped at the doorknob. When he looked in her face though, he saw that she hadn't meant it unkindly. "I guess it's different when you're helping out a friend. Uh, Ms. Minor. Have a great escape."

"You, too."

She watched him shamble out to the porch and down the hill. "Bye," she whispered and turned back to the bar and the view of the sea.

* * *

He found his car but decided he shouldn't drive. Instead he sat on the hood of his car and looked back up the hill at the dead cop's house. There were so many things he wished he had known when he was seventeen. He patted his shirt pocket again, checking to make sure it was there in a superstitious motion.

Marcus pulled out the bent check, smelling it as if it might be scented like a letter. He opened the check

134

and his jaw dropped. She had made it out to him for the sum of $1,000,000. The bottom of the check read, "For therapeutic services."

He sat frozen on the hood of his car for a long time, shaking his head and smiling. He folded the check neatly and put it in his wallet for safekeeping. Then he dug into his shirt pocket again and pulled out the small digital voice recorder. After a moment's hesitation he put the device under his left rear tire and, when he pulled away from the curb, he made sure he crushed it twice. "Coulda made two million out of that recording," he said to himself in the rear view mirror, "but how much does one guy need to start fresh...and let an ex-girlfriend escape?"

He laughed all the way down the hill and out of sight.

* * *

If Marcus had been looking in the rearview mirror behind him instead of looking at himself, he might have seen the bloom of flame that shot through the living room in the house at the top of the hill.

Asia Minor, silver screen idol to millions of B-movie fans and object of lust to many more, walked down the steep stairs to the dark beach below. At first she had thought she would rig a Molotov cocktail to throw into the middle of the living room but reconsidered. Odds were better than even that she would set herself on fire, as well. She had always feared dying in a fire so she wasn't about to attempt anything fancy.

However, Uncle Joe's well-stocked bar yielded several bottles of Jack Daniels and some high proof scotch so she threw them to the floor and tossed a flaming matchbook in the open door as she walked out the back. She didn't look back as the fire spread and climbed and clawed through the house. Instead, she kept moving, leaving a trail of clothes.

Periwinkles and sharp stones cut the soles of her feet but her straight course to the sea did not waver. As she waded out into the surf, the cold shocked her. She was glad of it. The cold would soon numb her wounded feet and she thought if she could swim out far enough, she could finally feel clean.

"Tonight I'm going to fulfill a dream I've had from when I should have only been sleeping with teddy bears," she announced to the whitecaps. The chill water was just below her bare breasts now. "Tonight, for the first time, I'm moving toward something instead of always running away from something, always looking back!" The sea floor dropped away suddenly. She went under and came up laughing and treading water.

The buzz in her head from all the booze didn't seem to matter anymore. She was a good swimmer, "a natural," her father said. She slipped under the waves into the dark and came up gulping crystal air. She pushed out into the dark in a crawl, legs and arms working smoothly, her stroke confident and strong.

This would be a binary choice, she told herself. Either she would swim until she drowned or until she felt clean again. Soon all the water would be all there was and she would leave everything behind her. Somewhere up ahead and hours away the sun was now reaching around the earth, coming for her and waking up the world to a new day.

She escaped to the sea. When she felt fresh and cleansed, if her mask fell away to the sea bottom, maybe she would have enough left in her for the swim back. The fiery reflections of the house on the hill chased her wake and she pushed harder. Soon Poeticule Bay would be far behind her, along with the weight of memory's burden. That was all the illumination she needed. Soon the cold would lift the burden of conscious thought.

Soon everyone she had ever known would read her love letters to Uncle Joe. They'd see what she was underneath her mask. She started to gasp and slowed her pace. She worked her arms and legs in a steady rhythm, going for distance. She felt lighter and lighter. She had the strength to keep going, straight toward the rushing, burning sun.

PARTING SHOTS

*A good friend of mine was dying. His faith
brought him great comfort. His faith
remained strong in the face of his illness.
Mine faded.
I didn't have the atheist versus Christian
argument with him. That wasn't an
argument I wanted to win. ~ Chazz*

Before he even opened his eyes, he groaned. Burt
could feel himself pulled up from blissful
unconsciousness toward daylight and damnation.
Genie was still dead and Audrey was still alive and
now he'd have to deal with it all over again.

The radio was on and Marcus, the morning DJ,
swam in behind his eyes and started prying the
eyelids up. Burt rolled over, hoping Marcus would
get to a song soon. Instead of introducing a song
Burt could retreat into, the radio guy nattered. The
radio dial was slightly off. Through the static Burt
could tell it was the regular DJ, though Marcus
didn't sound like himself this morning.

A stab of sunlight poked into his brain through the

curtain and he cursed as he rose from the bed unsteadily and made his way to the bathroom. For a moment, Burt thought he was going to fall but he caught hold of the podium sink, nearly ripping it from the wall. Wouldn't that have been a terrible tragedy? Old man trapped under own sink! *Nine of ten accidents happen in the home, so why not me?* he thought. It would be lonely, slowly dying under the weight of the sink, unable to get up. But dying could be an immense relief, too, wouldn't it?

After an unsatisfactory squirt, he faced himself in the mirror. Burt's eyelids were rimmed with bright pink and his nose looked like a tomato. He belched loudly and tasted gin. Gin made his stomach bleed. Good.

Audrey had thrown up so much blood, he couldn't figure out how it was possible God had delivered him the tragic miracle. Right now she was somewhere in Banff National Park taking pictures of elk so Japanese tourists could have a never-ending supply of fresh postcards. Audrey. His good daughter. Healthy and whole and a great weight on his heart.

Genie had always been Audrey's opposite. Audrey slept like an angel through the whole night from six weeks old. Genie had colic and seemed to keep it with her like a curse. Genie stayed cranky right up until her death.

Burt wondered if he should bother with the pretence of making coffee, head out for a double double at Tim Hortons, and pour in a little hooch? Or he could take a bottle of 90 proof in each crepuscular hand. His father, Silas, drank himself to death.

"Slow suicide is perfectly okay by the laws of man

and nature," his old man had said. "God gave us the grape and the barley and plenty of reasons to use 'em." Silas always concluded that and similar pronouncements with, "Burt! You're young and full of blue piss! Fetch me another bottle quick, before I sober up."

His father was a happy drunk, and gravely melancholy when sober. Burt decided he must have inherited the same taste for alcohol his father had, but regretted he didn't seem to enjoy the compulsion nearly as much. Now that Burt was an old man himself, the world had changed the rules on him. Alcoholism was a disease now and that new, ugly fact sort of made the fun spill out.

Silas — how come there weren't any guys named Silas anymore? — had taken pride in starting each day with a shave so Burt lathered up, too. Maybe that was the trick. Looking better might be the key to feeling better. Then he thought of Genie using his razor to shave her legs and how he had bellowed at her not to do it again. She'd run off for two days that time.

His wife, Helen, had always been the buffer. Helen worked as a librarian now. He saw her sometimes across the parking lot at closing time. He had assumed that she had put up with so much that her capacity to forgive was bottomless. Burt must have worn her out because after Genie died his wife didn't seem to have any energy left to make him feel okay anymore. He had begun to drink more after Genie passed, but he figured he was entitled. If you can't drink after losing a child, when was the best time?

Marcus blathered at Burt through the static from the clock radio.

"Shut up, Marcus!" Burt said, and kept on shaving. The razor was old and cut him several times. "The wages of sin are razor bucks," Burt said to his reflection. The haggard old face that emerged from behind the whiskers was little better than the mask that had grown over it while he dreamt. He missed half his chin but he had already put three dots of toilet paper on his shaving nicks so he decided he'd drawn enough of his own blood for the day.

The day she left, Helen's last words to him were, "Make God the center." He'd tried, but Burt was tired of apologizing. How much contrition did one man have to drag up before he could be free of eternal condemnation by a bunch of celestial busybodies?

God didn't understand how hard it is to be a man, Burt thought. *And sometimes, if you're very unlucky, He answers your prayers and in the end still gets it wrong.*

It was then that he caught a few phrases and realized Marcus was talking to him. He was sure he heard "eternal damnation" and the words "sorry prick." He stalked to the bedroom and finally tuned the radio. "What mischief are you up to, Marcus?" The static drained away and it was as if Marcus was standing in his bedroom yelling.

"...if you believe in reincarnation, let me tell you what that is, friends and neighbors," Marcus said. "Reincarnation in a hamster wheel."

"Okay," Burt said. "What happened to the usual mix of Johnny Cash, Stompin' Tom Connors and Elvis?"

"If you believe there's an old man in the sky watching your every move, how can you ever get naked or evacuate your bowels? I'll tell you what your fascist God makes you. You're a damned ant farm! And I use the term 'damned' not carelessly, but advisedly."

"Jesus!" said Burt.

"Jesus won't help you now," Marcus said, as if he had heard Burt. "Jesus died to get his Dad in a forgiving mood. Would you let one child, your *favorite* no less, die, just so you could forgive your other children?"

"Jesus!" Burt said. He almost skidded and fell as he headed downstairs for the phone.

* * *

Marcus figured he had less than a minute to go so he did his best to pour it all out before the station manager barged through the door to haul him off the air. He couldn't help thinking of his hero, Reverend Ted, who had been hauled away from the altar by a bunch of angry old men who hadn't appreciated the nuances of his drunken speech against religion. Ted had been dead for years now but people all the way from Bangor still talked about the Sunday the crazy reverend had gone off his nut. Marcus felt he owed the old minister something. Though his tirade from the altar had been lost on most of the congregation, Marcus counted that as the beginning of his journey from asleep and born again to awake.

"I'll get to our sponsors, Hankerson's Car Wash and Chigley's Roofing, in just a moment. By the way, the views of your humble radio host are exactly the same as our noble sponsors 'cause they know I'm only laying the beautiful truth on you!" For the first time since he spun jazz records for the one to five shift in college, Marcus was having fun at his job. Of course, the check tucked safely into his breast pocket had really kicked him into high gear. He'd use the money to get a tent and some supplies for the summer ahead. No need to touch the principle. A million dollars freed a guy up and knocked the shit of his boots.

"You know the beauty of these heavies I'm laying on you, brothers and sisters? The beauty is, you, too, can be godless and free to be dead forever. You don't have to feel guilty anymore. Say your child is dying. Guess what? It's a bad genetic bounce in a random universe. There's no one to plead your case to. If God's too busy to save your child from a horrible disease without you having to beg, what kind of monster is your god, anyway? I'd save your child in a heartbeat if I were omnipotent and I'm just a simple, know-nothing guy about to be unemployed. Think about that! If your God has less compassion than I do, what are you worshipping? You'd be better off praying to me and begging for my help and forgiveness and sending me lots of moolah! How about it folks? I can always use more. Maybe I'll pull a Pope and use the cash you send me to fill up my basement with fine works of art the world will never see! Sure, I could use it to feed the poor, but unlike religion, I'm not going to lie to you."

The board's red lights were blinking. "Our lines are jammed. Everyone wants to talk to their new god, the inimitable me, but you can call me Marcus!"

"This is Jim Chigley of Chigley Roofing," an angry voice came over the speaker. "I was just having breakfast and heard your show and I think I might just toss my cook—"

"No need to thank me, James. Enjoy your meal. I bless you for making this show possible."

"I don't — "

"Know what you did before I came into your life? In the old days, before me, you could beat your wife and feel terrible about it all the way to church where your priest said it was okay."

"Hey! I don't t know what you're talking about! I'm not even Catholic."

"Never mind that. Ask your *wife's* forgiveness. That, my friend, is the way to heaven right here on earth, right here, right now."

Marcus leaned back and looked through the glass door of his booth. His boss's door was closed, so he was sure Clarence Degal was still enjoying his morning nap. His boss made a great show of being the first of the day staff to arrive in the morning and the last to leave at night. Mostly Degal napped and ate chicken from the restaurant next door. On summer afternoons, everyone knew Degal would be out with advertisers on the golf course. He slept with his door closed and played golf under the guise of "making sales calls." Degal told everyone he was the hardest working station manager in the business because his car was in the parking lot the longest of any employee at the radio station.

"Next caller! Gwen, you're on with your new lord and savior, Marcus in the Morning on 95.4, almost 95 and a half on your FM dial. What's on your mind?"

"This is Gwen."

"Yes, we know. Go ahead."

"Do you mean me? This is Gwen."

"Next caller. Bobby, Bobby, lay it on me!"

"I'm a Christian, mister. Are you seriously saying God is a figment of my imagination?"

"Exactly, Bobby, you've got it right. He or she is a figment that's draining away your life energy. Which Christian god do you believe in, by the way? The Old Testament god who's always angry or the new testament God who took a chill pill who's all about love except when he's not?"

"I believe in both the God of the New and Old Testaments."

"That's no good. He's supposed to be eternal and unchangeable so you really have to pick one. Get back to me on that and we'll chat. Next caller!"

The secretaries from the front desk appeared at his door: Sheila and the other Sheila. The young one waved her arms while the old one slapped a pad of paper against the glass of his booth. He looked up and flashed them a grin. The paper read, "36 angry calls!" He gave both women an energetic thumbs up and shooed them away. As soon as they turned their backs he gave them both middle fingers.

"Next up, Roger's on Marcus in the Morning!"

"All I got to say is right on, man!"

"Nobody likes a suck up, Roger. I condemn you to the depths of hell for your impious thoughts about the hot check out lady at The Duck 'n Rush. She's over eighty and deserves your respect, you utter pig!"

Laughter. "Rock on, man. You're my new god —"

"Blasphemer!" Marcus said.

"We've got to whip through these calls, folks, because sometime soon Mr. Degal is going to wake up from his morning nap and I'll be off the air, so come on, Poeticule Bay, let's have a little intellectual rigor before I blow this town for a little place I like to call Anytown Better, USA! I can see by the jammed lines that you have the number so let's go to line 2 with Trish. Trish, what do you have to contribute to our religious discussion?"

Silence. Then he heard a tell-tale echo and hung up on Trish. "She's is in love with the idea that she'll hear herself on the radio. If you're going to talk to me, you'll have to turn down your radio. Trish, get over yourself. Buy a tape recorder and you'll be able to hear yourself all day without bugging the sh—um, bugging me. Whoops. With that breach of on air etiquette we go to, line 3. The queue says this is Burt."

"This is Burt."

"You're off to a slow start, Burt. My divine finger is reaching out, much like in that famous painting of God giving life to Adam. The difference is, my finger's over the button that will send you to oblivion. What's your story, Burt?"

"I killed my daughter."

Marcus spaced out a moment. "Tell me more," he said finally.

"You're saying God doesn't exist, but I made a deal with Him. I prayed like crazy and..."

"Back up there, cowboy. How'd you kill your daughter?"

* * *

Burt took a long drink from his bottle of gin. He

decided he was serious about getting the job done today and all that orange juice was slowing down the process.

"I had two daughters," he said into the phone. *Sending a message out to the living and the dead,* he thought.

"You have my attention, Burt. Lay it on me."

"My eldest, Audrey. She got cancer. Audrey was my daddy's girl. She couldn't do wrong and nobody loved a daughter like I loved her." He breathed heavily. He could hear it through the phone, but the more he tried to control it, the worse it got. He guessed he knew lots of things are like that.

"What happened to Audrey.?"

"The Big C."

"I'm sorry to hear it, Burt."

"Are you? I wonder. People find it so goddamn interesting, like they can't hear enough about it and can't think enough about it as long as it's happening to somebody else."

"I hear your pain, Burt, but I'm not going to apologize for you tweaking my interest. You called me. Now what's this about you killing somebody? Were you serious about that or are you just yanking me?"

"Audrey had the Big C and I...I loved her so much. I had another daughter. Genie. I dream of Genie with the light brown hair. You know that old song?"

"No."

"Well, I do. And I still dream about her. I killed her, or God did." Burt took another long drag of gin. "Genie was always wild. She was just born that way, like she was meant to be a wolf or something and there was some mistake along the way."

"What happened Burt, between you and me? It's just us guys, a good hunk of Maine and the South Shore of Nova Scotia listening."

* * *

Marcus wasn't sure if he should believe his caller and had his hand poised over the dump button, watching the clock hands skim around. "C'mon, Burt. Don't leave us hanging. Who'd you kill?"

"I like you better when you just let Johnny Cash sing."

"Johnny didn't sing. He talked his way through his songs and somehow nobody seemed to notice. What happened to your daughters, Burt?"

"Genie showed up at Audrey's hospital bed drunk one night after she'd disappeared for three days. Genie ran away a lot. Anyway, Audrey didn't mind, but Audrey was like that. Nothing phased her and she was just glad to see her sister. Audrey was always sunny...even acted pretty chipper fighting the Big C. Anyway, I chewed out Genie for showing up drunk and Audrey got all upset and I went to the hospital chapel and I made myself a prayer. I asked God to take Genie instead of Audrey."

"Interesting."

"Sure, it didn't happen to you."

"God doesn't answer prayers, Burt. Even if such a thing as God exists, and I won't grant you that, he doesn't interfere with our messed up world. If God cared about you, Audrey wouldn't get cancer — that's

148

what mature grown-ups call the disease, by the way, not 'The Big C'— and there wouldn't be so much suffering."

Burt took another ragged breath, remembering his church-going days. "I think there's so much suffering because there's so much sin everywhere."

"Sure, sure," Marcus said. "We're all sinners according to religion, which is like blaming us for having two legs and two arms each and commanding us not to have heads. I told you, Burt, we're all ants in the big plan, only there's no plan. God doesn't answer prayers, dude!"

"God answered my prayer that night." Burt said. "Genie dropped dead behind the wheel of her car that night at the look off over Poeticule Bay. Aneurysm. She was only nineteen and her brain blew up."

"I really am sorry to hear that, Burt. We all go one by one. We're all dying, some by feet and others by inches."

"That's a pretty way of talking about something ugly, but let me tell you, right after that, Audrey started to get better. It was like...suddenly she had The Medium C and then The Little C and then her scans were clear."

"You think your deal with God came through and you traded one daughter for another?"

"I know it. The doctor's couldn't explain it. They just said things like this happen sometimes, as if that was an explanation."

"I can tell you, Burt. You're an innocent man."

"I'm guilty. Audrey and my wife think so, too. They won't have anything to do with me. I don't blame them."

"Burt, it's all a big crapshoot. You got a bad bounce. Tell your wife and daughter that Marcus in the Morning forgives you your ignorance and they should, too. You're not a monster. You're human and we're all guilty of that."

Burt began to cry.

"Thanks for the call." Marcus pushed the dump button. "Well, look at us. We're all yak, yak, yak. Let's spin some Billy Ray Cyrus. I know you kids used to like his daughter's songs, but this is adult swim time now and I've got something here for Burt. Burt, I've got a gift for you. Genie died of an aneurysm because Intelligent Design is a joke. It was a genetic, organic failure of the structural integrity of a tube in her brain. Your daughter with cancer lived because cancer cells grow wild and sometimes they choke off their own blood supply and die off on their own."

Marcus took a sip of bottled water and thought for a moment. "Mysteries aren't divine just because we don't understand them...and one mystery doesn't explain another. Saying God did it means nothing. One day we'll know about the things we don't know about now and then we'll know we would have been better off doing good deeds on Sunday mornings instead of screwing around in church. Sorry, but that's the way it is. Hope you find peace for your achy-breaky heart."

He turned up the music and soon Billy Ray Cyrus was singing *Achy Breaky Heart*. Marcus's smile faded as he looked up to see Donegal's great red sweating moon face. Even through the thick glass, Marcus could hear his boss was yelling at Jimmy, the summer intern and Marcus's call screener, but the man's eyes were boring into Marcus' head as he yelled.

Jimmy was speaking to someone on the phone and waving for Marcus to come into the production booth. Billy Ray Cyrus's voice followed him out as he leaned out of the studio door, careful to keep the door between him and his irate employer.

"What's up, boss?"

"If you're going to change the format of my radio station, it would be a courtesy for you to let me know."

"Next time I change the format, I'll definitely let you know."

"The Sheilas are getting a lot of angry calls."

"Yes. Should I pack up my stuff?"

"Why?" Donegal said, suddenly looking more serene. "I was going to fire you because I didn't think anyone was listening to your show. Turns out you can turn up the heat. Just make sure you don't let the callers swear on air again. You let that last goddamn bastard say goddamn."

"Goddamn," Marcus said. "So, you're saying I'm not fired?"

"People are listening. That's all I care. You sucked last week because you were bored. When anybody's bored, they're boring. Get back in there and hit 'em again."

"I don't know what else to say. I thought I'd get pulled from the booth by now."

"Try slagging the government on taxes and gas prices. That always works. Tell 'em they need to pay more for gas and we need to raise taxes. That'll piss 'em off."

"You really aren't worried about ratings?" Marcus

said.

"People listen longer to people they hate than those they love. Look at Rush Limbaugh and Howard Stern."

"Shit," Marcus said. "That's the nicest thing anyone ever said to me since last night. You should know I really pissed off Mr. Chigley. The sponsor."

"Screw Chigley. He's a lousy winner when I have to play a round with him and he pays late. When he calls I'll listen to his complaint and then jack up the price. You keep up this intensity, your spots are worth more, anyway."

Jimmy got off the phone, his eyebrows high in surprise. "That movie star is missing and her uncle's house burned to the ground last night."

"Shit again," said Marcus. "Boss, I quit. Jimmy, you just moved up to on-air personality. You've got about fifteen seconds till that song is over."

* * *

Marcus didn't bother saying goodbye to anyone. He'd been the morning guy for years. so he was always at work before everyone else and left as soon as his time slot was over. Today, he walked out with a file box that contained his coffee mug and a bunch of stolen office supplies.

He paused at the front door, balancing the full box on one knee as he struggled with his key ring. He got the key to the front door off the ring and casually tossed it over his shoulder to the floor.

"I wanted to say something dramatic!" he yelled

back to the two Sheilas at the front desk, "but frankly, nothing occurs to me! I don't have a single cogent thought to share at the moment. See you!" He opened the door and was half way out.

"Bye!" the two Sheilas chorused.

"Oh, yeah," Marcus said. "One detail. You two were never very friendly but I always thought it would have been amusing if you both faked Australian accents."

The young and old Sheilas looked at each other and laughed.

"Especially if you did it while we had a threesome!" The young one looked angry. The old one blushed and gave him a smile and a flirty wink.

* * *

A sad old man sat in the back of a pickup in the parking lot pulling on a bottle of Jack. Marcus knew right away just looking at him, he had to be Burt. It was a small town. He'd seen him around.

"Hey," he said. "I'd love to chat but my ex-girlfriend is missing and the world is about to descend on Poeticule Bay. I'm thinking I don't want to be here when that happens."

"That movie star. She dead, too? You think that movie star burned up? It's all over the radio."

"I'm guessing probably," Marcus said. "God is capricious in His wrath, but I sure didn't see that coming. Maybe she just moved to Cincinnati. You okay, dude?"

"I liked you better when you let Johnny Cash

sing."

Burt looked at him with red, wounded eyes. "The problem is, Mr. Marcus in the Morning, you convinced me you're right about everything. My Genie's out of the bottle."

"Huh. I don't hear that often. Mostly when you argue with people it's my experience that they dig in their heels and are even more convinced of whatever shit they believe. Good for you."

"Didn't see that coming, huh?"

Marcus smiled and moved toward his car. Burt reached for the .22 caliber rifle in the bed of the pickup.

CORRECTIVE MEASURES

This is another story that has a root in real life. Many of us have run into trouble over a parking space, haven't we? I don't suggest this solution...but everyone has a revenge fantasy. Right? ~ Chazz

Jack pulled his car to the right, out of the way, so the woman in the green family van could drive into the Poeticule Bay Elementary parking lot. Instead, her car stood still at the mouth of the school's gate. Another car slid up behind her, yet she did not enter. He waved her in and she sat blocking the street, blinker blinking, waiting for what, Jack couldn't guess.

A horn honked. He assumed it must be the little white car behind her, urging her forward. The bell had already rung. The last of the kids who were on time had already streamed into the school. Jack glanced at the green numerals of his dashboard clock and huffed with impatience. Was she stalled?

He was about to pull forward and forget about being a good Samaritan when she wheeled into the lot and accelerated up beside him, frantically cranking down her window. "Are you deaf?"

"Pardon me?" he said, giving her a confused smile. He looked in her eyes and saw a savage animal. Her bright yellow peroxide hair was mussed, reinforcing the impression of something wild at the wheel.

"Didn't you hear me honk? You're in *my* way! I want to park right *there*." Peroxide Woman pointed at the empty parking space his car now blocked. Jack glanced in his rearview mirror. Half of the lot behind him was empty. She could park anywhere. Why hold people up for one spot that was no closer than any of the others available?

"No good deed goes unpunished," he said.

"*What?*"

"You win. I'll never do a good deed for a stranger again."

"I'm *trying* to park!" she screeched. "I want *that* spot right there." She pointed again to the spot behind him. We're *late!*"

He stifled the impulse to pull her out of her seat through her window. There still might be a few children straggling down the sidewalk, coming late to school. The van's windows were tinted, but he detected movement in the back seat. She no doubt had at least one child in there. There were too many witnesses. He took a cleansing breath as his therapist, Dr. Circe Papua, had taught him. "There are lots of parking spots," he said evenly, "and you're making yourself late. You, me and the poor guy behind you."

Jack glanced to the forlorn-looking guy in the little white car who sat waiting behind her. The swarthy man wore a hang-dog look on his face that told Jack

the man at the wheel was tired. He had the look of a
beaten man who expected a fresh beating every day.
Jack could see in a moment that this was a man who
had seen life and death. His intuition told him the
man waiting behind the ranting woman had, like
himself, learned the truth of existence in a war zone.
Jack recognized the haunted civilian look when he
saw it.

As he looked back in the woman's face, the
contrast was startling. She was the sort of person
who breezed through life with an air of entitlement.
Nothing really bad had ever happened to her and she
expected that nothing ever would. She could inflict
suffering on all those lives she touched, but never
experience a flicker of self-doubt. Pain was for other
people. She would never consider that she had ever
done anything wrong.

Peroxide Woman gave him the finger.

"You've caused several car accidents in your life,
haven't you?" he said, his face deceptively serene.

"Are you a fucking idiot?"

"You've got kids in your car, right? Nice mouth."

"Well, next time, *listen* for God's sake! I *honked*
my fucking *horn*!"

Before he could move his car, she did what she
should have done in the first place and tore off for
another empty slot behind him. His head heated up
and he clenched his teeth. Jack could feel the
pressure at the front of his head and there was a
familiar, angry tingle in his gut. The rage made his
jaws hurt. Before he left, he turned in his seat. He
didn't know what he was going to do with the
information then, but he memorized her license
plate — ATA 667. He'd remember it: 667, Next-door

Neighbor of the Beast. Then he vaguely remembered that some rabbinical scholars had said that the actual number of the beast was not 666, but 667. He'd have to google that.

And he would think a lot about the woman in the green van. He considered waiting to follow her home, but he would have to allow some time to pass. She had screamed at him. People had surely heard. The swarthy man in the little white car glanced over at Jack as he passed. Striking at her too soon would be a gift to the police. He would have to wait until the witnesses' memories had faded.

Jack could key her car in the night, he supposed, but insurance would take care of that, and a petty act of vandalism was something a teen in a tantrum might do. It wasn't creative or personal. Ditto, chucking a brick through her front window.

Driving on, Jack fantasized about following her home and doing things he had promised himself, and Dr. Papua, he wouldn't do anymore. At least, not unless she told him to do it. What if, in a bit of synchronicity granted by God, Dr. Papua called and told him she had a patient who needed deletion? He could tell her about the incident in the parking lot and maybe she'd say it would be okay to do a twofer? It would be delightful to confuse old Chief Rose by putting two murder victims on display in the same spot, by the steam-powered clock at the town hall, for instance. Usually he had to make sure his victims disappear, swallowed by the Atlantic forever. That didn't make news. Across America, lots of people disappeared. When he pictured Peroxide Woman, though, he wanted to make big news.

Last winter, Dr. Papua gave Jack the name of a

man who abused children. He drowned that man in a bathtub, over and over again until Jack couldn't resuscitate him anymore. It was a memory to cherish. Jack had always had a cruel streak, but if he channeled the urges the right way and went after only those people his therapist said should die, he deemed himself righteous in the eyes of the Lord. Lacking a conscience of his own, Dr. Papua guided him away from acts that would make him prey in a state that still had the death penalty.

Not that death frightened Jack. Dying's easy. Blending in and not getting caught is hard. Living among humans demanded a far higher price of Jack than Death could ask him to pay. To live, to pursue his calling, he had to wear a mask all the time. He breathed free only when he went through a cleansing ritual, and each ritual demanded blood sacrifice from a sinner.

Jack descended the back steps to his little basement apartment. He sat in front of the television, but all he could see was the woman's face on the flickering screen. He picked up a length of rope from beside his chair and practiced knots for the rest of the morning. He thought about how untouchable the woman assumed she was. What amazing first-world circumstances had come together to allow that privileged woman a life so secure she thought she could talk to him, a stranger, like that?

Later that week, when Jack arrived at his session, he wasn't his usual self. He needed no urging from Dr. Papua to speak. He recounted the details of the school parking lot incident to her. To his chagrin, his therapist focused more on his reactions than the evil woman's sins. He hated Dr. Papua a little for asking again, "How did you feel about that? What reaction did you choose?"

"I felt that there should be a little more random violence in the world," Jack lamented, "just to make bitches like ATA 667 more polite when talking to people she doesn't know."

Dr. Papua said it was not okay to kill Peroxide Woman, no matter how Jack hinted at the service he would be performing for humanity.

"This is the sort of social friction you must learn to manage, Jack," Dr. Papua said. "If you are ever to reintegrate into normal society, you have to — "

"Eat a little shit while ATA 667 goes through life tasting nothing but chocolate croissants?"

"Socrates said we should be kind to everyone we meet because everyone is in a terrible battle."

"Socrates never met the Beast, ma'am."

"She is not evil, Jack, merely stupid. This is much more simple than you imagine. You do not like being called an idiot. That is all this is. You are looking for my permission for a cleansing ritual. You do *not* have it," Dr. Papua said.

Jack sighed and nodded and looked at the floor, grinding his teeth.

"Do you promise *not* to kill this woman?"

Jack took a long time to nod his agreement.

"You are sure you can control your impulses?"

Jack's eyes were nail heads when he looked up. "Dr. Papua, you have given me several gifts. I have executed each mission — "

"Executed each *person*," she corrected him.

"Yes, ma'am, executed each *person*," he said. "I am thankful for your gifts. With God's strength, I will abide by your wishes."

"Good, Jack. Good. If you can control yourself, you are that much closer to feigning real human relationships. We must solidify your mask. Remember the credo?"

"I am what I pretend to be, ma'am."

The mask he wore looked like a human face, a rather handsome one with a kind smile. But it felt hot on his skin and tight over his teeth.

* * *

And here was The Beast again.

As the kids gathered around Jack on the soccer field, he spotted ATA 667 in the stands, sitting upright and rigid. He couldn't see her eyes through her sunglasses, but he knew her eyes were on him. She sat beside a child, a little boy, who stared at the ground looking miserable.

Jack took a cleansing breath that, by the pounding pulse in his ears, didn't seem to do its job. He asked the kids their names and checked them off on his list, wondering which one belonged to the Neighbor of the Beast. He ran his eyes over the list, examining the names, guessing which felt right for the child of a demon. She looked like she'd spawn a Tyler, Todd or a Chad. Poor little bastard. The kids were only seven and it was a co-ed team. If the bitch had a girl, what would she name her? He eyed the list again. Madeleine? Jocelyn, maybe?

He got them started on dribbling drills, encouraging the kids to keep control of the ball with little kicks. After a few minutes of getting them to move up and down the field, he played goalie and the kids laughed as they took shots on goal. He deflected a bunch of balls back to them, eventually letting them all through so they could move on to the next drill.

The late afternoon sun beamed heat on the players and the air was humid. The kids' faces began to glow red and their mops of hair matted to their heads. "Let's take a water break!" Jack said finally and the kids walked lazily to the side of the field.

Jack had brought a bunch of water bottles in a cooler at the edge of the field. The kids drank. Parents crowded around, voicing encouragement to their tykes. Peroxide Woman stayed in the stands, still watching his every movement. He imagined daggers, then lasers, shooting at him from her eyes. It was easy to imagine. Her body language was clear. She was stiff, preparing for battle.

A terrible thought occurred to him. What if this was a test from God or even from Dr. Papua? It took him a few minutes to convince himself that was impossible. Looking at all the people on the field, he caught himself dividing up the herd by category, doing precisely what Dr. Papua had warned him not to do.

"You must just see them as people. Do not look upon them as the sinners and the sinned against," Dr. Papua had said.

"It's a little more complicated than that. I am a predator, ma'am," Jack had replied. "The world is divided into *three* categories: The Prey and the Witnesses. And things like me. The Predators."

One of the parents, a bearded man dressed

entirely in red, descended upon him. The man was very concerned for his child's safety, he said. "You're not offering any snacks to the kids that have peanuts, are you? My kid is very sensitive to peanuts. Life and death sensitive."

"I'm just offering water but we'll let the parents know again. The notice is right on the snack schedule."

"People don't read."

Jack looked at him without replying. He didn't know what to say that would satisfy the man.

"Do you have a back up epi-pen?" the bearded man asked.

"No. That would be something you would have to supply for your child. We tell everyone the school is a nut-free zone."

"People don't listen."

"No," Jack said. "They sure don't."

He called the kids on the field with his whistle and they trotted out. He split them into two teams and got half of them to turn their jerseys around. "We're going to have a little fun practice game, guys!"

The kids moved in clutches, some distracted while others wandered the outskirts of the action around the ball. Others ended up kicking at their own teammates ankles, so anxious were they to get at the soccer ball.

A fat man at the edge of the field yelled encouragement to his son, jumping up and down in a ponderous pogo motion. Other parents clapped and shouted encouragement from the stands. Jack found his gaze wrenched back to the stands, hoping to see Peroxide Woman having a seizure and choking to death on her tongue. Or spontaneously combust.

That would, by God's grace, be a very good thing. Every time he glanced over, she stared back at him. Jesus was not going to reach down from his throne at the right hand of the Father and crush her into dust. A thought passed through his mind of which Dr. Papua would not approve: *The Lord helps them that help themselves.*

Jack looked away, trying to focus on the action of all the little witnesses kicking clumsily at the soccer ball. He willed himself not to look at Peroxide Woman, but at every break in the action, he glanced over. He peeked at her so often, he worried the witnesses would begin to see him for what he really was.

"I am what I pretend to be," he said under his breath, over and over. But each assertion was instead a reminder that his mask was slipping. The herd might see his teeth.

A very old woman who watched everything with a massive pair of binoculars — so big they had to be Navy issue — sat beside the man in red. She was obviously somebody's grandmother. As she watched the action, she spoke to the pretty young woman beside her. They smiled placidly back at him and he found their presence calming. He tried to focus on the old woman and her stack of curly white hair rather than the vibrating presence of The Beast. He felt like his chest was full of violin strings, shuddering and singing to match The Beast's vibrations.

Jack encouraged the kids to pass to each other. One boy, taller than the rest, hogged the ball and wouldn't pass it. He was talented, so much so that Jack thought he was too precocious for this age division and should be moved up to a more competitive level. Jack blew his whistle and broke up the play, telling the kids again the importance of teamwork and passing the ball.

On the very next play, the tall kid moved the ball up the field all on his own again. With a strong and straight kick he scored a goal. Everyone clapped and he gave the kid a high five while yelling to the tiny goalie who had been scored upon that his was an excellent try. "I don't think it would be easy for anybody to stop that kick," he said.

"What's your name again?" he asked the tall boy.

"Chad."

"Chad. Right. I want you to take over for goal for your team, okay?"

The boy nodded and ran back to take over for his team's goaltender.

Peroxide Woman rose from her seat and stalked toward him. She pulled her big sunglasses down her nose to reveal eyes like shiny blades. She stood in front of him as if fighting a strong wind, her arms wrapped tight around her chest. "Chad's the best out here. He doesn't belong in goal. Fat kids go in the net."

He felt the tingle in his gut again and his jaw tightened. "We're just trying to spread the wealth around, ma'am. Everybody gets a turn in net. Now if you'll excuse me, we're in the middle of a practice game."

"*We're* not trying to do anything. *You're* trying to screw Chad over just because you drive about as well you coach."

His eyes flicked away to all the little witnesses. "Lower your voice and exit the field, please."

"You haven't got over our little parking lot drama, have you, Coach? Just yank him out of the net, put him on offense and I'll go sit down."

"This is just a practice and it's for everybody."

"If he's stuck in net, it's a waste of his time. And mine."

"He's in Under Seven Soccer. At this stage, it's fine to waste his time."

"I'm over seven," she said.

He looked around, embarrassed. The kids were standing still, watching the argument. Murmurs and whispers came from the assembly of parents in the stands. He called for a break early and directed the kids to the cooler full of water bottles at the edge of the field again. The kids melted away slowly and all the while she stood in front of him with her arms crossed. Jack wondered if anyone had ever refused her anything.

Before he could speak she spun and started heading back to the stands. "Stupid bitch," she said, loudly enough for all to hear.

She was only two steps away. He hissed his message out to her in a whisper the breeze brought only to her ear. "A-T-A-6-6-7," he said slowly.

She spun again and headed straight for him, less than a foot from his nose. "What did you say?" Her hands were fists. He expected that at any moment, she would punch him.

"I said, 'A-T-A 6-6-7.' "

"And what am I supposed to think *that* means, dickhead?"

"It means I know your car. With that I can find your house. In fact, I can find *you* anywhere."

She blinked and her mouth dropped.

"Are you actually threatening me?"

She was judge and jury. What she didn't know was that he was the executioner. Dr. Circe Papua herself had praised him for his skill. He didn't have the doctor's gift of persuasion, but perhaps he could borrow a page from her book with effective results.

"You must listen very carefully," he said.

"Yeah? I must, must I?"

"Shut up. Let me explain something to you."

"Anything else?" she looked amused.

"People don't listen," the bearded man in red had said. And he was so right. People walked around in civilization as if the world had been made safe for them. Nervous little squirrels eating frantically while keeping their eyes sharp for hawk shadows? They understood the world so much better than human prey.

He wanted to slap Peroxide Woman across the face and wipe the blood from her nose on her bleached white sweater.

"I know you," Jack said. "I see you lots of places. You're the kind of person who has one attitudinal setting." He kept his voice low so the kids and the other parents could not hear him. "You don't have a lot of varied responses. You're either satisfied things are going perfectly your way or you're a bitch."

He was sure she was just on the edge of hitting him then and he wondered what the societal etiquette was. If a woman hits you first, can you defend yourself and hit her back? And what if you lose control, say, and accidentally crush her windpipe in the process with one strike with the heel of your hand? Just because you're the kids' friendly soccer coach now doesn't mean you aren't also a guy who's wound so tightly you can hardly wait for Dr. Papua to call on your peculiar talents again.

His head began to throb. He could feel the pulse pounding loudly in his left ear again. It was a danger sign the shrill woman in front of him could not see or hear. If she knew, she'd scurry back to the stands and grab her children and keep running. If this went badly, his mask could fall to the ground. He could turn into the other thing right here and he would be of no use to Dr. Papua in her exploration of the mysteries. He had to tamp down his natural impulses. *I am what I pretend to be.* Or, like he told the kids in his charge, *Use your words.*

"You have two choices," Jack said.

"Get you fired for threatening me or get you arrested for threatening me? I think I'll do both!"

He stepped close enough he could smell bleach. "It's just you and me out here, ATA 667. Go ahead and call the police. Then when they let me out, I'll wait. I could wait a year, maybe two. All the time I'm waiting for my time, you'll be sweating and wondering. All the time you'll be checking your back seat and looking over your shoulder. Anything could happen. Your car could blow up or I could come by for a visit over a long weekend when the kids are off on a sleepover. I could just show up with a big screwdriver one day."

"My husband — "

"Your husband is a minor factor in the equation. Guys who marry women like you? They're used to taking orders. They don't get an opinion. They get told. You'll have beaten him down every day long before I start in on him. I could bend your husband over and do him in the ass while I watch you burn in battery acid. He and I could both enjoy that."

She made a choking sound. She turned white.

"See, what you don't know about me is, not so deep down, I'm a pretty angry guy. The world is full of us. I'm the postal carrier you stiffed on a tip last Christmas. I'm the homeless guy with the sign you pretend you don't see. I'm the miserable poor slob you married who can never do anything right. Right now that poor bastard is surfing porn and dreaming of the freedom he'll get after you're dead. At this very moment he's dreaming of the day you are paralyzed by a stroke so he can have the joy of parking your wheelchair by the remote control and slapping you across the face every time you drool. He doesn't have the balls to divorce you. Men who marry women like you never leave, but he's hoping every morning that you'll fall and hit your useless head and drown in the bathtub. I've watched a guy drown in a bathtub. It's slower than you might think and very interesting to watch."

Her mouth moved but she made no sound.

"Do you read me?"

She nodded.

"I said, 'Do...you...*read*...me?' "

"Y-yes."

He glanced at the crowd. They were watching but he was satisfied there was no way they could hear anything he said.

"I said you have two choices. You want to know what the other one is?"

She said nothing. He didn't need her to reply to anything he said now. "You can run to old doddering Chief Rose and he'll come talk to the sweet coach who's great with the kids — everybody says so — and it will be a he said, bitch on wheels said situation. Then, I can assure you, at some point, something really bad is going to happen. Something so bad you can't even imagine it yet. Something so bad, I'll have to take some time to think it through to make sure it lasts a long time when I come calling."

She was bug-eyed and mouthed the word "Jesus."

"The second choice — and I bet you're going to love the second choice — is you turn around and sit back down and let me coach your kid. It's a long season ahead and I don't want to hear another fucking peep from you."

"Okay...okay." She was shaking. A single tear slid down her cheek.

"Wipe your face. I won't hurt you as long as you keep your mouth shut. You are a burden to all who know you. I suggest you call Dr. Circe Papua. Call her and make an appointment. She's an excellent therapist who helps people like you. In fact, I insist you go see her or bad things will certainly happen. If you fuck up and fail to turn your life around, I'll find out about it. I really hope you do fuck up, ATA667. I want to show you things you've never dreamed in your worst nightmares. I'm talking horror movie-level shit storms and rope that bites your wrists. Read me?"

She turned around and began walking back when he hit her with, "Oh, yeah, and clean up your driving. Maybe you should take a defensive driving course to remind you to be courteous to other drivers."

She slunk toward the stands, her head down.

The rest of the practice went smoothly. He kept Chad in goal for the rest of the game and finished with passing drills. When he blew the final whistle, the humidity had taken its toll and the kids went to their parents soaking wet, their jerseys plastered to their bodies.

Jack watched Peroxide Woman go. He was reminded of Lot's wife in the story of Sodom. When she ran, her two children in tow, she did not dare look back upon him, the force of God who had chased her away, lest she turn into a pillar of salt.

The pretty, young woman appeared at his side. "Hi, I'm Gina. I'm Maddy's mom." Jack gave her a smile and shook her hand. I got your schedule in e-mail and I'm first to give out snacks. Any recommendations for what I should bring?"

"Something cold," he said. "And please, no nuts."

"You bet," she said. "We certainly don't want any *nuts* around our kids." She smiled at him and, in some small seductive gesture, she touched her long brown hair and they both felt self-conscious. "And this is my mother," Gina said.

The old woman with the stack of curly white hair and the binoculars smiled up at him.

"Oh, hello, ma'am," he said.

Gina's hands flew in a mixture of signs Jack had no hope of following and after a moment both women laughed. When they looked at Jack, they gave him kind smiles and he could see the resemblance between the two, despite their age difference. The old woman must have been a beauty once, too.

"Never mind me," the old woman said in a dysphonic, nasal voice. "I'm just an old deaf woman." She gave him a wink and clapped him on the shoulder with a surprisingly strong hand. "I can't hear you, but I read you!"

One of her eyes was shot white with a cataract. The other was dark and pierced him with a knowing look that said conspiratorially, "Hello, brother. Does my mask look right?"

His words to Dr. Papua returned to him: "The world is divided into *three* categories: The Prey and the Witnesses. And things like me. The Predators."

We are everywhere.

OVER & OUT

Through several stories, you'll see that tinnitus recurs. There's a reason for that. I had it. At one point, I was sure it was a brain tumour and, if it didn't kill me, I was sure it would drive me insane. I used stress reduction techniques and after a long time, it went away. I guess it wasn't a tumour. ~ Chazz

My two-year-old son wailed, "No!" from his crib. His cry told me he was asleep. It was another bad dream. I rubbed his back, my touch so light I just smoothed his pyjama top. Frankie sucked his thumb hard. One eye rolled open for a moment, like a vacant nod to a passing stranger. He was on his way back to deeper sleep, though the intensity of his self-soothing hardly abated. He bears the mark of a dedicated thumbsucker — a tough little red callous at the knuckle of his left thumb — and I worry that he might screw up his teeth if he keeps it up too long. If Josy were here, he would be toilet trained by now.

Emily slept through Frankie's nightmare.

173

Teenagers seem exhausted all the time, or maybe that's just Emily. The alarm clock by her bed doesn't even wake her for school some mornings. Even when she is awake and getting ready for school, she seems distant, as if she is still dreaming in a small, warm place. She is stronger than me, but fathers don't have the option to act sullen.

I tip-toed into the bathroom, avoiding the squeakiest floorboards. When Josy and I bought the slouching house on Seaside Road, she and the real estate agent went on and on about how great the old floors were. Now with two kids, it seems the bare, shiny floors are for sliding and banging up knees and elbows. I can't walk the floors at night without thinking I'll wake the children.

When Josy still lived here, I don't remember worrying about the noise the floors made. It was as if two adults roaming a creaky house cancelled each other out with the white noise of living. Why is "antique" so valued when "old" sucks so much? Why do we hold on to things we should have thrown out long ago? Do our atoms mix so much over time with other people and things that, in some unseen way, we mistake the things we own for ourselves?

Noise first became a problem when I began fighting with my wife. Sometimes Josy and I would take the baby monitor out to the car in the garage so Emily wouldn't hear us yelling. We cooperated in that, at least, so we could hear Frankie if he woke crying, catching our discordant vibe through the ether.

I can't sleep, except in stolen snatches of disturbing dreams I can't quite remember on waking. The rest of the night I disappear into a book or escape into late-night infomercials for products I would never use.

At three in the morning, television becomes a time machine. I revisit my days of eating cheese sandwiches while watching the paramedics from *Emergency!*, Johnny Gage and Roy DeSoto. The cops from *Adam-12* are still keeping the streets of L.A. safe. *The Six Million Dollar Man* is still running at 60 miles per hour, though the special effects, so impressive then, make me giddy now.

At Josy's urging I tried an anti-depressant for a few months, but I didn't feel any different and I would wake in the middle of the night biting my tongue, sometimes till it bled. After Josy left, I flushed the rest of the prescription down the toilet in a rare moment of certainty and righteous anger. I told myself that Josy finally getting out might be the only anti-depressant I would ever need.

The only time to have a long, hot shower is after the kids are in bed for the night. I tell myself it's relaxing, but lately it seems less so, like the running water is an excuse to sit on the bottom of the shower stall and cry without being heard. I am an actor during daylight hours, but I have no script. My audience of two wants to believe everything will be okay, almost as much as I do, but I don't know how much longer the show will go on. Improv is so much harder than saying the lines someone else made up for you.

When the hot water runs out, I step out of the shower stall's steam cocoon and examine my body's aging topography carefully. I probe the inside of my upper lip for that bump that comes and goes. It's down now, but who knows what it will do by morning? I examine my neck with my hands slowly, like a man selecting coins from his pocket, going only by feel. I find no lumps. I wipe the mirror clean of fog with my towel and examine my throat. It looks too red to me, but that hasn't changed in a long time. I wish now that they had taken my tonsils, almost the size of golf balls, when I was a kid. I came along just when that operation was going out of style.

I take a deep breath and hold it. My respiration used to be much deeper and slower, I think. I was a lifeguard during my summer breaks from college. I used to be able to hold my breath for much longer, swimming underwater all the way out to the line of buoys that roped off the common area for beach goers.

I feel a familiar ache down the right side of my abdomen. It's like a flashing red light in a car dashboard that won't shut off, reminding me that I'm getting too stressed. Soon after my wife left, I was diagnosed with Irritable Bowel Syndrome, which was a tremendous relief because I was almost sure it had to be bowel cancer. My entrails tie themselves in knots, though I'm not sure what the ratio of figurative to literal is in that statement.

"I know what the problem is, now, honey!" I told her after my colonoscopy confirmed the best case scenario. "Everything is okay!" I smiled as if I was looking right at her, though she held a phone to her ear on the opposite coast. I live in Poeticule Bay, Maine with a window to the Atlantic. Josy had run as far away as she could from me and our kids, all the way to the Pacific, short by nine blocks.

"No, Pierce. You don't know what the problem is," she said.

That was the moment I knew she wouldn't be back. I really was playing the part of steadfast, even courageous, father in a made-for-TV movie with Bill Pullman or Bill Paxton. I'm never sure which is which. "Us" is now just Pierce and Emily and Frankie Murphy. For a long time I thought that Josy was my solution. She opted out of that equation.

Bob, my doctor, is more understanding than my soon-to-be ex, which really cemented my feeling that "us" — Josy and Pierce — was over. Understanding is the greatest service my doctor has done for me, though that's not his fault. I don't have any problems Bob can solve with pills.

Oddly, telling yourself you have hypochondria, rather than a respected, telethon-worthy disease, is no comfort. All hypochondriacs are eventually right. Even the word hypochondria confuses me. I know "*hypo-*" means "less." I don't know what "-*chondria*" indicates, though I'm guessing "time." Josy said it meant I had "less spine."

The pulse in my left ear became much louder one morning. It was annoying, then worrying. I listened to my pulse like a clock ticking down, like my heart's works were unwinding. I got up from the couch where I had been watching TV and plunged into the medical books I'd bought at a garage sale. How common could cancer of the eardrum possibly be? I found nothing much there and was getting anxious so I called Josy about it, forgetting the time difference and waking her up.

"Is it a whiny tone?" she asked, her voice raspy and, I had to admit, sexy.

"No, I think that's tinnitus, a steady high-pitched sound in the ears." Then I realized what she really meant. "Thanks anyway, Josy. Go back to sleep."

I went to see Bob about it. The fact that I was suddenly aware of my heart pounding with each beat didn't seem like a good sign, but he seemed unconcerned, careless even.

"This kind of thing just happens," he shrugged. "There isn't anything to be done."

The room suddenly came into sharp focus. Bob's stethoscope seemed shinier and the floor seemed dirtier. This possibility of there being *no* possibilities was a new idea to me. We are so drowned in our self-empowerment and self-help culture, we're sure we can overcome any difficulty if we just concentrate and...what? Be magic? Fish don't see water, but we are deluded, self-help fish in a daydreaming sea. We do not notice the illusions through which we swim.

"There isn't anything to be done," I said, as if trying to find my bearings. "There isn't anything to be done." Like testing an unfamiliar phrase from a guidebook.

Bob quirked an eyebrow as my face lit up. My ear still pounded, but I was happy. The cure for the melancholia of the abandoned and soon-to-be divorced isn't a nervous fling with a new date discovered on an Internet site. That's distraction, not displacement. My listening ear began to heal my broken heart in that moment. In between the beats, I heard the words: The cure is to first, give up. *Beat.* Give in. *Beat.* Let go.

I felt light.

Soon, I promised myself, when I hold Frankie, I won't wish Josy were here to hold him, too. I'll keep him to myself and love him twice as much. When Emily comes down to breakfast, sullen and looking for a fight, I'll be ready with pancakes, sweet maple syrup and a smile. Soon, I won't be faking that smile.

The self-help fish pretending to be a brave man will write his own script. Not all old things are treasured antiques. Some things, once broken, can't be fixed.

Maybe I'm wrong. Maybe I'm still a deluded fish, but the hook is out. Josy never called me so I finally stopped calling her. If happiness stays out of reach, I'll settle for dignity.

THE SUM OF ME

I read this story at an open mic night at a writing conference in Victoria, BC to enthusiastic applause. For the remainder of the conference, people looked at me sympathetically, asking if I was okay. If they had been willing to buy me dinner, I would have milked it. Since all they offered was sympathy, I assured them I'm a fiction writer and suggested that, ultimately, this is a hopeful piece. Writers are never identified with their heroes, but blow up a few cars in fiction and everybody has a sneaking suspicion you're a homicidal maniac. Okay, they aren't necessarily wrong about that last part.~ Chazz

Stay-at-home dad.

40.

Broke.

This is not the future I did not plan. The future I did not plan, but thought somehow would take care of itself, is not taking care of itself. Squeegee kids aren't broke like me. They aren't still paying for a vacuum they bought on credit last Christmas. Credit card debt is kicking my ass, or was, until my dad intervened and I discovered there are prices to be paid which are much higher than the interest on VISA.

I have no excuses and, like the rest of my generation, no clue. My wife, Cecelia, has a nursing job at an old folk's home and I take little freelance editing jobs here and there. My main occupation is to watch our two boys and rub Cecilia's feet when she gets home after a long shift. We have her tiny retirement investment plan. The statements go unread because neither of us read Bewilder, an alphanumeric language only understood by people in the financial services industry. We hope it works out.

My father learned his financial skills from his parents during the Depression. Grandpa was an Episcopalian preacher in Poeticule Bay before the roads were paved, when everything arrived by boat. The congregation often fed the minister's family with cod and lobsters rather than feed the collection plate a few coins. Dad scraped up a little money here and there and somehow became what it seems no one can be anymore: The mythic Self-made Man.

Dad would lie in bed and plot his escape from poverty while his brother counted pennies into a mason jar each night. Childhood was so short then, it was almost imperceptible. They did escape. My father's generation had smaller dreams and the discipline and savvy to make those lies true. They made something of themselves and I have no idea what that might feel like. Instead of selling things, my wife and I had kids and bought stuff off the TV because that was our little slice of the American dream. We trusted the Future, but the banks killed it and the government never arrested anyone for Future's murder.

My uncle is still alive, too. He gambles his ample retirement fund with various Vegas casinos and heart by-pass specialists. Dad and Mum were snowbirds. After she died, he gave up on Poeticule Bay, Maine permanently and moved to Boca. He watches the sunrise and the sunset, takes pictures of pelicans wheeling over the water like pterodactyls and ponders his only son's squandered potential.

"We never needed much, certainly not near as much as kids today think they need. I still don't need much," Dad says. "If it comes down to it, I could live off a greased rag for a month."

Dad's speaking to me over the phone, but he sounds like he could be talking to himself. I guess that's true since, while he talks, I'm thinking of my boys and how all their friends have iPods now. The technological future is finally here and the party rages on without my kids.

Dad graduated from pennies to folding money, mason jars to stock portfolios. When I was a kid asking for a few dollars to buy something, his answer was always the same. "Why do you think you need that, boy?"

I was not deprived exactly. Dad provided clothes, food and shelter. But my wants? My wants eclipsed the sun. I wanted to fill my room with books and toys and music because that is how you buy happiness. Less is not more. Less is less.

My father wanted my childhood to be as short as his was and my room to be as bare as a monk's meditation chamber. I denied him that satisfaction so long, I still don't feel like a man. And yes, he still calls me "Boy."

Dad owned Poeticule Bay's only hardware store. Early each morning he went off to work freshly shaved and optimistic. Each night he shambled home to supper, miserable. By the last spoonful of dessert he resolved that tomorrow would be better. What I did not understand then was that the tomorrow he was thinking about was the far-off tomorrow, the arthritic future wandering Floridian beaches alone collecting shells.

Retirement is not in my future. I have fitful dreams of being a writer. That is the same retreating mirage I saw on the distant horizon when I was eight. There are haphazard moments of clarity when I compose eagerly. Then I turn on the TV and fall asleep. Words with promise have died. Clever lines form skeins of sentences. I reach in spasms. I worry I'm already too late. The bills mark time.

Awake and rubbing my eyes, I am smack in middle age on the brink of last chances. I am halfway between those early promises and the sum of me. That distant horizon still recedes. I am not a bestselling author whose book is soon to be a major motion picture. I'm not even a grown-up.

Yet.

In this frame of mind, I made excuses to Dad why I could not load the whole family in a jet and wing off south for a visit. I let slip that I could not come because my wife and I had to pay off credit cards. I said too damn much.

Dad called back at seven the next morning. My debt had been gnawing at him through the night.

The kids were still in bed so I was, too. "Time you got up, boy! I suppose Cecilia was at work an hour ago!"

He's not big on preambles. Why don't I have call display on the phone by the bed?

I didn't tell him I was up till three last night writing. That would just be another mistake to hold on to and bring up at Christmas. "Is the book done *yet*? When do we see it in stores and how much will you be paid? How much, boy? *That* doesn't sound like much."

I thought about telling him the kids were painting each other with glue again and that I had to hang up. I didn't, though. I listened because he was talking about giving me money. His was a generous offer of an interest-free loan to kill the credit cards and raise the possibility of a future without debt.

I'll owe *him*.

Instead.

Again.

I said I'd think about it, like I still had a choice and pride.

Later, when I looked upon my innocent boys' debt-free faces, I had to remember how to build a smile. Each grim facial reconstruction soon fell from my lips and I had to rearrange my face again. When they want the latest robot dinosaur, will my card be maxed out again? Will their memory of me be The Failure Who Always Said No? How different is that from the Self-made Man who says, "Why do you think you need that, boy?"

What will happen when they grow up? When they go to college and fall into the same — or a deeper — debt trap, I will pull them out of that hole *if I have a rope*. No money? No rope. No hope. There lies the soul of shame's pain.

Each New Year's Eve, Cecilia and I say *this* will be the year we "get some breathing room." We'll save money...somehow. We'll win the lottery or I'll sell my novel or...something. What's likely to change since we aren't doing anything different? We never speak of this secret aloud for fear that, like some magic curse, the danger will only be made real in the speaking.

I'm worried about the slow, spreading stain in the bedroom ceiling. Will roofers even *accept* a credit card? How much will new eaves troughs cost? Will the furnace die this winter?

"How much?" Dad asked.

"Ten thousand," I said. I braced myself but he did not say anything. The weight of the silence on the phone line stretched out. His disappointment was that heavy. My scalp burned and my body felt skinned by rusty carrot scrapers. "Five hundred a month okay?" I ventured.

"Yeah," he said. "Promise you'll cut up your credit cards?"

The next pause was mine, the startled kind.

"Yes," I lied. What if I have to rent a car or get a hotel room for some ugly, unforeseen reason? I think about the roof, the furnace, the eaves troughs, the latest dinosaur robot and the look on my boys' faces when a classmate gets a new computer. My father will not understand why I will never cut up my credit cards.

I must have that safety net for emergencies, even if it could hang me. I *could* try to explain my situation, what my real life is like. That's definitely what I should do.

"Um...Dad?"

Go ahead, I say to myself, sweating and now out of my body. *Tell him!* Tell him that the best things in life *aren't* free! Tell him iPods buy love and happiness. Explain how you're asking for $10,000 because that's all your stupid pride can bear to ask but you could ask for twice as much and still not cover your debt! Tell him there's little hope but you wish he shared your dreams for success, anyway. Give him another reason to call you "Boy."

"Yeah?" he says.

All he's got waiting for you is the sucker punch of a loan, judgement and condemnation.

"Thanks, Dad."

"Yeah."

I hang up the phone, my head hot and pounding. The kids are watching a *SpongeBob* rerun. My wife won't be back from work for another hour. I could steal a nap.

Instead, I sit down. I dream big.

I write.

VENGEANCE IS #1

Fact: My wife is a psychologist and she must not be happy with all I ask her to edit, especially this story.
I also approached her with trepidation when I asked her to read the chapter about Group Therapy in *Higher Than Jesus*. She's a sport.

What intrigues me about this story most is the voice of the character. It's sort of my tribute to Jay McInerney's book, *Story of My Life*, a book the critics didn't appreciate. Later, McInerney wrote books I didn't get but I loved his first three books: *Ransom, Bright Lights, Big City* and *Story of My Life. Bright Lights, Big City* influenced me especially. It gave me a lot of false hope that kept me going as a very young worker drone in the publishing industry. That book also inspired me to write *The Hit man Series* in second person, present tense. It worked out well. ~
Chazz

* * *

Fact: Most shrinks — like 99% of them — are pretty much nuts. Psychos are attracted to the profession. Here's how I think it happens: Neurotic parents breed and send their neurotic kids for treatment. They get sent to therapy when they're young. At first, nobody wants to talk to some useless stranger about why their parents hate them (why else would they be there?)

Then kids end up sitting there spewing about how miserable it is to live at home when a couple of hundred years ago, you'd be out of the house and free from domination much quicker. A couple thousand years ago, there would be no Xbox but you'd be off on your own by the time you were, like eleven or something. After awhile —after all that review and scab-ripping — once the hate is really ingrained, the patients notice that listening to nuts go on about how fucked up their parents are (fifty minutes at a time for a whack a money) looks like a pretty sweet job, if you have to have a job.

Psychos become psycho-counselors. That's when they're officially cured. Turning patients into colleagues, picking the fruitcakes from the crazy orchard (yeah I know what a mixed metaphor is) is like, the greatest success the fields of psychology, psychiatry and social work is likely to ever have. I know. I've sat in enough of their waiting rooms looking at old magazines. When I started out, none of the waiting rooms needed new paint jobs. Mama wanted to start at the top. When the best and most expensive didn't work out, we went down the ladder.

For instance, we're standing in the kitchen. Ma is in her PJs with a coffee cup holding her up even though it's after school. Ma is big on appearances when she goes out the door, but inside the house, it's housecoats and the fuzzy grizzly bear slippers she gave me for Christmas and then decided they were warmer and cuter if she wore them all the time. Ma's looking at me with this perpetually surprised look on her face. It's hard to figure out what she's thinking because she always has that bat-right-out-of-the-fireplace look since she tweezed her eyebrows so much they don't grow back anymore.

She's standing there with her bare face hanging out saying, "Oh, Georgie, I was talking to Mrs. Whositz at Sobeys and she said her Tanya's psychotherapist really helped her with her anorexia."

"Damn it, Ma! You were talking about me in the goddamn Sobeys!"

"Don't swear. And perhaps you could supply me with a list of what places I'm allowed to speak about my daughter."

"Sure. It'll be a fuckin' short list."

"Don't swear." Ma always says that in the low tone —"well-modulated" three therapists back called it — which makes me think she's back on the Valium. If you take Valium for a long time — I googled — your lungs someday don't work anymore so maybe it is a long-term solution. "Well-modulated" is supposed to calm me the fuck down but it doesn't seem to work, or maybe it's supposed to keep Ma relaxed, I'm not sure.

Anyway, back to my for instance: "I don't know what you're so upset about Georgie! I wasn't blabbing about your mental health. We were talking about Tanya's success."

"Tanya's a bitch."

"Yeah. So? You can be, too, dear."

"Goddamn it, Ma! What does Tanya's anorexia have to do with me? I don't have anorexia. I wish I did. I tried it and it made me hungry."

"Well, eating disorders are all on the same rainbow, Georgie."

I should get tips on puking from Tanya but she's got a thing about fat girls. Can't really blame her for that. I mean, everybody's got a thing about fat girls. Especially me. I read that if you have fat friends, it makes you feel like it's okay to be fat, too. Of course, there are people who want us to accept ourselves, love ourselves no matter what. That seems unreasonable to me. I mean, the people who say that are either old, fat broads who are tired of trying and just want to drop out of the popularity contest we call Life, or they're experts who are these skinny bitches who have somebody else do their makeup. I mean, it's just ridiculous, you know?

I know. I've been over 200 pounds since I was thirteen. I don't even know what I weigh now. I decided when I turned fifteen that I wasn't going to look at the scale until I felt like I'd be happy with the numbers. That was almost two years ago and every time I go to the bathroom I feel like the scale in the corner by the bathtub is looking back at me, all judgy.

Summer's coming and there's a misery but at least I won't have to suffer it at school. You know the drill. Everybody's been to school and you're either the moose or the hunter. Guess which one I am? Yeah, fat and in high school is like walking around with those huge moose horns that don't fit through a fucking door.

Robert Chazz Chute

Hey, maybe if that bitch Tanya is cured, she'll go from skinny bitch to moose, too. We could be friends for a while there while she's just overweight. Then when she gets to be too moosey, I'd have to stay away from her and laugh at her in gym class and bitch her out in the cafeteria for having something to eat. Like I said, I can't have fat friends. I can't get any bigger. I mean, *Jesus!*

Last week I had a different kind of counsellor — the stupidest species. The guidance counsellor scheduled a meeting with me (right in my free period without even asking. Math would have been much better.) Anyway, this guy who used to be the phys-ed guy, before he got arthritis or something, starts asking me about my goals. I said supermodel just to watch his face work through it. He couldn't help himself. He glanced down at my belly and made a face like he's got gas or something. Bitch.

Then he asks me what I want to be when I grow up and I say, "I dunno" and he says "Me, too," and smiles like that's clever instead of pathetic. He was probably relating to me at my level or some shit that 50-something guys say, thinking they're at least as cool as when they were 45.

He talks to me about university and safety schools and shows me a few brochures to get me hot and bothered. I wonder what I'm supposed to do because there aren't any fat girls in the brochures. There are happy black girls and smart-looking Chinese girls with glasses and all the guys look like they're on some football team. No nerds, dweebs or fat girls need apply.

The ex phys-ed teacher (I refuse him any title with the term "guidance" in it) says if I write some essays,

I'd have a shot at some kind of scholarship because my marks in English are so high. That doesn't seem all that impressive to me. It *should* come easily. Everybody speaks English.

I'm good with a camera. That could have been cool since I could have assistants and look like a photographer all the time. I quit photography, though. I was getting some good action shots for an in-class assignment, taking photos of these two pretty girls who probably will end up as models snorting coke off each other's ribs. Anyway, I was kneeling in front of them (it makes them look even taller when the camera angle is aimed up) when some assholes made fun of me because my ass crack was popping from my jeans. Then I had trouble getting up quick and the boys were just howling mean.

The teacher, Mr. Call Me Mike Sandling was a good guy I guess, saying "Alright! Alright! That's enough!" and I looked at him with my big, watery, cow moose eyes and we both knew I wouldn't be back in that fuckin' door.

I wondered later if that's why I got scheduled to see the guidance counsellor. Maybe Call Me Mike thought I should get some attention from the crippled up, phys-ed teacher, get some guidance and maybe some diet advice so I don't come into school one day with home-made pipe bombs strapped across my moose belly. Didn't get any diet advice and that's fine because I'm sure I know more about dieting than any idiot who studied it in school but never actually had a weight problem. The closest he gets is, on the way out, he puts his fucking hand on my shoulder and says (real soulful you know) "You'll figure it out, Georgie. Everybody's got something going for them."

"Yeah, I can see you've got it all figured out," I said.

Then he goes back in his office, shuts the door, takes out the gun he keeps in his desk drawer to protect himself from the hockey team goons he's scared of and blows his brains out so the back wall of the guidance office is always like art no matter how much the school custodian repaints. Well, I *imagine* that's what he does, anyway. I would if I were him.

I've been eating more pizza pops since my chat with the phys-ed teacher. I think what a useless bitch he is, pop another one. I think about how, even if I get some kind of bullshit English scholarship, it's like four more years of being stuck in a bigger high school. Then I eat another pizza pop. Nobody's going to give me a scholarship for going to a cabin on a mountain so I can commune with my moose brothers and sisters, watch TV, order in more pizza and read *Twilight* (in perpetual twilight ha ha) and graphic novels for the rest of my life. Then I think how all life is like being stuck in high school forever and I finish the fucking pizza pops and I'm sick of pizza pops now. But that kind of hate always wear off.

I guess I'm looking for a rescue helicopter to haul my moose ass out of here in a big moose net. That's why I tell Ma to call the new therapist. Look at me, so weak and young and full of hope, huh? I keep forgetting the helicopter never comes.

I forget how many counsellors I've seen. Dad lives with his new and improved family now but Ma says he's got excellent insurance through work so I can go as much as I want.

So back to the whole psycho cult thing where, if you become one of them, you're cured. I refused to become one of them, of course. I'm not a joiner. Ever see more than one moose at a time? Me, neither. I don't know how they ever make moose babies.

I think if you're a guy moose, it's pretty hard to even look at a cow moose so you close your eyes and think of fucking a pretty deer with slender flanks and long eyelashes. When you're done, you're off on your own again pretending it never happened, not even looking at the cow moose as you pass her in the hallway outside of Chemistry class or look her way even though your locker is only twelve lockers away from hers. I digress.

Anyway, my psycho psychotherapists would see me once a week for a while and then one day they'd sigh heavily and refer me to someone else so I'd have to dump my guts on the nice rug of the next therapist all over again. And the next. And the next.

Sometimes they'd call me "difficult" or "combative." That's what they put in your file when you aren't "cooperative." One old Freudian called me "truculent and intransigent." I had to look those words up. They weren't nice.

I'm just looking for answers. I wasn't abused. I had a pretty boring and uneventful childhood. No priests in my deep, dark background. My parents didn't even believe in spanking, though sometimes they couldn't seem to help themselves.

I remember one therapist said it was hard to help me because she couldn't bring herself to like me. She complained that I smelled bad and the clients who came into her waiting room were turned off by the smell. She was pretty fed up, I guess. She topped it off by saying she was just trying to help me. Then she told me I was terminated.

"What does that mean? Are you going to have me killed by a robot from the future?"

"It means I'm dismissing you."

"Like in the military?"

"I'm firing you as a patient," she said.

"That's odd," I said. "My parents pay you, so I thought you worked for me."

"Goodbye."

"Can we discuss this? I'm not super fond of you right now, but I don't want to start this all over again."

"Get out," she said.

So, yeah, she was kind of a bitch about it. We got a letter of termination later that week (together with a bill for all the services she had failed to render) and a list of three other psychotherapists I could piss of next. (I assume she picked three colleagues she hated from Psycho School.)

However, the next one wasn't so bad. Her name was Circe, which I messed up when I tried to pronounce it. It turns out you say it, "sear-say" which is pretty cool. I liked this new one at first because we started with her name and ended up talking about mine.

Georgie is short for Georgette, which Mom chose because I was the cutest little blonde fat baby she'd ever seen (I must have been dropped on my head and face repeatedly later on.) Anyway, I was named after some character on *The Mary Tyler Moore Show*. I've never seen it, but apparently I was sickly and sweet, so Georgette it was. I told Circe that it sounded to me like I was stuck with a fat girl's name so she suggested I change it, just like that. We batted a few ideas around and I said, "What's the thinnest girl's name there is?" and without hesitation she answered, "Gidget."

That's what we accomplished in our first session. I came home and announced my new, improved name and Mom was pissed so I was sure I was finally on to the right therapist. The important thing in judging how intelligent someone is, is how much they agree with you. If they agree with you a lot, they must be very intelligent.

I should have known it wouldn't last. That first session Circe must have deked me out, disarming me with her snake charms. I never liked her so much as when she came up with Gidget. Not only did she give me the idea for my new, non-fat name, then she expected me to make over my life so I'd come up with a whole new personality to match the new name on the package.

I was willing to try at first. I was supposed to make like my whole life was a movie script I had to write as I went.

"Gidget is a new character," Dr. Circe said. "What is the new you going to be like? You don't like Georgette, so how are you going to be different from the old you?"

The process sounded good at first, especially since it was tied up in a slogan with a red bow: "Fake it till you make it." There was an awful lot of work wrapped up in that little phrase. It was catchy and I tried for almost a week. She had me drinking lots and lots of water. I took a bottle of water with me everywhere and that was okay. It felt like I was living in the bathroom but I stuck with it, at least until one of the skinny bitches at school started in on me about how I was killing Mother Earth with all my fucking water bottles.

I told her Mother Earth was on my kill list, but I planned to start small by murdering my own mom in her sleep. "Let's see how that goes," I said. Singlehandedly taking on oh-my-aching-ass "Mother Earth" sounds like a huge project.

I also didn't want anybody to think I had a bladder infection or something so I cut out the water at school but   kept pounding it back at home.

Trying on a new identity felt right at first. I was sick of being me and Dr. Circe and I had worked out the differences. For instance, Georgette was pretty surly and called her therapist Dr. Circe because she was still acting like a girl.

Gidget called the therapist by her last name, "Dr. Papua", because she was "a grown up young woman." I played along, though I didn't think it made that much difference and I was still surrounded by the same bunch of assholes as I had always been.

Dr. Circe insisted the change would come when I chose my reaction to stress instead of being a victim. That did sound good and she was the first therapist I had who actually gave me stuff to do. Everybody else just wanted to talk about my feelings until, presumably, I'd figure it all out for myself. That sounded to me like an awfully lazy way for somebody to make a living, sitting there listening to me spew.

There were other requirements ("commitments" Dr. Circe called them.) Gidget was supposed to get to bed early, start the day working out for half an hour and then showering every day. I'm a teenager. Morning doesn't work with my biorhythm, which I told my therapist the next week.

She told me to work out after school but by then I was tired and just wanted to sit on the couch and read or watch TV. She told me she didn't have any patience for patients who had a problem for every solution.

A few weeks went by and she kept asking me if I really wanted the life Gidget was offering since Georgie was still on the couch plowing through chips. I said it was hard and she called me a whiner, which kind of devolved the therapeutic relationship, I thought.

When the letter came, I can't say I was totally taken by surprise, fired again by an employee. Still, I thought she'd have me come into the office one more time so she could at least charge for one more session and tell me to my face how much I suck.

"Oh, Georgie!" Ma said. "I mean...oh, Gidget!" Ma hadn't completely made the transition to the new me, but I guess I wasn't the only one who wasn't committed to the therapeutic process. She read me the letter, which used the phrase "impediments to therapeutic process" twice, which I thought was excessive as a euphemism and poor English composition. With a name like Circe Papua, obviously English isn't her first language.

"It means I'm not enough of a robot for her treatment to work," I explained.

"It means you have to want to change," Ma explained back at me.

"I know that, dumb ass," I said. "But apparently

198

I've got so many issues I need a magazine rack here. Fuck! If I'm so broken these people can't fix me, what does your excellent insurance pay for? I mean, shouldn't part of the therapeutic process be that the therapists make me want to change?"

"You said you wanted to change," Ma said.

"Sure. But not enough to actually change. Not yet. Isn't that what all this counselling is for? To make me see the light...or something?"

I went up to my room and didn't eat until supper and then decided Dr. Circe was the closest thing to somebody useful I'd seen so I needed to get back together with her. Ma threatened to make me work in the back of her sewing shop after school to keep me out of trouble (here I think "trouble" means "fridge.") Anyway, psycho girls do not need to spend more time with their mothers if improved mental health is the goal.

So that Friday afternoon I went to Dr. Circe's office to try to make up. If that didn't work, I was prepared to settle for a terrible vengeance. You've heard hell has no fury like a woman scorned. Well, look out if the woman is young and prone to mood swings and impulsive outbursts. (And did I mention I'm a cutter? Yeah, my forearm looks like a road map of downtown Detroit. Fuck you, don't judge me. It's one way to feel something besides fat.)

I go in late Friday hoping to catch her and there's this dude sitting in her outer office looking fidgety. I never saw anyone else in the waiting room since you go, you wait, and about the time somebody's coming in, you're going out the back stairs so you never have that awkward moment of looking into another patient's eyes and thinking, *In what perverted way are you all fucked up? And in what perverted way are you assuming I'm all fucked up?*

He sat there in a suit that was obviously way too big for him. I wanted to ask him what his diet secret was but I figured starvation was probably involved so fuck that. I tried that and it made me hungry.

There's a desk in the outer office. It's always empty except for a little hot plate and a tea pot. I sat down at the desk and pulled my journal out of my backpack and looked through it, looking urgent. "I'm sorry. I don't seem to have you scheduled for this afternoon."

He looked up like he was surprised I could talk, as if the fern in the corner had suddenly sprouted lips. "Excuse me?"

"I'm sorry, there must be some mix-up. I don't have you scheduled for this afternoon."

"I'm here to see Dr. Papua."

"Well, obviously."

"And?"

"Dr. Papua cancelled your appointment. One of her patients is on the South Street bridge and she had to talk the girl down...I mean, so she'd take the slow way down." I almost laughed but his look stopped me.

His eyes went wide and for a minute I worried that he was some kind of anger management freak like me. One of us in one room focusses the mind. With two, matter meets anti-matter and the universe explodes. Instead he started to tear up. "Th-that's t-terrible!"

"Yeah." Beat. "Well, I'm sorry you didn't get the call. There's probably a message on your voice mail or something."

He nodded and spent a full minute fishing some stiff, grungy tissues out of his jacket pocket. Great. He'd bought it, but he wasn't getting up to leave, either.

"Um, what should we do?"

"About what?"

"Well, can I reschedule with you or — "

The longer he stayed there, the riskier things got so it occurred to me that pretending to be a secretary would get iffy quickly. "Hey, I usually just clean the office and water the plants. Dr. Papua will call you as soon as she's done convincing some wingnut that life is worth living."

He went white. "That's not very — "

"Sorry. Look. What do you want?" Then inspiration struck. "I'm just here to water the plants and uh...lock up the office. Circe must have been in a big hurry. You know, it's like, an emergency. Maybe that's why you didn't get her message to cancel."

"What should I do?"

Jesus! No wonder this guy needed shrinking. "Go," I said, "home, I mean. She'll call you."

I looked at the clock. Five minutes to four. A therapeutic hour is only 55 minutes long. That's just one more way they cheat you. Whoever was in there with her right now would be finishing up and going out the rear exit. Dr. Papua would soon emerge from the inner office and find the crier and me sitting there. If that happened, I was willing to bet the crier would throw a sadness tantrum, which wasn't part of my plan.

He finally got up and went for the door. "You shouldn't call people wingnuts," he said, another tear sliding down his cheek. "We come here because we're troubled. Life is very difficult for some of us."

"Yeah. Sure is," I said. I'm troubled by people who can't leave fast enough.

Finally he did leave and as soon as the door whispered shut I dumped the anti-constipation medicine into the tea pot and gave it a swirl. Well, the box say it stops constipation but it's really pro-diarrhea. I was still swirling the tea around hoping the stuff would dissolve faster when Dr. Circe came pumping out, all dressed up.

"Got a date?" I said.

She paused in mid-stride and I could tell she was taking me in and doing the cleansing breath thing like she'd taught me. It gave her a minute to rearrange reality now that I was back in her life again.

"I don't believe we're scheduled for today," she said. Had to hand it to her, she slapped her mask on tight after the initial surprise.

"I need to see you," I said.

"I have another patient right now."

"He left."

"Oh?"

"I popped in hoping I could talk to you and there was a guy sitting and waiting."

"And he just left?"

"Yeah. He looked really angry. Pissed off."

"That doesn't sound like the person I was expecting." She walked over to the desk and filled her empty tea cup. I'd put an awful lot of the stuff in the tea and I worried she'd taste it. I'd watched her drink her tea over many therapeutic hours and knew she liked it strong, always with four tea bags in the pot. I'd thought of testing it at home with some of

Ma's tea but, for obvious reasons I didn't want to try it out on myself and Ma brews her coffee one cup at a time and stands and watches it.

My ex-therapist didn't look like she believed me, but maybe that was because I couldn't help but stare at her teapot. I must have looked shifty.

"He got a phone call,." I said. A text from somebody, I think. Then he just got up and left."

"Hm," she said. "Georgie — "

"Gidget!"

"Gidget, good. Gidget, did you not receive my letter?"

"Yeah. That's what I wanted to talk to you about." I took out another water bottle from my backpack and drained it. I wanted to show her I was still doing something she'd asked me to do. Maybe we could compromise so I could change a little more and she wouldn't put me through the hell of breaking in another therapist.

"I don't think that's a grand idea. I think we've taken our therapeutic relationship about as far as it can go. We've tried over many sessions to get you to a place where you're ready for the commitments of the process. Perhaps you'll find better luck with another therapist who can provide what you need. Not every therapist is for every patient...and vice versa."

"So, what? You only work with the people who aren't very fucked up, is that it? I've got to find a new therapist because...why exactly? I don't make it easy enough for you?"

"I didn't feel we were making progress, Gidget. I'm concerned that if we aren't making progress then you aren't getting the help you need."

"I want another chance."

"We've had this conversation before."

"I want another chance."

She was giving me that kind smile of hers, very much practiced, like she was talking to a fairly retarded little kid. Then I noticed her smile went a little sideways. "Oh," she said softly and put a hand over her stomach.

"Are you okay?" I said, smiling now, too.

"Georg — Gidget. I don't think this is appropriate and if my scheduled client isn't going to show up then I should finish up here. I have an engagement right after work and I'm really not feeling well, so... Oh! Excuse me!" She ran out the door and down the hallway toward the women's bathroom.

Awesome.

I hadn't expected my plan to work that well or that fast. I had hoped that she would see that I'd bothered to take a couple buses to get to her office and welcome me back. If that had worked, I would have accidentally knocked over her teapot with my backpack.

That would be embarrassing but I'd be back in and by the time she figured out what I had done to get rid of Mr. Tear Stains, she'd forgive me because I'd demonstrated a real commitment to getting therapy from her. I'd be a story she could tell at cocktail parties for years. She'd act mad at first, but then she'd see how funny it was and how much I clearly need her and she'd forgive and forget and soon I'd be her favorite patient and she'd see she'd been totally wrong about me and someday soon I'd be skinny and she'd admit we'd made a lot of progress and I was a fine young woman and she'd be really sorry, apologizing all over herself for ever ever thinking she should get rid of me.

But it hadn't worked out that way, so Plan B was to get a terrible vengeance on that bitch. The trouble was, I wasn't sure what to do next. I really thought Plan A would work. I mean, how many patients dared to come back and face her after she sent out her fucking letter railing on about "positive therapeutic outcomes"?

I wandered into the inner office. I'd spent so many 55-minute hours on that couch, spewing on about Ma and her boyfriends and how nobody seemed to like me much and here she was, still not liking me much. It was like she didn't get me at all and I really thought Circe did at first. What's up with that? I thought she liked me a *little* bit. Sure, I'm quirky but if your therapist won't cut you some slack, what the fuck?

I went over to her desk and sat behind it. I still had no idea what I was looking for, so I looked in the drawers. I thought maybe she'd have a vibrator in there for the boring stretches between patients but I couldn't find it. If I'd thought to bring some superglue, I could have really fucked up her desk and phone but, like I said, Plan A was supposed to work. I did a full circle around the office. Every time I came in here I told her the flowery wallpaper really sucked and that she should change it but she never had, so I guess I wasn't the only one unwilling to change.

How much more time would she be in the bathroom? I was running out of time and between all the water I had been drinking and the fear of getting caught in here, I really had to pee.

In all the girl detective stories, the young heroine

"casts about" for clues, so that's what I did. I cast about for a way to fuck with Dr. Circe Papua. The filing cabinet behind the desk was closed but the key was in the lock. I stopped casting about.

I peeked out into the outer office. No footsteps running my way, so I ran over to the tall fining cabinet, opened the lock and yanked open the bottom drawer. If I'd had time, I would have looked for my own file. I wondered how much she doodled in the margins of her notes. Would there be little drawings of dicks and vaginas? Would there be pages and pages of her handwriting, over and over again: "I hate this fucking fat, little bitch. I hate this fucking job. I should have been a librarian so if somebody started crying and whining I could just tell them to shut the fuck up. I have got to get rid of this fat little bitch." I would have looked, but I didn't have time.

The bottom drawer was U – Z. There weren't many files in there and I noticed an old phonebook was tucked in behind a few file folders. Y is for Yellow Pages. I took a squat and pissed in there, letting go and feeling scared about getting caught and having a very positive therapeutic outcome in about equal parts. Being scared apparently helps you pee harder.

I pulled my pants back up and slammed the drawer shut with my foot in one motion. I had just finished buckling up when I heard footsteps. I flew over to the couch, feeling warm and light.

"Gidget," she said, like that said it all, like an accusation.

"Are you okay?" I said, all sweet concern.

"No. No, I'm not. I had t-to...uh...vomit."

"Maybe you better sit down."

She did and here we were in our usual spots,

206

except now she had a filing cabinet drawer full of bright yellow urine. Not bad for a Plan B inspiration.

Her face looked pale, like it had fallen in somehow. As shitty as she obviously felt, she would leave soon and the piss would ripen in her phone book all weekend, and it was supposed to be a hot weekend. By Monday morning, the whole office would smell strongly of piss and she could explain that to Mr. Tear Stains and I'd be sitting at school feeling happy happy happy about my brilliant fucking vengeance all day. Maybe she'd have to start over on all her files. Maybe that shitty flowery wallpaper would absorb the smell enough that Dr. Circe would have to close up the whole office and redecorate. Maybe my leak would leak through the bottom of the cabinet and soak into the rug and through the floor and through the ceiling into the office on the floor below. Maybe she'd get in trouble with her landlord and have to move. Maybe she'd get so teary about it she'd quit being a shrink altogether. One way or other, she would sure be fucking sorry.

"I was supposed to go out tonight," Dr. Circe said. The way she said it I wondered if she knew.

"I wanted to talk to you."

"I thought from my letter you would understand that our talking should be done. I'm not the therapist for you, Gidget. My letter was clear in that regard. What did you hope to accomplish coming here?"

I felt my fat face getting hot. I wondered how long before the smell would waft our way. I wondered how she could be so mean as to kick me out in the first place. I still wanted to stay, but the piss in the filing cabinet might become apparent any moment so I wanted to run out of there, too. I wanted us both to get out of her office to let my revenge percolate and ripen.

"Gidget," she said. "I'm feeling very unwell and I've got a massive headache coming on so I think we both better leave."

"Okay." I used my small humble voice.

She looked at me with sad eyes. Instead of moving to get up she said, "You know...I think I made a mistake with you."

My heart rose up and rubbed against the insides of my ribs and I straightened up.

"Ending it wasn't the mistake," she quickly added.

"Oh."

"But I should have had another session with you to discuss why I had to terminate treatment. Not every therapist is for every patient and I felt that we weren't a good fit. For this to work, we have to be able to trust each other and I never felt comfortable with you alone in the office with me. I'm sorry about that. You never gave me any reason I could put my finger on. It was just a feeling. I'm all for logic but I'm a psychotherapist. I have to trust my intuition, too. All you seemed to bring to your sessions was anger and I didn't see anything else."

She had been wrong about me. Then she kicked me out of treatment and made herself right. *Shit!*

"I'm sorry I couldn't help you. We talked extensively about strategies you can use in your life which I hope you will act on. I still think those strategies will benefit you." She held her head with one hand, like she was countering pressure that might push her forehead out. "We're all just trying to get through life the best we can."

I swallowed a stone that hit my stomach when she

said that. "What? What did you say?" I'd heard her, but I wanted to hear it again.

"We're all just doing the best we can."

I didn't expect tears. Not from me. Never from me. It broke me open. "I'm scared, Dr.—Dr. Papua."

She looked at me with forgiving eyes then. She looked at me like she saw something new and hopeful. That really made me feel like shit on a shoe, piss in a drawer. I cried in stupid sobs that I hated myself for but couldn't stop.

"What if this is the best I can do? What if this is it? What if I'm never any less miserable than I am now?"

Her shoulders relaxed a little bit and she softened. Somehow she made me think of Ma when I was really little, when I was still a skinny kid. "Gidget," she said. "You're showing me something instead of useless anger."

I didn't answer. I just slipped sideways on the couch and wrapped myself around a pillow and cried and cried. I felt like that skinny little kid again, letting go like that and letting the big, fat, hot baby tears just roll and roll. When it finally stopped, Dr. Papua was looking at me with a kind, gentle smile that killed me.

"You know, Gidget, maybe we do have some more work to do. I'm thinking I was harsh with you. I should have worked this out with you instead of taking the easy way out. You've been through a lot of therapists, I know. I think that prejudiced me. I expected that I was just the next in line, but you showing up here..." She spread both hands out in a gesture that said, "Welcome back."

I felt cold and got the first whiff. "This is excellent.

I really, really want...uh, but first...this may be hard to explain..."

HIGHER POWER

Three things about this story first:

1. The incident with the light in this story? It happened to me. Weird wiring inside and outside my skull.

2. Burt and Marcus attended the same church years before they met again in the short story, Parting Shots. Here's the basis for Marcus's lack of belief.

3. My grandfather was a Baptist minister. He was a good man, but sadly I only remember three conversations with him.

In the first, he's trying to listen to the radio and tells me to be quiet. In the second, he's giving me some answers to my questions about capital G God that do not satisfy me. In the third, he helps me put my letter to Santa in the big red mailbox. He examines my poor scrawl on the envelope before he hands it to me. Just as I stand on my tiptoes and slip my wishes, dreams and hopes into the mail slot with a mittened hand, he says, "With your handwriting, I doubt the Post Office will accept it." Oh, Grampy! ~ Chazz

It started in the middle of the night as Sunday morning was growing roots and slowly rising from the ruins of Saturday night. Ted awoke, groggy, but dimly aware of his wife Birget's soft snoring beside him. He had to get up to urinate. He shouldn't have had the coffee so close to bedtime. Or was this one of those early signs of prostate cancer he'd read about in *Reader's Digest*?

Ted struggled out of bed, his low back aching — or was this kidney cancer? — and felt his way to the bathroom in the darkness. Once done, he perfunctorily ran his hands under cool water. He was waking up and didn't want to. He made his way to the top of the stairs when lightning struck.

Or he thought it was lightning. The sudden brightness came from directly overhead. His eyes had adjusted to the darkness so he was dazzled by the sudden brilliance. He froze for a moment and all was dark again. Confused, he took the five steps down to the living room and looked outside through the slats of the window blind. No storm, no rain. No lightning.

He moved to the couch and lay down. It was 2:30 in the morning. He suffered insomnia a few nights a week and a move out of his warm bad to the cool of the leather couch was often enough to allow him to settle down again. He looked around the living room, making out the dim outlines of furniture, the bookcase, the television. He briefly entertained the notion that someone had broken into the house silently and had set off a camera flash but dismissed that as ridiculous.

Then it happened again. His jaw dropped open and he almost laughed. The globe light at the top of the stairs in the hallway outside his bathroom flashed on.

Ted got up and climbed the stairs again, flicking on the light switch as he went. The globe light shone down brilliantly again, a steady beam. He reasoned that the cumulative vibration of the household had loosened the light bulb. His grandson Tyler bounced around the house on his Saturday visits and he recalled with his own daughters that occasionally the light bulbs needed to be tightened when they went through their gymnastics phase.

However, he wasn't going to get a chair to stand on in the middle of the night at the top of the stairs. If he fell and broke his neck, Bridget slept so soundly she might not discover him dead until morning. Uncertain of his purpose, he reached up and was able to twist the glass globe over the light. It did not move. The beam stayed steady.

Puzzled he reached out and flicked the upstairs light switch off, then on. The circuit responded normally, dark, then light. He shrugged, flicked it off and returned to the living room couch.

He lay down and considered whether true insomnia had really set in and should he give in and search for the TV remote? Birget had been the last to bed and her habit was to leave the remote wherever she was, never returning it to the little wooden stand he had made for it in his workshop. He had presented it to her as a solution to his daily search for where she had left the device.

"Jesus was a carpenter, Ted," she had said. "You need to stick to spreading his word because I don't want that sad little stand cluttering up my décor."

Ted had responded by putting the stand on the table by the TV with some force and she proceeded to ignore its existence and function ever since.

The upstairs light flashed again.

Ted stared up into the darkness, waiting for the next flash. Within a minute it came again, not as brilliant but there nonetheless. Wait a minute, he thought. I shut off the circuit! Both switches are turned off, so how is the light getting any power at all?

Then Ted's big moment came. The globe light flashed an answer to him, spoke to him. Ted didn't sleep the rest of the night and he got up early to get ready for work. They had been married for twenty-one years this June, so their mornings had settled into a routine long ago. She always woke in a mood only caffeine could cure. He often joked that before nine she was a stereotypically mean 1945 German. After coffee she came up to the 21st century standard.

At this, she often replied that if they were Unitarian, she wouldn't have to do without a newspaper on Sunday morning. However, she was stuck married to a Baptist minister so she couldn't get the paper like a normal person. Even though the Sunday paper was completed by Saturday night, she said, the only heathen who refused to respect the Sabbath was the poor, doomed paperboy who would be eternally alight and screaming for his transgression. "Doesn't seem fair. You only work Sundays and you've supposedly got the key to the kingdom."

"Shoulda married that other guy." Ministers, no matter which variety, are on call all the time and summoned to the ER to bless every broken toe. Birget knew the demands of his calling. On those nasty mornings, she was looking for a fight. None of that nonsense today. While she made her coffee, he dawdled over his cereal in silence. When she came to the table, he got up and headed for the door without looking at her.

"What's the rush?"

He paused at the bottom of the stairs and looked up at the hallway light for a moment. It did not flash. "See you in church."

"It's only just nine and I'm not dressed yet — "

Ted was already out the door. He walked across the yard from the rectory to the side door of the church and unlocked it. John Castillo, the organist, was warming up in the sanctuary. The front door would be unlocked and the choir would arrive soon. John seemed to be alternating between scales, Rock of Ages and the tune played at baseball and hockey games that ended with the crowd yelling "Charge!"

Ted squirrelled into his tiny basement office. His predecessor, Rev. Ditko, who retired eight years previously, had left a bright yellow "Do Not Disturb" sign on the inside doorknob of the office door. "At some point you're going to start using this," the old man had said, "and then you'll wonder why you didn't always use it."

For the first time in his career, Ted stuck the sign on the outside doorknob and slammed the door shut.

He spun the old skeleton key, locking it. It was the first time he had done that, too. Ted headed straight for the cabinet that contained communion wine like a looter in a riot. The bottle was dusty, a gift from a young Catholic priest he'd met years ago at a non-denominational conference. He should have known better than to give wine to his brand of Baptist. Ted had never been drunk, even in college. It seemed imperative now.

He fell into an empty stupor, seeing only the globe light's flash between each swallow of acidic wine. The bells in the steeple rang so Margaret Cillian, the choir's ancient soprano was undoubtedly in the sanctuary. One Sunday last summer, a young alto had dared to push the button to ring the steeple bell recording in her stead and the old woman had chewed him out for trying to steal her honor. A headache began to form deep in the center of Ted's skull as the fake bell rang out to call the faithful, as if all city dwellers needed was a reminder. As if they were village peasants who would pull themselves from their straw beds at the insistent pealing.

The clock crawled closer to eleven. The congregation trickled and then clambered in. Ted drank faster, wincing at the taste of the horrid stuff. The old wooden floorboards creaked and thumped above him with every footstep. His dread grew. He took longer drags of wine. Something built inside him along with the growing headache. Whatever was going to come out, he couldn't keep it in its cage.

The choir started up above him, their singing barely muffled. Ted shuddered. Someone knocked on his office door, at first hesitant and then with growing conviction. Two female voices parried with each other. One of the women ran off while the other continued knocking on the heavy old door.

"Ted? Are you in there? Are you alright?" Birget, of course.

Ted let her pound on the door and made sure the wine bottle was empty before he pulled himself up and turned the lock. He yanked the door open to find Marcus, the kid they paid to be the church handyman. He held a large screwdriver, apparently about to exercise his mechanical options in popping the door. Birget, looking pale, stood at his shoulder.

"Ted! Are you okay? We called and called. What have you been doing in there?"

He grabbed his robe hanging on the back of the door and breezed past them.

"Ted? Ted! I asked you a question. What have you been doing in there?"

"Jerking off," he said. "I just found out that's all I ever do." He didn't look back and steamed up the stairs to the dais.

The choir climbed lazily through an old gospel, perhaps stalling for his benefit. When Ted burst through the door, John mangled a few notes at the organ. Usually he sat off to the side while the choir stood and sang but now he stalked in front of them and grabbed the sides of the altar. Ted's knuckles grew white as the choir pressed forward through another chorus.

His headache burst then into a pressure he had never before felt. He waved the choir off. Most sat immediately, though the choir director, Brad Cherney, kept waving his arms, oblivious to Ted's warning. Only Margaret Cillian, that old crone, kept singing, apparently seizing on this moment of confusion to take a rare solo.

"Siddown!" Ted cried and John stopped playing in the middle of a discordant note.

A murmur went through the congregation. People leaned toward each other, whispering all at once. Ted spotted Birget at the back of the church. The combination of her complexion and her white dress made her look like a terrified ghost. Marcus stood behind her, the screwdriver still in his hand. The boy had an amused smile on his face and that gave Ted the courage to smile, too.

"Aren't you just *sick* of these old songs?" he said too loudly into the microphone. "I mean, really. These songs really suck. We should celebrate more. You want a church meeting that rocks? We should play some old Springsteen for you and get your blood going again."

He looked over the crowd as the shockwave hit. All the regulars were there, each family in their accustomed pew. The church board members sat in the front row. Six old men looked up at him with red eyes and their blue veins throbbed through their paper skin, lips tight and jaws clenching. They were businessmen who were getting ready to die so church was very serious business. In private, and only to Birget, he called the church elders The Blue Hair Crew. In meetings, they called him Pastor and he called each of them "sir." They didn't appear sensitive to sarcasm.

Ted felt his skull pound further and wondered if its beat would ever crescendo. Ted's own physician, Chad Bradshaw, sat just a few rows back with his pretty wife, Alicia. The doctor sat with his arms crossed and watched him intently, his forehead wrinkled. Ted thought briefly of going straight to Dr. Bradshaw. He felt like he was on the first long uphill climb on a roller coaster. Then he remembered the message he received from the light and gripped the altar even harder. As his headache banged on, Ted closed his eyes and listened to the mass of voices babbling at each other. It sounded like a gaggle of geese on fire. "*Sh!*"

No response.

"Shut up, you robots!" Ted yelled and the congregation fell into silence.

"You know what I see here? I see a bunch of people who smile on Sunday and shoot you on Monday! I see a bunch of people who haven't received the message of the light!"

More murmurs and nervous rustling.

"I have a message for you from the light!" Ted paused and had no idea what he was going to say next but was pleased to find that the headache receded as he spoke. "I got a pressure in my head and preaching you the good news is apparently the valve that's going to release that pressure."

Birget walked briskly up the middle aisle. "The Reverend is not feeling well today. This is...most unusual."

"You siddown, too, you old cow!"

"Ted!"

"I've got something to say and you're going to hear it before this headache starts up again." Dr. Bradshaw stood, apparently ready to jump forward if needed in his professional capacity, but his eyes were full of doubt as to what he should do next.

"Don't you folks worry about me," Ted said. "Something came to me last night in a flash and...

wow, I realized a few things. I've been down in my office for the last couple hours knocking back a little wine and thinking about it. It couldn't be more clear."

"Oh, my God!" Birget said, and turned to walk out the door.

Ted smiled and looked behind him to see the choir looking at him with hard eyes. He looked to the back and Marcus, standing there in his cheap sports jacket and blue jeans.

"There it is. I've been married to that woman for years but I dare to step out of the mold just once and she's looking for the door!"

A group of parents with children stood up as if some silent parental alarm known only to them had gone off. They moved as one toward the exit following Birget.

"You folks with young children should stay because, today, I'm going to stop the lies and we'll save those little tykes a lot of time and guilt. We're going to save those kids all the time I've wasted! They're young so they might get it!" Ted gestured to the line of hard-faced men directly in front of him with their blue-haired wives. "The Blue Hair Crew are too scared and too close to the grave to take the truth up the ass now but for you it's not too late!"

He heard a thud behind him. Margaret Cillian had fainted. Ted glanced back and smiled. "I never like that old bitch. And from now on, anybody who wants to push the button to ring the steeple bells can do so any time they want, day or night! We've got to tell people the truth revealed to me in the light!"

Dr. Bradshaw moved forward then. "Ted, I think you better come with me. You're either just drunk or something is terribly wrong with you. Major changes in personality are a symptom."

"Screw off."

Another wave of murmurs went through the crowd. Ted's headache started galloping again to match his heart's pace. More people got up to leave while others appeared to settle in, fascinated and titillated with the changes to his usual, staid Sunday service.

One voice pierced the din. Marcus yelled from the rear, "Give us the good news, Rev! What's up?"

Ted could have kissed him. "The good news? The good news is you sorry bastards can stop grovelling! I'll tell you why, too! You ever read any old stories? Look at any Greek tragedy or Homer, say. The Odyssey and all that. In all those old stories, a hawk or two would fly off to the right and it would mean one thing. If they flew to the left, it would mean another thing. Prophets would tell kings some shit they saw in a dream and it would all mean something. It's modern times now. Now we know those prophets were schizophrenics! The voices were just in their heads! If there's drought, it's because the earth's weather is messed up. It doesn't mean anything beyond the fact that you drove Hummers too long and the pollution screwed something up in ways we don't quite understand.

"While we're at it, a groundhog who sees his shadow in the spring? It's just a big rodent. Spring comes at the same time every year no matter what. A rodent is not a meteorologist! Why do you pay attention to that? And...and I'm just a rodent. I have not seen my shadow. I have seen the light! I can't get you into heaven! I can't even get you a bargain on winter radials!"

Murmurs flitted amid the crowd — it was no longer a congregations per se. Many were listening to his slurred rant instead of going straight to their default: taking offense at the unexpected. He let out an appreciative, growling laugh.

"Last night, a light in my house flashed and for a brief moment I thought it might mean something. Then the light said, 'Bullshit, it's an electrical anomaly!' It said, 'It's a short that will cost you a bundle of money for an electrician to fix. My flash of light doesn't actually mean anything. It's a wiring issue, a faulty connection. Wires heat up, make a tentative connection and the connection breaks as the wires cool. That's all. And you know what came to me? We're all bullshit, electrical anomalies!"

"Tell it, man! Teach it, brother!" Marcus yelled.

Dr. Bradshaw made a motion for Ted to calm himself, which the pastor ignored.

"This is good news!" Ted continued. "It means an evil god didn't give us September 11th because of our wicked ways! It means homosexuals don't get AIDS because God hates them. If you based who He hates on who gets AIDS then God must *love* lesbians... though Jesus knows we all love lesbians, don't we? Lesbians so hot." His eyes fell on Cybill Shipman in her best denim overalls two rows back. Ted blurted, "Well, you know. The lipstick lesbians, I mean."

More gasps of horror. Marcus doubled over and let out a shout of a laugh.

"Holy shit!" Burt Messier, the Blue Hair car dealer, blurted out from the front row. His wife and two daughters sat beside him. He tried to cover the ears of the nearest girl. She leaned away from Burt, desperate to hear Ted's message.

"*Exactly*, Burt. This is *all* holy shit. Let me tell you something — "

"Somebody call the police!" someone in the congregation called out.

"Call an ambulance!" Dr. Bradshaw yelled back

"Burt, let me tell you something before the cops show up," Ted continued on smoothly. "You're here because you're trying to bargain your way into heaven. Your best years are over. You're stuck with that toothless bag of bones beside you and you want another shot. Someday soon you're going to wake up with some incurable disease and you want to hope that your life means something. Or after you die you want another life that means something since you pretty much screwed up this one. Am I right?"

"You son of a bitch!" Burt said, growing purple with rage.

"You're a good Christian, Burt, so I know you'll forgive me."

"Bastard!"

"Careful, Burt. You're still in church. If you're right about your view of the universe, you're really fucking yourself over...now, where was I? Oh, yeah, I was talking about the horrible incurable disease Burt is scheduled to get any day now."

Burt looked like he was about to get up but then sat down, stricken.

"Tell us the good news, Rev!" Marcus said again. "Don't stop!"

"The good news is that if you hear my message today, the bargaining is over. It's going to be such a comfort to face your final days knowing that no evil god did this to you. You're just a fluke, an electrical anomaly. You don't have to try to pray so hard you thwart the determination of an all powerful god to kill you off. There's no negotiation to be done. You can finally, for the first time in your entire meaningless existence, be free of fear. You're coming from nothing and headed to nothing! You! You can be godless and free like me!"

Dr. Bradshaw tackled him and brought him down. "*Et tu, Brute?*" Ted said. "And you, a man of science! I'm so disappointed. You, of all people, should get it. You're a high priest of society, too!"

"Shut up, Ted —"

"The good doctor explained."

"Shut up!"

The headache was gone and Ted couldn't remember ever feeling so well.

* * *

The doctor was right about one thing and he had proof. The shadow in the CAT scan, he told Ted a few weeks later, indicated that something was very much wrong with him. "It's a brain tumor, I'm afraid, Reverend. Inoperable."

"Just call me Ted and don't be afraid."

"It's a brain tumor, Ted."

"Okay."

"Okay?"

"Sure."

"This isn't a normal reaction. That tumor must be pressing on something. This is not appropriate. Do you feel euphoric, Ted?"

"Nah, don't worry about me. I'm not wailing and crying and throwing myself around because...well, this is just the Circle of Death, Simba — no guilt or doubt required."

"Um..."

"You'll come around once you think about it for awhile. You're a smart guy."

Dr. Bradshaw looked at him for a few beats, his face solemn. "I'm smart enough to know that I'd rather be happy than right."

"That's a choice. This is all about choices. I suddenly find I've got a lot of choices. Birget's moved in with her mother so I can watch sports on TV. I don't have to fake being patient when Birget says I should watch something more worthy of my time. And I always know where the TV remote is now."

"What will you do?"

"I'll do the logical thing. Publicly recant, claim disability, blame the tumor for going off the rails, squat in the rectory until my new friend in my skull kills me off. Or maybe one of these days I'll wander down the highway and throw my carcass in front of a semi. Given the choices modern medicine offers, that would be the logical thing to do."

"Have you thought about moving somewhere? I can't do much for you, but you may have some time to see something of the world before you go."

"Nah. One part of the world is pretty much like any other and I don't want to be far from the light bulb in my upstairs hallway. It might have something else to say before I'm done."

"Ted, if you need anything — "

Ted shook his head as he got up. "Having a god to answer to is such a demanding thing. The standards are superhuman, but we aren't that super. It's unfair, like asking a dog to type. People are easier to deal with now. They don't expect perfection anymore. I'm relieved."

He paused to throw his troubled doctor a smile before he strolled out the door, out of the waiting room and into bright sunlight. He could do whatever he wanted. But what? What mattered now?

I'LL TELL YOU WHAT THEY WON'T

You'll notice a crossroad here with Asia Unbound, so it's nice to see the story from another perspective. Isn't it strange that people get so offended where sex is involved, but violence is fine by them? Baffling. I was surprised to find that one of my most trusted readers, oldest friend and consiglieri, Peter, declared this story the saddest he'd ever read. "Pete," I said, "I'm writing fiction, not an instruction manual." He warned me not to publish it so, naturally, here it is. I don't judge my characters. That's up to the reader and your visceral reactions. Bad guys are fascinating in one particular feat: They don't think they are bad guys. ~ Chazz

Plan A complete. There's just enough light leaking under the door to pick out the outlines of shapes on the floor. I can't really tell which is which, but the trail is predictable. It always ends in a pile of shorts and panties at the edge of the bed. Take the socks and shoes off first or you look stupid, that's my advice.

I wish someone had told me the way things really are, so I'm thinking this through, sorting out what you need to know. Somebody's got to tell you the truth and it's down to me. I take this responsibility very seriously. I'm going to get this all straight in my head and later I'll write it all down for you. Feel free to pass on joy. It's the only way to stop the conspiracy.

Wait. I'm listening to her breathing. She's an athlete. I can tell by her long slow breaths as she dreams. Also, tonight's games were exhausting and, if not for the little blue pill — not that I need it, you understand, but I do want it. The night would have ended too quickly and nobody wants to go home from the county fair before they say you have to go home. Besides, if not for the extra exercise, she would have kicked me out of her apartment and then Plan B would fail. Happy, happy! The vital part of Plan A had to include some pretty energetic gymnastics to make Plan B possible.

She's still dreaming and restless so I stay put and listen till she settles down into deep sleep. She — what was her name? —was a real sport. Don't jump to the conclusion that I'm a pig just because I didn't catch her name. We were in a meat market. She was dressed for trawling. Lots of guys were drooling at her but none of them understood The Platinum Rule. Let me educate you for your future happiness.

The Platinum Rule really boils down to one admonishment: To get the pussy, don't be a pussy. You see who you want. You stare at her. She'll look at you and then look away. Look at you and look away, look at you and look away. You don't break your appreciative gaze. You are staring at a buffet table and you are starving. Then you strap on your nuts and walk up to her. When you play tennis, do you think about each shot or do you just see where the ball is going and react? Of course, you keep moving forward and you plant your feet and you say your name like she should already know it.

Then, hot damn, you're in business. If you're hanging out in the club all night screwing up your courage instead of screwing, you're not a man. You're afraid of what you want, afraid of somebody saying no, as if that draws blood. Forget that strategy. That approach makes you spend your time dancing (which makes men look, at best, undignified and sometimes stupefyingly ridiculous.) Don't be a pussy. Pussies spend too much money on drinks.

If your dream girl tells you to take a hike you haven't wasted the night. Tell her that if her lesbian lover is also into men, maybe you could all enjoy a threesome. If that doesn't light her up, walk away. The worst thing that can happen is that she takes you up on the offer. Telemarketers have it right. It's about volume. Make your pitch and keep pitching. You'll never walk out of a club alone. If you aren't in business right away, you set your sights on the next woman, starting with the most gorgeous creature you see, of course, and work your way down the chain until you get a nibble on your ear.

Don't worry about whether you're in her league, either. You're both human and she has needs, too. I know, everything you're told is that she wants romance and flowers and three dates before you hold her hand. Everything you're told is wrong. Let the girl know everything she thinks she's supposed to want is wrong, too. The number one line that's gotten me the most chicks is, "Hey, you seem like a really nice girl. Too bad. I was really looking to hook up with a bad girl tonight."

Number two is: "I've got a small dick so you need not be intimidated plus I can breathe through my ears. I'm really hung if you count the length of my tongue." If she's disgusted, move on. She was never really in play. If she laughs, you've got the hook in. Give her permission right off to be as complex as she really is.

Everybody really wants to drop the façade and loosen up and howl. I don't smoke, but I've always got a pack beside me and a lighter at the ready. To a woman who's willing to risk lung cancer every day, what's a one night stand? Alcohol lowers inhibitions, but don't drink too much or you'll be useless when it counts. You can get sidetracked with the means to the end. A sloppy drunk is crap next to an enthusiastic partner who doesn't have to be drunk to let loose her inner freak. A flashy Rolex knock off and cufflinks on a crisp shirt will take you farther than most guys appreciate.

Oh, and dude, never wear sneakers to the club and think you'll get laid. Sneakers are for the gym and for children. You need real shoes, preferably Italian but definitely something that will give you height and a nod to fashion. Ask your gay buddy and he'll help you find what you need to wear. You don't think you have a gay buddy? Ask the guy with the shaved chest who is always going to or coming back from the gym. That's your gay buddy.

There are three other rules that are key in making

for happy nights with exotic women. The Bronze Rule is smile with your mouth *and* your eyes. It's the cheapest way to improve your looks and a happy guy always gets to the starting line faster than a guy who thinks he should look tough or cool. Smile like you mean it, not like the wolf you really are. That's the Bronze Rule. You, my future Olympian, are so going to get laid.

The Silver Rule is, be a man. None of this stuff about being yourself. If being you were really so great, the shebas would be coming to you, not the other way around. Unless you're a Hollywood star or a pro athlete in a sport that matters (basketball, baseball, football and maybe hockey in North America, soccer everywhere else) don't be you. You are the hunter and you're looking for fresh game. Girls in bars are in bars for one of two reasons. They either get to feel good by rejecting men and dancing and drinking with their friends or they are there to hook up. If they are there for the former, find out fast and move on. There's plenty of fun to be had in the city. There's no need to buy drinks all night for some uptight wench who's laughing at you with her coven every time you get up to get her another drink. No free rides on this train.

The Golden Rule: do unto others as they would do unto you. In other words, get away clean. Every woman has one flaw that kills the ideal long-term relationship. That one flaw is that they aren't every other woman. It's biology. You want to spread the seed because there are so many women and only one lifetime — and for the last three fifths of that all you've got are those happy memories of all those chicks who got into your car. Seize the night, for soon you'll be watching reruns of TV shows that weren't really worth watching the first time around.

Getting away clean is essential to living another day to go hunting without encumbrances. Occasionally you can turn an ex-girlfriend into a casual sex partner but eventually she's going to find somebody and start shopping for picket fences. Leave them behind so you don't get left behind. Don't fall in love. That's God's trick to make you perpetuate the species, the same power who gave you so many nerve endings in the tingly bits and then condemns you for wanting to use those tingly bits. That's the divine bait and switch, like when you end up wondering where your sex kitten of a wife went and how she was replaced with another version of your mom.

So you reject the paradigm and become Bond, James Bond...or whatever name you like. Don't give her your real number and don't tell her what you really do. Whatever you choose, your profession for the night must at least sound glamorous. If you're a cost accountant, who cares? If you have zero imagination, at least have the gumption to tell her your Will Smith's cost accountant. Firefighter is always good. Troubleshooter for a foreign government — as long as and especially if you can fake an accent — is surprisingly effective panty remover. Model scout is cliché and worse, they won't believe you, so refer to The Silver Rule again. You're not a schmo, you're a man. Be one and failing that, act like one and maybe it will take.

You are not interested in making friends. Friends make more money than you do and have greater career success so when you go to their house you're reminded how shitty your life is. It's like being stuck at a perpetual high school reunion where everyone but you is an astronaut, a surgeon, an orthodontist or Paris Hilton. If you get a really good friend, your grand prize is he asks you to help him move and if he's your best friend ever, he'll hit you up for money.

A real man stands alone but never lies down alone. A real man does not give a massage without the expectation it will lead to sex. He does not want to be friends. He wants everybody naked. Now.

Tonight, she returned my hungry look and had her tongue in my ear a couple minutes after I walked up and asked if she wanted company. The club was loud so when she told me her name I tried to read her lips, failed, and let it go. After a girl has her tongue down your throat, to ask her name is bad form. It makes her feel like a slut and you feel like an idiot and once she's heating up you don't want to slow her momentum.

Ah. Lesson's over for tonight. She's down to a slight snore now. Karen? Taren? Marrel? Maris? Dunno. Any of the above. All of the above. Who cares? Time for Plan B.

I slip out of bed as quietly as I can. This is the toughest part of the plan and if it's going to go sour, this is where it happens. I gather up clothes as I go, including hers. There's a puddly trail from the door to the bed and I gather it all up. If I need a quick getaway, I don't want her pulling up her handy jeans, chasing me out to the apartment parking lot and cracking the windshield with a garbage can. Yeah, that happened, but Daddy learns from his mistakes. Even while she was screaming at me in Spanish and hammering on the glass, she was still naked from the waist up.

I step out into the light of the hall and quietly close the door, but not all the way. I turn the hallway light off with an elbow as I head for the living room. It was kind of a blur when we came in. She'd wrapped herself around me in the elevator and I thought we were going to have lift-off right there until I pointed out the elevator might have hidden security cameras. They never do, or if they do, no one's watching. Still, it cooled her down enough to dig out her keys as she dry- humped me up to the 30th floor.

The living room is coordinated everything. She must work in the financial industry or has a daddy who does because, despite her youth, she does not live like a student. There's no cinderblock and plank bookshelf and the couches don't look like they're from the slightly damaged department. There's a leather chair under a reading lamp that looks so nice I can't resist running my hand over it to feel how soft it is. Then I pull on my underwear.

My god! There's even a bar! Who has a bar in an *apartment* anymore? Have I slipped and fallen into 1966? I thought bars in apartments were for raging alcoholics who were members of the Rat Pack. Maybe she's a *Mad Men* fan.

I look at her books. All that shit about the eyes being the windows to the soul is just romantic stuff to get you hooked into breeding and anchoring your life in the productive harbor of ordinary citizenry. The media is trying to make you into a tax-paying robot. They don't know any better. They've just swallowed everything that's ever been taught them about what it means to be responsible and nice and soulless like everybody else.

Karen Taren Merrill Maris Whatever is an intellectual. She has a stack of The Economist on the floor by her reading chair and at the bottom of the bookshelf holding it down is about 70 pounds of books about culture and politics: Noam Chomsky-type stuff. Karen Taren Merrill Marris Whatever is not without redemption. On the middle shelves, she's kept her college reading and some good ones, obviously from her electives. Nietzsche, Spinoza, Dostoevsky, Sartre. Ooh, I could so go for a girl like this if I weren't an emancipated man. She wouldn't care for my philosophy. Libertine has fallen from favor with all the media's counter-programming.

The top shelf tells a different story. Her latest reading is disappointing. I pull out a few and scan titles that disgust me. There's a lot of self-help stuff here that denies who we really are as humans, emotional animals driven by hormones and ruled by fear. There's so much less to us than The Secret. Self-help stuff uses home-spun corn to make complex things simple and simple things complex. As if you can stay attracted to one woman by sheer force of will and forget your raging hormones. Ha!

I slide back into my shirt and go to the kitchen. I go slow. Bang around through the cabinets at all and next thing you know she'll be at your shoulder asking if you want eggs. It's easy and quiet since Ms. Whatever is efficient and sensible. The coffee can sits beside the coffeemaker. I find the filters after a little hunting and set it up so the coffee will begin to brew at 7:15 AM. If all goes well, she will wake to the smell of fresh coffee percolating. Before she even opens her eyes, she will think of me and smile.

I put my shoes out in the hallway. They go on last because I've got to move like a cat now. I am an animal already, so predatory feline is a short trip. I am stealthy. I am a spy. I am the master. I am all these things because I know the secret: I am complex in my simplicity. I steal around the apartment. I don't know what I'm looking for until I find it. When I do, it's an ah-ha moment that gives my brain's pleasure centre — already so happily stimulated on this fortuitous night — an orgasmic tingle.

Don't judge me. Some guys are into feet and some guys love nothing more than to screw the back of a girl's knee or bone her armpit. I'm just being me. This is better than all that.

Got it! I slip out the door and Plan B is almost complete. I put my shoes on in the elevator. There is no camera in the elevator. I'm golden.

Half an hour later, I'm down the street from my house changing into fresh clothes in the car. I'll wash these skunky clothes myself. No evidence is left behind. Lights off as I turn in the driveway. I'm back to the lair. I key the automatic garage door opener and slide the car in. I'm pulling my prize out of the trunk in the dark when the lights pop on and there she is. She's got a look on her face like a sour plum and if this were an old comic strip she'd be carrying a rolling pin.

"You're late," says the warden.

"I pulled a double shift. Didn't think you'd mind me doing some overtime."

She looks down, pulling at her ratty nightgown. How old is that thing? I think I can still make out the stain from some baby puke. I'm going to have to get her a really nice robe to wear, but robes are hard.

236

Women keep robes in the bedroom. Still, I take my responsibilities seriously, even the ones I don't buy into.

"Bobby's got a fever. I called the plant twice," she says. She says it like maybe she's saying something else, like she's got a question on her mind. She's afraid if she says it out loud it will contain the magic word that breaks the spell she loves. Suspension of disbelief is so hard.

"I was in the yards working on a boxcar linkage. I didn't hear the page. Those speakers sound like the teacher on a Charlie Brown Special, anyway."

I shrug. She shrugs and the light cast from the bare bulb above makes us both look yellow and older than we are. Maybe it's not the light.

"Is he okay now?"

"Better since he threw up," she says. "He's sleeping."

"I'll look in on him."

"Don't wake him."

"I won't wake him. I just want to see him." I stop and pull out my trophy for her. "Hey, I got you something today."

She brightens a little. She always brightens a little when I bring home a prize. That little bit of hope and excitement and expectation reminds me of old times. I love that little fire in her that's not quite snuffed out. There's a fragment of a look in there that got me to break the Golden Rule.

"You got me a vacuum cleaner?"

"It's a Dyson. Awesome sucking power. You know my policy. Overtime money goes to luxuries for my baby's house and home."

"Thanks. It's very nice."

237

"You bet," I say and she leans in to give me a kiss as I pass her. She brushes her lips against my cheek. Our eyes meet for a moment and I think she knows, but I give her the smile that goes all the way up to my eyes and keep moving. She stands aside and, as I squeeze past her, I'm thinking I should have a shower and gargle before I let her this close. It doesn't matter. We've been living like sister and brother for...when did I realize I'd been scammed? I forget. It's been years now.

I go to your room and you are sleeping soundlessly. Even in the dim light from the hallway I can see you're flushed red, glowing like a stop sign. You must have eaten something your body didn't like, but you'll be fine.

You'll be even better when I write all this down. I don't have much money. We rent the house and the car's a lease. Still, one day, when you start dating, just a few years from now, I'll hand you an envelope. You'll learn the Bronze, Silver, Gold and Platinum Rules. You will always be free.

Maybe I'll divorce your mother before then but I doubt it. Momentum is what carries us through, and downhill, when the engine is out of gas. Think what you will about me, I do know love because I have you. Women come and go. Friends move on. Wives can stay or leave but fathers and sons can't divorce. I am your constant guiding light and I won't let them indoctrinate you. You will live in Eden where all the naked chicks will play with your snake.

Your first girl will tell you love is more important than freedom. You'll know better. I better go have a shower and then write all this down. That's Plan C.

When you finally do get snagged, and eventually

everyone trips, your new wife will think I'm a monster if you tell. What I am is nature. I am real. I'm not the monster. Everyone and everything that insists you stay in your cage and be fake? They are the monsters.

THE DEEP REACH

My grandparents lived on an island. We visited them via a ferry named the Joshua Slocum. It's the same ferry used in the movie, Dolores Claiborne, based on the book by Stephen King. When the tide was low, taking the car down the long, slippery, seaweed-ridden ramp was terrifying to a child. I think it makes anyone with an instinct for self-preservation uneasy. A little seed planted long ago led to this story about choice and memory. ~ Chazz

On good days you could smell it on his breath. On bad days, most days, the sickly sweet liquor smell boiled out of his skin with his sweat. My father was propelled forward by instant decisions and compulsive actions. He announced we were all going to visit Grampa for a week on Slocum Island the same night we left. Dad burst into the rec room. You can live with someone who drinks too much and expect surprises, but you are never any less surprised.

His eyes shifted back and forth, taking in the scene: Me, sitting on the floor surrounded by the toys his work as a carpenter's assistant had bought. It was as if a timer in his head had gone off without warning and now we were moving briskly to the next phase of my life without delay or ceremony. "Every day I come home from work you're playin'. It seems all you do is *play!*"

"I'm nine years old," I said. My army of soldiers surrounded me, but toys were no defense. I had placed pillows on the floor for hills and draped a blanket over them. I deployed my forces across the wool terrain, each green plastic figure carefully placed. My father kicked the blanket and my troops went flying and the small unnamed, unspoken something I felt for him just because he was my father? That drained away.

"Put away the toys and pack," he said, dismissing my choking protests with the wave of a calloused hand. He stalked up the stairs to the kitchen. I heard the empty clang of a pot thrown into the sink. "This week we're going to the farm." Without a sound my mother scurried to pack.

I gritted my teeth and my eyes felt big, boiling with hot water. "Mom and me are toy soldiers, too," I said, but not loud enough for anyone to hear. "Just toy soldiers."

The trees along the coastline turned their spines to the cold, salty onslaught, their spindly limbs pointing inland. The wind and the sea molded their forms into skeletons miming fear and anguish. The trees seemed to be reaching for us as we sped past. I rode in the car's deep back seat glimpsing the trees from a well with brown vinyl walls.

"I don't want to see Grampa!"

"Shut up and keep digging!" My parents said in unison. They cackled like crows over an old joke that never failed to amuse them. Bored and car sick, I tried to lure them out of the spell of the car radio — "Old-time radio and golden oldies!" — which seemed to make them drift away.

"Why does Grampa live on Slocum Island?"

"It's where he used to work," Mom said, not looking back at me. "His old congregation are his neighbors now. They take care of him."

My father laughed. "He retires from the church and they're still tithing." I knew what tithing was. Dad gave me ten dollars a week and made me give back eight. "They give him tinkers but shell 'em first so he won't be breaking the law. Like he couldn't tell they were tinkers by the size of the claws!"

"What are tinkers?"

"Tinkers are undersized lobsters, sweetie. You're supposed to throw them back so they get to grow up."

"Who was Slocum, Dad?"

He shrugged. "Somebody dead, most likely."

"Doug! You don't know anything," my mother said. "The island is named for Joshua Slocum."

He looked at her sideways and raised an eyebrow in that aggressive way he had which said, "Oh yeah? Big deal." I knew that look.

"Joshua Slocum was an explorer."

"And he's dead, right? Right, Charlene? Right?"

"Yes, of course," she said. "Right."

"Well?" His tone said neither of us should ask any more questions.

"Sorry." My mother looked at the road ahead. She

pulled down the passenger side visor and checked her make-up in the little mirror. I could see her jaw muscles working but she swallowed down whatever she might have said. Mom's motto in life may as well have been, "Oh, please let's not fight." Her job was to keep Dad calm. When that didn't take all her time she took care of me.

The road wound down the steep slope and ended at the water. The ferry to Slocum Island waited far below us at the pier, dancing in a restless back and forth pattern. The waves pushed the boat at port so the starboard side bumped against the wharf. When the tide was low, the water pulled and dropped so far away that the dock was a high wall of brown and black timber encrusted with sharp, black barnacles. The slimy seaweed reaching for the ship's hull was a green cloud in black water. I thought of horror movies with creatures made of otherworldly green and black tangles of unknown plants rising from deep places. No one knew what the stinking monsters did when they weren't above the surface, breathing air and crushing and eating humans. My guess was that the water dwellers spent most of their time telling their kids what they were doing wrong.

My father inched the car down the steep ramp to the ferry, probably a little too carefully because he knew he'd had two too many beers. The soaked ramp was slick under the wheels. I held my breath, convinced that if I lost concentration for a moment we would be sucked into the water. My mother saw my face in the mirror on her sun visor and gave me a half-smile. She said the trip across the channel would take only a few minutes. My parents looked straight ahead, silent. Our eyes never seem to meet each other.

The ferry's engine rumble rose and fell with the mechanical effort of carrying us through the chop. The channel looked dirty green. Only the sea gulls seemed oblivious to Slocum Arm's moods. I pictured my bathtub toys capsizing.

I squeezed my eyes tight but we were already tipping and sliding away. One side of the car lurched up as metal screeched against metal. The hard heavy scraping sound stopped and a brief cotton ball pause passed over us. All I could hear was the wind as we fell. The moment before we hit the water felt like letting go of a swing at the high end of its arc. The sound of the splash came, first low and dull and then rising quickly to high and light. We rocked back and forth.

For a brief moment, our car floated on the surface and I looked at the horrified faces of the sparse ferry crew. The frames of the movie stuttered and slowed. Someone blew a whistle hard and wouldn't stop. The shrill note was the only sound that registered in my ice-fogged mind. A bearded man in a red plaid jacket on the deck of the ferry pointed at me. I felt the cool glass against my forehead, my nose squashed flat, as I watched the man rise. Sea spray licked the glass. The man's mouth moved in slow motion. I think I saw his lips form "back seat" before the green murk rose past the glass and over the car roof. The whistle stopped abruptly, replaced by the roar of the water claiming its prize. We were sucked down.

Cold water rushed in, filling all the empty spaces between me and my parents. The shock of the water at our feet and rising fast made us move. We clawed at our seat belts and pulled at the door handles and pushed at the doors. We were cemented in a brick, pointed down at a steep angle. We plunged into deepening gloom.

My mother said something and reached back toward me. I'm not sure what she said, but her tone was desperate and aching. There wasn't time to say goodbye. There really wasn't time to talk. My father said something I couldn't make out but his tone was almost calm. He could have said anything but his flat tone said, "I give up."

I couldn't hear their last words because I was screaming. I was screaming about how we had to get out — which had occurred to them, too, I'm sure — but panic reduces us to helpless babies. We sank. How deep could Slocum's Arm reach? I wanted to scream more but the water bubbled past my chin and I held my breath. I could feel the pressure against my eardrums. The pressure kept coming.

Cold, silent slow-motion panic made us clumsy and stupid. I wanted to get out fast but water mixed with the panic makes simple things, like pressing a button on a seatbelt, nearly impossible. The icy water enveloped us so that we failed to save ourselves and, another insult, we knew we were failing and failing slowly. What air there was in my lungs burned fast.

My eyes were wild and blind in the thick night of watery places the sun can't reach as we sank. Somehow, I finally unbuckled my seatbelt. There was a little pocket of air by the rear window to tantalize me and give me hope but the air would be gone in less than a minute. My face pressed against the rear window. I gulped oxygen.

I'm making this last longer, I thought. Why am I making it last longer?

The air disappeared and, through the glass, I glimpsed the surface shooting up to heaven in a trail of bubbles. The water pressed on me, trying to get inside.

We're going where the fish have to make their own light. No one will find us. The Coast Guard would give up and Grampa would perform one last service, blessing the spot in the sea where we were swallowed. Our car will be a gruesome aquarium. Our bodies will rot down here. We are contorted fish food with surprised looks on our faces. Tinkers will feed on us and they will get to grow up. They will be big lobsters.

When I began to drown in earnest, I flailed and I kicked. As my lungs filled and burned with salt and need, everything began to go black. In swirling eddies, I could feel my parents writhing in their seats. All things closed up, final like the snap of a steel-jawed, knife-toothed trap.

The water is hungry for us. The end was deep Black.

Eyes squeezed shut, I reached for my mother, but she was too far away. My hand closed on nothing.

Silent panic.

Desperate, I reached for my father.

And then I stood on my grandfather's farm, or what was left of it. It no longer produced food. The farmhouse became my grandfather's cottage. My father had long wanted to buy the 200-year-old farmhouse. When my grandfather became too old to keep it from crumbling, he started to call the ramshackle house "Bethany." This was a sign to my father that he had to offer a few thousand dollars more to put a balm on my grandfather's surge of sentimentality. The farm became ours, complete with all the antiques, the hole in the kitchen floor and the barn that would soon collapse under the weight of age, the ruin of weather and gravity's pull.

To "work the farm" meant to do all sorts of menial labor that was too much for a nine-year-old boy (or at least too much for the lazy little boy I was.)

The first owners of the farm painted all their furniture with a tar-like substance. My first job was to paint chemicals on a child's desk covered with a brown lacquer so thick, it was soft. I slowly scraped, peeling away years of layers to loosen the lacquer's grip. The chemicals burned my hands and forearms and the fumes stung my eyes. I experimented with cursing. The wood of the desk revealed itself and slowly rose up clean from the layered brown muck. I discovered a secret hidden in plain view: It was pine, smooth and fresh and pure.

"The barn will have to come down," my father announced, just as a hired bulldozer rolled up the lane to meet us. He knew I loved playing in the barn. "It has to be pushed down before it falls down, Tommy." He walked away before I could protest. A few minutes later, my last playhouse was a flat pile of rubble. The dust cloud reached into the sky.

We pulled all the boards we wanted to keep from the destroyed barn. Years ago, there had been a few cows, a large space to hold hay and a little farm equipment. A small workshop had once stood at the end of the barn. No it was a clear space with a dirt floor amid the rock foundation's rubble. My father motioned me to where he stood, bent and pulled on a rusted piece of metal protruding from the soft, black earth at our feet. It came up easily, as if relieved to emerge into the light.

I didn't recognize the object in his hand and looked to my father, my face a question mark. "It's a shoe for oxen. You've seen horseshoes. This is a shoe for the hoof of an ox. The animals pulled the plow in the old days." He was quiet for a moment, examining the ground at our feet with a new intensity. "You know, I bet there's more."

We knelt, facing each other on the old workshop floor and dug with our hands. "Things get absorbed and buried. Give it more time and the frost brings it up through the soil again."

A glint of sunlight off steel. A barrel hoop came up in his hands and his smile was beatific. "Beatific" was the word they used in church to talk about Jesus's smile in the stained glass window. Digging up memories from black dirt was the only time I could remember my father displaying pleasure at something I could agree was fun.

I felt something smooth under my dirty fingers. In another moment I held up a square glass bottle in triumph. Soon we laid out our treasures: a rusted ax head, horseshoe nails, several more barrel hoops and a full set of ox shoes. There were four glass bottles. They looked like they might have held medicine.

"I feel like we're on an archeology dig!" I said.

"Me, too!"

Neglected things pushed down for years revealed themselves. We became not one, but two nine-year-old boys. Something sweet passed between us, a father and son who enjoyed each other's company, meeting each other across time.

I wanted to stay in that moment forever. It was better than Christmas.

"Tommy? Are you okay?" my mother asked. "Are you carsick or seasick?"

"How's he supposed to know and what difference does it make, Charlene? You puke in this car, you're cleaning it up, boy!"

I fell from Heaven. I rose up from the Black.

Exiting the other side of the ferry crossing, the car crawled up the steep, narrow ramp of the wharf on Slocum Island. Once on dry land, I realized I had been holding my breath as we climbed away from the ferry and out of the sea's grasp. I felt the uncomfortable pressure of something at the center of my head as we drove inland to safety. I looked through the back window as we climbed up hairpin turns and away.

That was a long time ago. I am now the age my father was the day I panicked and blacked out in the back seat on the ferry crossing to Slocum Island. Was that a glimpse of future oblivion or Heaven's prelude? I don't know. We all find out in time.

Today, he, too, became buried thing.

Despite my father's storms, I kept that moment of elation safe from the intrusion of darker memories. I choose to think his spirit will rise to catch sunlight. I choose to remember my father as he was amid the powerful magic of discarded totems. No one *deserves* Grace, but it can still be given. That is our power.

THE SCARECROW'S STAND

Love is the answer no matter the question,
unless the question is how to come up with
a story like this. It's another story that
posits, what's real? We are fooling
ourselves, certainly. The question is, by how
much?
~ Chazz

He dreamed of bales of sweet-smelling hay under a blood-red sky. Fresh fields stretched out forever and caressed his naked skin. A warm breeze carried whispers through leaves and grasses. He couldn't quite make out what the voices said, so he walked toward them. The voices were as elusive as the wind but soon he came to a clear spot where deer had huddled together for the night. It was as if he'd been called to their sleeping place, where the hay lay flat in a rough circle. He understood now that the voices weren't whispering but sobbing. In the center of the circle, a stag lay on its side with a vast gash in the side of its neck, its head more off than on. The acrid stench of copper rose from the broken deer.

As he looked closer, the pool of blood around the deer spread, growing as if from a spring. He stepped back to avoid the red tide, but it grew in all directions, flooding his perfect field of sweet hay. He turned to run for shelter, too late. Smeared with foul, sticky blood, it rose farther, surprising him with its heat as it climbed past his waist and toward his heart. In a moment it would fill his mouth and nose and get into his lungs. He became a writhing tower of blood, gagging and blind and full to bursting.

He opened his mouth to drown and awoke shrouded in sweaty sheets, wrapped tight like a cloth trap, a noose tight as wire around his hips and legs. He put his hand to his face. It came away wet with a smear of blood. He shouted and bolted. In the bathroom, he wretched but nothing came except a single drip of blood hanging in the toilet bowl water.

Washing up in the sink, the nosebleed had ended. When he was done, he threw the facecloth in the garbage can. He didn't dare close his eyes, afraid he might see a bloody scarecrow, its misshapen head rolled back at angle impossible for a human. Beneath the scarecrow's tattered rag face, he knew he'd see his own face, the torn mouth gaping in a silent, agonized howl. The gnawing need had returned.

He took comfort in the bright bulbs around the mirror that drenched his naked body. Sweat still glistened on his torso. He looked fit enough, though he had noticed that, despite his regular trips to the gym, the six-pack he had been so proud of a couple years before had receded beneath his flesh.

"Fat shit," he said aloud. He studied his face and pulled at the bags under his eyes. He wasn't sure, but the look he had on his face might be...worry?

This wasn't who he wanted to be, this skittish coward suffering a broken child's nightmares. This couldn't be what he really was. This mask he wore, had been wearing for years, suddenly disgusted him. The cravings, so successfully ignored and pushed down, were back. They gnawed at him with jagged pangs like a three-day hunger strike. The night waited for him. He had something to prove and he wanted so much to make that nightmare go away.

The dream always started out so softly but ended in blood. This was the third time in a month the nightmare repeated. Tonight it would send him out into the city to see if he was still the man he used to be. Like an old man who knows he has an appointment to get CAT scan results, he didn't want to know the answer but he had to find the truth.

He gathered his morning clothes from the stand by his bed in a flurry. Crisp and ironed and clean, the suit was supposed to be for his morning meeting. Barely past 11 p.m., he stepped into the street. Always early to bed, the night stretched out before him like yawning jaws. He had to find a safe outlet to block the visions of sweet-smelling hay and the warm wind over his naked body and the neat bales. These were dangerous, seductive thoughts he had to stop and replace.

If he wasn't careful, he would find himself driving out to garden markets in Amish country again. He'd wake up in a bed and breakfast with fancy quilts and stroll the farmers' markets, his gaze lingering too long over the amputees, the Amish farmers with prostheses for arms and hooks for hands. That path had one bloody end.

It had rained while he slept and he was grateful for

the freshness on his face and in his lungs. The sharp sound of his dress shoes on the concrete pleased him. The sidewalks were usually dirty and the people pressed too close in daylight, but in the dark after rain, he didn't mind the city so much. He missed the stars you could see when there wasn't a street light in any direction for miles. That was another country joy he had forbade himself.

The streetlights and Fate guided him. The important thing was to keep moving. Where the crosswalk commanded him to walk, he walked. When he encountered a white flashing hand telling him to wait, he turned on his heel and went another way, letting the path of least resistance take him. Like a shark, he had to keep moving to live.

The rain had driven most people indoors, leaving the city to him. It was a calming feeling at first, but when he closed his eyes he saw a row of neat bales with blood spreading out from them in a gory Rorschach. That drove him on, pushing himself to walk faster until his shins ached and he knew he would soon give in to his cravings. It was inevitable. A dam cannot hold forever.

He slipped into a bar and made his way through the crowd. They were a young bunch and he felt out of place, like he had returned to a old house that was now someone else's home. He took his time getting to the bar, making eye contact with several young women, letting his eyes linger and letting them see his hunger. Not one returned his look and by the time he got the bartender's attention he felt old. His suit, which had made him feel so sharp and dangerous a short time ago, now felt too tight and too formal. As he surveyed the room, he realized he was the oldest man and the only one in a suit. He downed a beer in three gulps and fought his way back out to the street and the cool air to see where Fate took him next.

The next bar's patrons were slightly older. Returning to the nightlife, he felt out of practice, like doing the butterfly stroke after not swimming for years. He ordered a drink and surveyed the bar. The music was some kind of warmed over '80s west coast rock-a-billy. Lyle Lovett pulled this shit off with clever lyrics and the force of his intelligence and personality. Whoever sang the stuff now had none of those attributes. There didn't seem to be any women who had come alone. An earnest clutch in splashy dresses sat in one corner, their heads together, but their circle faced inward. The group's message was clear: "We're here to talk to each other. All others keep out."

Nonplussed, he turned to ask for a Glenfiddich. He hadn't paid attention to the bartender. As he caught the eye of the man behind the bar, he realized he knew him. It was Joey. Older, but Joey. It seemed impossible, but there he was. He even wore the stupid mint-green bow tie he had worn with his matching suit to the junior prom.

"I said, what'll you have, sir?"

It wasn't Joey. He had been Joey. Now he wasn't. He wore a bow tie — bright red — but the bartender was bald and wore an earring. He had a crooked mouth with not quite enough teeth and a blue vein pulsed prominently at his temple. His nose, pushed to one side, suggested he had once worked as a bouncer before wising up and learning how to mix drinks.

"Sir?"

"Glenfiddich."

He watched the bartender's hands as he worked. What had he been thinking? Red was a primary color, but so what? It still looked nothing like green. It must have been the bow tie that set off the memory. Joey looked stupid in that mint bow tie, his ears sticking out and his pants hemmed a couple of inches short to expose white gym socks. The last time he had seen Joey, they were both sixteen. Joey didn't get any older.

He didn't look at the bartender's face again. He left him a twenty and didn't take any change and downed the scotch on the way out the door. He craved fresh air, but he heard himself say, "Country air is what I need."

He steamed down the street and tacked right through a small park, ignoring the sign that told him no one was allowed into the park after dusk. There was still enough orange city shine in the sky to light the path. A silhouette of a man leaning against a tree spoke up in a gravelly voice, taking him by surprise. "Evening, Chief!"

"Hey," he said and kept going, staring straight ahead. The silhouette emerged from the gloom and fell into step with him. "Gimme a dime, man."

"No dimes, no change," he said.

"Nothin' changes, huh? No change at all?"

"I have nothing for you." The man was shaggy and it seemed to take him a lot of effort to match the quick pace. A sickly sweet smell wafted on his breath.

He recognized that smell. "You're a diabetic. You drink too much to be a diabetic."

A startled intake of breath. "You magic? Are you a

magic man, changeless man?"

"Go somewhere and sleep it off and don't bother strangers."

The man continued, undeterred. "That's good advice, changeless man. Strangers can be dangerous. I know all about that. I'm a stranger and I'm dangerous. Suppose you give me that dime and spare me your white boy bullshit."

The temperature changed between them. He could feel a crawling sensation under his skin. An animal wriggled under his muscles and it repeated one word: "Yes! Yes! Yes!" The trees parted above them a little and a cast from office buildings at the edge of the park suddenly illuminated their faces. He was glad he didn't see Joey. The man had a rugged face. He spent all his time outdoors, no matter the weather.

"I said gimme that dime, white boy. Don't say no just 'cause I'm Indian."

Yes! Yes! Yes!

He took one step forward and punched the larger man in the throat. The trick, he knew, was not to try to hit the target, but to move without hesitation and hit a spot behind the target. You had to throw your weight, shoulder and hip, behind the punch.

The man collapsed in a heap, grabbing at his throat and uttering a sickly, gargling sound. He watched the man writhe, twisting and drumming his heels on the pavement, a wicked horizontal dance.

"The last two people I killed were white guys," he said. With a faint smile on his lips, he watched the man struggle for air. "It's not about your race."

The mugger went quiet, though probably not dead. He didn't stoop to check. Instead, he merged with the shadows behind a massive tree trunk and listened for a full minute, straining his ears and vision to make sure he was alone. His pulse was steady, which pleased him. He still had that special something...or lacked that special something. It was fascinating to him how quickly a man could become a thing. Still, he felt cheated. There had been no planning or joy of anticipation. Making the man who asked for a dime suffer had been a taste that, instead of slaking his thirst, had merely whet his appetite. He had controlled his impulses for years and now this idiot had come along, a gift of Fate, and it wasn't nearly enough.

He moved when he heard voices at the far entrance to the park. A loud, drunk couple were attempting, and failing, to sing a melody he thought vaguely familiar. He was several blocks away before he realized their futile wailing was an old Mariah Carey song he liked. Somewhere from farther uptown he heard church bells: 12 a.m.

He quickened his pace and midway down the next block he found a little basement jazz club that looked promising. A huge black guy dominating a small stage played the saxophone. Behind him, a drummer worked a lackadaisical rhythm with brushes and a bass player plucked, a cigarette with a long ash plugged the side of his mouth.

The paltry audience was a scattered array of depressed people whose lives were orchestrated with a soundtrack that always played the blues. None of the men look like they owned a suit. The women were all paired up, except for one beautiful redhead in a red dress at the end of the bar. She wore unflattering cat eye glasses. The frames were bright red as well.

She watched him in the mirror behind the bar. Why not? Fate had delivered him the gift of a homeless guy harassing him for a dime and now, traffic lights and crosswalks had sent him to find her.

He sat in a stool two seats down from the redhead. A harried, older woman dressed like a waitress but working the bar said, "Kitchen's closed but the drinks are all night long," she said.

"This doesn't look like a place I'd eat, but I'll have a Mojito."

"This isn't the sort of place that serves a Mojito. No mint leaves."

"Rum and Coke?"

"Rum and Coke."

He got his drink, put a fifty on the bar and watched the big black guy blow. He had an ear for music so he knew the guy working the sax was good, really good. The big man, his face made blacker by the luminous white of his dress shirt under hot lights, finished his set on a high note. Before the saxophonist left the stage he announced the band — Louis with an 'S' — would be playing again in twenty minutes. The musician's smile missed several top teeth. He watched Louis with an S leave the stage. The drummer seemed to have trouble getting up and the bassist grabbed him by one wrist and pulled him along, stumbling.

He thought of the man in the park. If he was really in control, he could have just knocked out a few teeth. That alternative hadn't occurred to him at the time. He could feel the pressure building in his chest and head. It had been so careless of him to strike the mugger's windpipe. The fight, if anyone could really call it that, was over too quickly and the event had passed too casually. It was like knocking back a fine wine instead of savouring the moment and making it last.

He had played trumpet in high school, but on graduation he tossed the trumpet over the bridge rail and into the river as he walked out of town. He had liked playing the instrument but he had made two quick decisions. First, the trumpet was too heavy to carry along with his sleeping bag and rucksack. Second, he needed a gesture that said he wasn't coming back and his high school days — and everything else that entailed — lay behind him.

It might have been more fulfilling, but when he tossed it over the rail, careful to look care-free as he did it — there was no splash. A particularly hot spring brought the water levels low and the trumpet case smacked into a brown island of mud beside an rusted overturned grocery cart.

"You haven't offered to buy me a drink yet."

He didn't turn all the way to look at her but instead turned just enough to speak to her reflection in the mirror. Her eyes shone green, which contrasted with her red hair so well it occurred to him the hair color must come from a bottle and her contacts were too bright to be real. Except for the cat-eye glasses, she was too good to be true. Wearing the green contacts just for the look and compounding that with fancy glasses smacked of trying too hard. With her body, she didn't have to try at all. Her pleasant, sing-song voice suggested English wasn't her first language but the accent wasn't identifiable.

He looked her over in the mirror for some time,

watching to see if she would look away. She held his gaze. She bounced one crossed leg in a way that suggested she was impatient, not fidgety. "You haven't offered to buy me a drink, either," he said finally.

"Have you just arrived on the planet? That's not how these things usually work here."

"Yep, just fell off a turnip truck from Planet Zoof."

She gave him a smile. Her red lipstick was painted on shiny and thick in a way that mothers don't approve and men love. With lipstick on her teeth, she looked like she had been drinking blood. Perfect.

"How does a man treat a lady on Planet Zoof?"

"Ladies, I don't know. But you? We'll find out in a few minutes, I guess."

"You don't mind pissing me off, even though I'm your only shot at the only 21-year-old in this bar?"

"I'm a risk taker. Women respect that."

"I don't know whether to kick you in the nuts or —"

"Kiss me in the nuts?"

She laughed. Her laugh sounded unpracticed, like his own. "You a comedian? You're in the wrong club if you are."

"Bond trader."

"Slumming tonight? Does the wifey know you're out here trolling?"

"No wifey."

"Odd," she said, looking him over carefully. "You don't look flamboyantly gay but maybe you're in het mode tonight."

"No wifey, no husband-y."

"Nice to meet you, Mr. Bond, Bond Trader."

He raised glass in a salute but gave her nothing

more. She looked impatient again, like she'd found out she wasn't as good at something she'd thought herself expert. "What if I told you I manage the band, that I'm not just hanging out looking for action? This is a pretty unlikely meat market," she said.

"It is an unlikely meat market, or maybe you just like coming to a market where there's no other competition."

"You're not talking like a newfound friend."

"I don't want to be your friend. That's for guys who don't say what they really want."

"Which is?"

"That's a question for a woman who pretends she doesn't know what the biological score is. But you know the score."

"You're really starting to piss me off," she said with a smile.

"Really? I thought I was paying you a compliment, letting you know I think you're too smart for the ordinary mating rituals. Maybe you aren't that smart."

He turned to look at her and lowered his eyes to her breasts and then up to her eyes and gave her his best predatory smile.

Her eyes narrowed as she twisted a red curl around long fingers. "How do you treat a smart woman who knows what she really wants and is tired of average schmoes?"

"How she wants to be treated once we get past the bullshit dancing around, I guess. How do you like it, Red?"

"Does this approach ever work, even on your Planet? I assume you reproduce asexually, like plants or something."

He gave her a smile to show his white, even teeth and to let her know he was unflappable. "You approached me. I just put myself close enough to give you the option so you wouldn't have to get your ass off that barstool. Otherwise, we'd be here all night playing coy games. And yeah, this works very well, Red. I'll tell you why. A woman like you with all that red hair and legs up to there and cleavage down to there? You aren't here to go home alone. The crowd looks pretty thin tonight but I'm guessing you've already shot down seven guys."

"Eight."

"Okay, eight. Bravo. They all buy you drinks?"

"Mostly, but I started early. I've been doing business here since four."

"So are you ready to be serious about leaving with me or are you just trolling for another free drink? I don't like going to bed with a sloppy drunk. Lack of inhibition is great. I'm a huge fan of losing inhibitions. I want to lose my inhibitions every day. However, if you've had so much you're going to throw up on my dick, maybe you should get your band to call you a cab."

"I'm not really their manager," she said. "I sell the drummer hash."

"That explains why he can't keep time worth shit. If you're really friends with anybody in the band, you should get them to lose Ringo."

She picked up her clutch purse and rose from her stool. "You coming?"

"I will be soon. Is your place far?"

"You've got money for a cab?"

"I guess I didn't piss you off too much, after all."

"You interest me, like an ugly bug in a jar."

"So this is charity, huh?"

"Let's not fight. Let's say I'm curious. Your mouth's writing big checks for an old guy."

"Ouch. That's your first real jab."

"Now that I'm taking you home, you're going to act nice?"

"Why not? Now that I know the bullshitting is over, I feel my mood lifting. See, I just wandered in for the Blues."

* * *

He slammed the door behind them and groped her breasts before he kissed her. She grabbed his hands and slowed him down. "Easy! Easy," she said. "You can only read a book the first time once. You can only unwrap Christmas presents once." He acquiesced. He understood savouring anticipation.

They undressed each other, going slower as each piece of clothing hit the floor. They took their time getting to the home stretch and then it was a sprint and then it was a tie as they came together. He hadn't done that before. It made him feel close to her, like there was something different about her compared to all the others. Maybe if she lost the stupid cat-eye glasses, he would keep her around. Maybe there was a way out of the cycle, after all.

"Not bad for an old guy?" he said.

"Don't do that," she said. "It was okay. I am used to younger guys, though. Have you got another ride in you tonight or is the well dry?"

"Are you getting even for earlier or are you just a

bitch after?"

"If you got to know me better, you'd find I'm a bitch before and after."

"Then I look forward to catching you again at the only time when you're at your best."

She laughed, but it sounded real this time. He thought it was pretty sound, something he'd like to get used to. "You're very clever, Mr. Bond, but too old for me. What are you, forty-five? Fifty?"

"Jesus! I'm only thirty-eight!"

"My God! My dad has friends your age!"

"Oh, hell. You're messed up," he said. "*I'm* the mean one. You're the silly bitch who wears red like you're a brand of soup."

"Ouch. You are a *nasty* old man, aren't you?"

"I'm not old."

"Too old for me," she said.

"Is this buyer's remorse?" He got out of the bed. On impulse, he took one of her cigarettes from the top of the cluttered dresser.

"Mr. Bond. Let me share with you why you're here." She sat up in bed and held out her hand, demanding the pack. She let the sheet fall to her waist as she lit up and hit him with a smile that was ruined by a curled lip.

"You wanted to get laid and that's why I'm here," he said.

"No. You're here because you pissed me off and you had your moment."

"You were there, too. I'm sure you were the moaning chick under me, bent over and begging me to pound you harder."

"That was my parting gift." She took a long drag on her cigarette, lay back into the pillow and raised her arms over her head. "Now, this? This is my moment."

He watched her. Without the stupid glasses, she was a ten. She looked good enough to eat, a porn star with a hot fudge pussy.

"Take a good look. You don't think you're old? Men never think they're old until they're shopping for coffins. I'll fix that for you. I'm the last, and hottest, 21-year-old you'll ever have. You pissed me off walking into that bar like you owned the place, like you were some young stud model who could say any shit to anybody and get any girl. I gave you your shot, but your dick's too short for this ride. Time to grow up and act your age, old man."

He stared at her, said nothing and smoked. He memorized her breasts because she was right. He should have brought a camera, but there would be time for that later, under different circumstances. He would have to wait for some time, until whatever DNA and fingerprints he had left behind had been wiped away with time.

The bartender had seen them leave together. He might even kill the bartender first, as a warm-up. The ache was still in his belly and head but, with every word, Red put another burden on his shoulders and he knew there was only one way to lift that weight. Sublimating his rage by drilling women in one night stand after one night stand was not going to assuage that gnawing, grinding ache anymore. Sex instead of violence couldn't hold back the tide any longer. He knew that now.

"Grab your pants and get out," she said. "I'm done. I'm content to know I'll be starring in your empty masturbatory fantasies until the Viagra fails. That makes me very happy. Maybe you'll be nicer to women — much older women — from here on, but assholes can never fake nice for long. Older women won't put up with your shit, anyway. They know their value. Guys like you end up lonely and wondering what happened. Now you know the truth about yourself. You are fucking cursed, man."

He stepped into the bathroom to change. He didn't want her to see his flaccid penis. On his way out, he stopped by the door and looked back. "If you're going to be this mean, I'd like to buy some hash," he said.

She let out a long stream of smoke. "How about an eight ball?"

"I've just got cash left for the cab. I'll come another time for the hash, Red."

"Come with your little tail tucked between your legs," she said.

"You're right, Red. You sure are a bitch before and after."

"I faked it during," she said.

He was done with this part of his life and it was time to go back to the beginning. Despite her curse, he left smiling. He felt...what? Free? Yes, that was it. He hadn't felt this way for a long time. He hadn't felt this way since his   last hot, jobless high school summer.

* * *

In the beginning, the sky stood gray, fading to black with rain on its way. He debated about whether to boot it back to town or find shelter under a tree. Farmland stretched out in all directions, but there was nowhere to hide if the clouds opened up on him.

266

He could pedal to town, of course, but wasn't the bike a lightning rod? He stopped his ten-speed at the side of the road, refusing to scurry.

A vast chestnut tree stood just outside the wooden fence. If the tree hadn't been struck apart by a hundred years of storms by now, he reasoned the lightning wouldn't find him. If he were killed, it was just God being capricious and no one can stop that anyhow.

He crossed the ditch, carrying the bike in an awkward grip. He carefully stood the white ten-speed against the fence a number of posts away, perhaps one-hundred feet. If the bicycle did act as a lightning rod, it would be far enough away that he'd probably only catch a little jolt through the ground and he'd have something to brag about to Cherry when she got back from her family's cottage. He sat beneath the tree and waited for the storm. No one could see him from the road. He braced his feet against the fence and thought how private this little hollow felt. Yes, he'd definitely have to bring Cherry here.

Her real name was Cheryl. The nickname annoyed her father and he thought he knew why. It made her father think about what boys do with girls. It made her father suspect he and Cherry had already done it. Her dad was right about that, though he probably didn't think they'd done it in her parents' bed. That made him smile. Everything about Cherry made him smile — except when she wanted to talk instead of do it.

He suspected Cherry's Dad took her to the cottage to get her away from him. He'd wait. All the other girls in town were ugly or thought he was creepy or went out with other guys.

A stab of lightning flashed across the sky. Thunder rumbled again but then took on a thinner, higher-pitched chug. The sound of a large engine melded with the distant thunder. The engine headed his way across the field of tall hay. Minutes passed and the whine of the engine hit a higher register and the rumble grew taller and wider until it seemed someone must have somehow spotted him from far away and was now coming right for him.

A tall glass booth rose above the hay. A thin figure drove toward him. He recognized the odd mushroom cap of the outsized roof of the thresher. Disembodied above the reaching hay, the machine looked like a telephone booth hovering over the field. He watched it grow and grow until he saw the boy at its helm. Joey Pasternak steered the machine, focused on his work.

In hungry fascination, he watched the machine's whirling blades gather hay like a vast maw filled with knives instead of teeth.

Though drawn to the big machine, he had no interest in speaking to Joey. He made himself smaller against the trunk and used a trick he practiced every day at home. "I'm not here. I'm not here. I'm not here," he said in a low voice. For a perverse moment he thought the thresher might come straight at him, break through the fence and sweep him up with the hay. Just before it reached the edge of the field, Joey wheeled left in a neat turn. Bales of hay stood in perfectly spaced intervals in the thresher's swath. He had no use for farming, but enjoyed its neatness. He knew real farming had lots to do with dirt and stinking fertilizer and shit, but he could respect the baling machine. He relaxed and watched the thresher retreat, watching with interest as another bale emerged from a spout in the rear and slipped down to the newly shorn field.

He liked order. He made his bed every morning and folded his clothes "like a girl would," his father often said. His dad was a slob who came home from the factory each night filthy with grease that a perfunctory shower never quite washed away. His father oiled gears in the works below the line all day, keeping the cars inching forward as an army of union men swarmed with power tools.

His father might like the thresher. He liked cars that made a lot of noise and the big diesel on the thresher was the loudest thing he'd ever heard. His father would respect Joey. The boy was bewildered at school, but he looked like he knew what he was doing up in his high perch harvesting hay.

The thunder rumbled on but the rain held off and he was glad of it. Once in a long while a car would blast by behind him with a doppler's blare of country music. No cops patrolled these remote roads splitting farmland, so everyone barrelled along, free to speed, free to do anything.

Around noon, Joey surprised him by stopping the thresher nearby. The gangly boy jumped from the ticking machine and walked to where he sat. "What do you want?" Joey stood in denim coveralls, hand on hips. The rest of their class still looked like long versions of children, but Joey looked tall and filled out like a man even though they were the same age.

When he didn't answer, Joey swung a leg over the fence in a smooth maneuver. Until now, he had only known Joey from a few shared classes. In school,

Joey was as useful as a goat underwater. Here, amid the clods of earth and the tall hay cut low and long fences stretching out on each side, Joey was home.

"I said, 'What do you want?'"

"Nothin'."

"If you're here for a quiet place to jerk off, go the fuck home."

He looked up at Joey and arranged his face into what he thought might look puzzled. "Relax, man. I'm just watching you work. You ever write your name in the hay with that thing? I betcha you could write out 'fuck you' in the field and somebody's grandmother could have a heart attack reading it from a jet flying over."

Joey's shoulders relaxed and he allowed a laugh. "No, I never tried writing my name or nothin'. I'll wait till I own the farm or it'd be my dad having the heart attack." His hands were still on his hips, like Joey thought he was an adult catching a naughty child.

"You could always say it was aliens. Aliens are always taking shit kickers like you up in their spaceships and raping them with anal probes, right? Then they leave crop circles to let the other aliens know there's some good farm boy ass around here."

Joey looked like he would get mad for a moment and then burst into another forced cackle, as a crow might laugh. "Shit, city boy. You got way too much time on your hands. You been thinking that up all this time?"

"Nope, it just springs to my lips naturally, which is what the alien crop circles say about you, by the way."

"You're a funny little faggot, city boy."

"We go to the same little high school in a tiny town that's really just a village of 1,200 people and you call me a city boy? Pasternak, it's a good thing you can drive that thing."

"Thresher."

"Yeah, I know."

"Yeah, you know everything."

"You're one of those guys that make knowing things sound bad."

"You know what happened to Bug Freily?"

"Everybody knows what happened to Friely."

"I'm asking if *you* know, city boy."

"Do you know something everybody else doesn't?"

"My dad's cousin is a cop. I heard that he was hanging by a tree."

"He hung himself in the woods out back of his place. A tree was prob'ly the most convenient thing around."

"I heard his pants were down around his ankles."

"Yeah?"

"So I thought of you, city boy."

"You think about me a lot that way, Pasternak? Next time you're giving yourself an enema in the shower, make sure you don't turn the water on too hot, alright?"

Joey didn't smile. "Bug was a friend of mine."

"So, are you confessing something?"

Joey looked at him a long time before he answered. "He said you were going to come over that afternoon to look at his bike. The day he died."

"The day he hung himself. You tell that to your dad's cousin?"

His answer changed Joey's face. His cheeks flushed a brighter red. Pasternak choked and seemed

to struggle to find his voice. "Bug had a little dirt bike. He said you were thinkin' 'bout buying it. He said you were going to meet him by the quarry and try it out that day."

"I changed my mind about Bug's bike." He nodded toward the ten-speed leaning against the fence. "I've already got a bike."

Pasternak took another step toward the thresher, walking backward.

"I wasn't gay for Bug. Nobody could ever want Bug's pants down. My dad's cousin says it looks like somebody was trying to make it look like an masturbation accident, chokin' and stuff."

"It's called autoerotic asphyxiation and it's very common. Parents like teens to be troubled and suicidal at the funeral, not freaks like Bug."

Pasternak balled his fists. "Shut up! He was a friend of mine!"

"Every loser has another loser friend. It's not special."

"Fuck you!"

"You jealous, Joey? Is that what this is about? You think I did your boyfriend? Maybe the cops should be talking to you."

"They found footprints! They took molds. They just don't have anybody to match up the shoes with!"

"That's too bad."

"You did it, didn't you? I didn't want to think you could do that. We've known each other since kindergarten but — "

He leaped the fence easily.

Pasternak saw him coming and broke into a run for the thresher.

He wasn't in track, but he was fast. Despite the

other boy's lead, he closed fast, his long stride stretching out farther, predatory. His heart rose in his chest and he felt that rush again, like if he wanted to, he might fly.

Pasternak beat him to the thresher and climbed into the seat. The engine roared immediately and he wheeled the machine around to head for the farm. The Pasternak boy had thought he could escape in a big slow piece of farm machinery simply because it seemed safe and familiar. It really wasn't either of those things. The cab's door did not lock. Joey Pasternak was a big, strong farm boy, but the young man who pulled him out of the thresher's seat and fed him to the machine's teeth was stronger.

A cardinal, bright red, darted by. Red is his favorite color. It reminds him of summer, the sweet smell of hay and warm breezes ferrying the scent of copper. Red tells him of how neatly a body can be baled.

* * *

The wind sighed through the fields, bringing the yearning sobs and whispering voices. The ghosts say it is wrong to allow such potency and power to wane. Power must be used or it is lost. Age and time is no excuse. In blood, he comes home to his true nature. He was wrong to resist so long. The womanizing bond trader is the mask. Markets collapse and bellies sag, but murder is forever. He will make up for lost time.

He is the Scarecrow.
This is his gift.
This is his stand.

NEW THERAPEUTIC APPROACHES

Over & Out was a character study. This follow-up to that short story gets into some action and we see how giving up was a temporary solution.

It's a strange thing reading this story after a long absence because I see echoes of the chapter called Fight Club in my crime novel, Higher Than Jesus. There's even a character named Crystal in that chapter, too. Our brains work in tracks. The challenge is to make sure the brain doesn't fall into ruts. ~ Chazz

We are arranged in a circle in a high school's multipurpose room, after hours. The chairs point into a claustrophobic hole of desperation. I don't have a lot of choices about where I look. When I look up, I see gray ceiling tiles stained with brown, rusty water leaks. Down is old green lino, the color so bright under the fluorescence that I'm reminded of baby shit. People drone and mutter but all I really hear is the incessant thumping in my left ear. It's so hard to concentrate on what anyone is saying, but I try. I try really hard to pay attention but all I can think about is myself and the drum pounding in my ear.

Crystal, the woman immediately to my left, would be pretty except her next dye job is three weeks overdue. Her bright blonde roots under brown hair make her look like a doll dipped in a mud puddle. With bright red lipstick she could look really great, but her mouth twists into a sour face, like she's eaten a lemon. She's telling us she finds it hard to concentrate. Since the God of Irony is nasty, we all try to listen but she's hard to follow above the cacophony of tinnitus.

At first, her eardrum wouldn't let her read, she says. Now she can't follow anything on TV so she spends her days listening to the beat, bored and terrified she's always going to be stuck this way, and trapped in this room with the rest of the condemned. "And it's only in one ear. What if I wake up tomorrow and it's shrieking at me in both ears?"

We're all scared about that and a hush falls over the circle. With no ambient sound, my tinnitus is worse, so I'm grateful when anybody's talking just to have something else to hear. The kids complain the radio is always blaring too loud, but I can't handle silence.

The therapist, Dr. Percy, breaks the quiet and kicks in a few reassuring words. However, he's a gray man who doesn't sound like he possesses any conviction that he can help us. When he talks, our eyes search out others in the circle. We're an irritable bunch. A few have their eyes trained on Percy like he's got all the answers but most of us discreetly roll our eyes and stare at the baby shit floor.

There are two people I really don't want to look at: Jack and Jerry.

The first is the big black guy in the camouflage pants straight ahead of me. He doesn't conceal his boredom like the others and his size makes me think the camouflage isn't just a fashion faux pas. Everyone else gave us a little biography of the people they used to be before tinnitus hit us in the ears. When his turn came, he told us his name was Jack and shut down. The rest must be too ugly to say aloud.

Jack shifts in his seat more than most and sighs loudly. It's clear he'd rather be anywhere but here. His open rudeness to Dr. Percy makes me shift in my seat, too.

Jack is at 12 o'clock, so I have to concentrate on the baby shit or my eyes naturally drift up to meet Jack's gaze. He's looking at Crystal. She has a great body and I'd like his seat so I could stare at her, too. I'm too shy to steal glances unless she's speaking.

Dr. Percy, lounging at three o'clock, has the circle's only reclining chair and his upper body is almost horizontal, like he's riding first class and the rest of us have the hard, cheap seats in couch. He explains at the beginning of each meeting why he rates the big chair, a little guilty I think, that his back bothers him so he needs the recliner. We glance at each other when he says this, more disturbed. If he can't deal with a little back pain, what hope do we have that this wet sack of stinking therapist can help us with our problems?

At nine o'clock is Jerry, the guy with the hairless

scrotum on his nose. It's one of those facial deformities that makes you think, why don't you just get that cut off? Can't medical science fix that hanging, swinging thing?

Bad things happen to people and sometimes a lot of bad things happen to one person. That's Jerry. He doesn't say much but he ends each sentence with "... hey, what?" It sounds like something somebody old and British would say, but he has no trace of an English accent otherwise and he can't be any older than I am. I assumed he was horribly retarded, though at the breaks he whips out a romance novel and reads until the group settles back into the circle again.

Everybody wants to stare at Jerry but they don't, except for Jack. That's another reason Jack makes me fidgety. He seems immune to social conventions. He does what we all want to do. He stares into the chaos of Jerry's lopsided fang-filled grin and the ball of skin hanging from the end of his nose. His face is an accident you feel guilty for gawking at so you peek and look away, peek and look away. I get queasy if I look directly at Jerry when he talks, but fortunately his utterances are rare. We steal our glances, are revolted and feel guilty for the sick pleasure staring brings. We look and become fascinated with our wristwatches. Moments pass and we look again with fresh horror.

In the circle, most of us have pale, drawn faces which, I think, reflect my thoughts. We all need more sleep. We can't keep a job but our insurance doesn't provide enough money. We look for meaning in our affliction but, unlike other diseases, there's never much to be found.

If you have a heart attack, that's God telling you to live more, get off your ass and take better care of yourself. Cancer? Live deeply and savour life's joys and contemplate the mysteries. Extreme tinnitus doesn't have much meaningful to share. All I've come up with is, "Oh my God. Oh my God. What if the noise gets worse? I'll kill myself...but at least I'm not Jerry. Hey, what?"

Dr. Percy gazes at me. His face says he's asked a question.

"Sorry?"

"I said, we haven't heard from you since your first meeting. Why don't you share with us?"

Oh, sweet Christ. Crystal nudges me with a sharp elbow I assume she thinks is good-natured encouragement. It's the first time a woman has touched me on purpose in two years. I flush and try a joke but it doesn't come out like a joke. "Well, it's not a brain tumor. The doctors ruled that out."

Percy stares at me, unsatisfied. "That's true of everyone here. Why don't you share something about your feelings, Mr. Murphy?"

"I'm in the middle of a divorce, so...I guess I kind of feel like I'm dealing with this on my own."

"Back up. What kind of tinnitus do you have?" a youngish guy in plaid golf pants says from the edge of my peripheral vision. He's got a braying voice that spends too long on the vowels and he always speaks with authority, like he's in charge.

"Pulsatile tinnitus."

"Well, that's much better than sirens. I got sirens. Sounds like a fire engine in my head. I'd take your kind of tinnitus any day."

"It's not a competition," Dr. Percy says.

Golf guy bobs his head and says "Of course," loud and long, like some other bonehead — not he — had suggested it was.

Percy gives me the nod and I stumble in. "I've got two kids at home, a little boy and a teenaged girl. I feel like if I can learn to deal with this, maybe I can deal with all the other stuff better."

"Other stuff?" Percy says. He fixes me with his eyes and sticks a fist under his chin in a way that suggests he's bored but has adopted the "This Is My Listening Pose." I wonder how bad his back pain is. I hope it's pretty bad.

"Well, you know. The divorce, the kids, the mortgage. I gotta pay lawyers and we'll probably lose the house. I'm out of work and...I guess I'm feeling overwhelmed. Getting out to group is the only break I take."

Jack sits up like he's at attention and, for a second, I see the soldier he was. "You get one night out a week and you come here? Jesus."

Percy has no doubt caught Jack's vibe and looks offended. "Do you think Mr. Murphy is wasting his time here?"

"That's up to him, but if I were him, I'd be heading out to a peeler bar. If I only got out one night a week, I'd be using more imagination and make time for fun."

I can feel Crystal beside me shift in irritation and she kicks her purse over in the process. "Easy for you to say. He's got kids at home. It's really not easy to get out for single parents."

Jack looks back, unimpressed. "He manages to make it here. And he said he's got a teenaged daughter. Let her babysit. It'll keep her out of trouble and get divorced dad a life."

I jump back in, hating that they're talking about me like I'm not here. "I'm not divorced yet."

"That's interesting," Percy says, adding his Thinking Face to his Listening Pose. It's surely meant to convey that something profound is coming, but instead I think of shrinks as depicted in newspaper comic strips. I wonder if his back pain feels like a serrated steak knife twisting into his vertebrae.

"You say you aren't divorced yet. Do you think it's not going to happen?"

"Well, no. She's moved a couple thousand miles away, so that's it."

"She abandoned you and her children, correct?"

"Yes."

"Was this after you developed tinnitus?" Percy says, leaning forward. "She left you because of this?"

"No. The tinnitus came afterward. We'd done a lot of fighting before then, mostly about money. She left to go live with some guy who owns a beach house."

"Oh," he says. The bastard actually looks disappointed, like if Josy had left me because of the tinnitus, it would have had significance to the group. As it was, I didn't fit the script so I was a therapeutic dead end.

"Bad bounce. Bad bounce, hey what?" Jerry says and Dr. Percy shrugs and looks at Jerry and looks his watch.

We take an early break. The donuts are stale and the coffee is burnt. We mill around, talking little and mostly listening to the unique sounds that only each of us can hear.

After the break, we go to the high school's

language lab. We sit in rows of little wooden booths and wear big headphones. At first, the empty headphones seem to amplify the drumming in my ear. Then Dr. Percy's voice comes through and he talks to us in a fake, breathy voice he must imagine is soothing. We're about to hear music played at very low volume. We're supposed to ignore the sirens and the shrieking and the pounding in our ears. Instead, we focus on the music playing quietly below the din. I wonder if Dr. Percy has cancer of the spinal cord and if it's eating him, not yet diagnosed, but rotting him to a puddle until he is boneless.

The music is there, like a slow moving whale swimming deep, oblivious to the typhoon raging above it. An hour goes by and at first all I can think about is the pounding in my ear that matches my pulse. The pounding comes so hard that it's not just an irritating noise that's always there. I feel each beat as actual pressure and I wonder if the doctors got it wrong. Maybe it is a tumor. Maybe it's not just Dr. Percy who will die crying in a place of relentless pain, in a misery beyond what drugs can reach and ease.

I concentrate on the whale and, for a little while, the pressure recedes. Just when I think I'm getting the hang of it and the pulsing is going away, Dr. Percy is in my ear again. "Thank you for coming in. See you all next week and we'll pick up where we left off. For any of you who want to stay, the chronic pain group next door has invited us to join them for their potluck night. Apparently they all brought too much to eat and have generously invited our group to join them down the hall in Room 222."

Before Dr. Percy clicks off his microphone, there's

a protest of electronic feedback that sets my teeth on edge and several people shoot up, clawing their headsets off.

"*Gee-zuzz Chriiiiist!*" Golf Guy brays.

I hate Golf Guy and, despite the pain in my ear, I grin. I get my face back under control when Jack and Crystal stand and they catch my pleased look. I try to cover up my sadism by being mean to Dr. Percy.

"Bravo, doctor!" I say heavily and give him the slow clap. The others join me and I can see him waving at us from the glass booth at the end of the room, proudly accepting our applause, oblivious to sarcasm.

"Moron," Jack says.

"Shithead," says Crystal.

"Hey, what?" Jerry says, bobbing his head in agreement and making the hairless scrotum bob and swing independent of his head. My stomach is a sick acid clump so I'm not in the mood for Chronic Pain Potluck.

The others seem to move as one slow amorphous glob toward the promise of free food, but Jerry, Jack, Crystal and I head to exit. Jack hangs back a little, maybe to watch Crystal's tight ass as she sashays out. Jerry's right behind me, treading heavily under the weight of his massive backpack. I feel like he's chasing me out.

"Hey, Murph!" says Jack.

"Yeah?"

"I hope you didn't take what I said too personal, man. I mean, I was just saying that you should get out more besides coming out to Percy's circle jerk."

I blush, shrug and mutter, "I dunno." I keep my eyes on the door and keep walking, falling in step with Crystal. It's a thrill to walk beside her.

"Jack's right," she says. "You should get out more. We should all get out. I've got a little girl at home. I know it's hard to be a single parent, but if we don't take care of ourselves, we can't take care of our kids. Like the oxygen mask on the airplane: Put your mask on first so you can help your kid so everybody can be awake for the fiery crash into a mountainside. We don't want to miss that. Life's too short for this shit."

"Life's too long for us to put up with this shit in our ears forever," Jack adds.

"Yeah," says Jerry, so lost in thought he doesn't seem to have the energy to add his tagline. We all wait for him to say it and, as soon as it's clear he won't, the three of us chorus, "Hey, what?"

For a moment, I hold my breath and then Jerry starts laughing a long, gasping, seesawing wheeze and we join in. The sac on the end of his nose shudders with each hitching gasp as he laughs harder and harder. It's as if we're seeing the guy behind the gruesome mask of affliction for the first time. We're seeing past his nose.

We're still laughing — Crystal has a fetching snort — when we hit the parking lot. We slow down, anxious to get out of the high school, but not so anxious to leave each other and separate into the night.

"Tonight's the first time we've laughed here," Crystal says.

"Percy's useless otherwise, so we should be going to a comedy club instead of to group," Jack says.

"Then the peeler bar," Crystal suggests. She looks my way as she says it. Warmth washes over me, mostly embarrassed but titillated, too.

"You know what I think?" Jack lights a cigarette. "I think we should try to act as normal as possible. Percy's therapy — the talk therapy, anyway — feels like a bath in the pity pool. We'd do just as well looking for some fun and forgetting our troubles. That, or I find a new therapist who gives me something more to do."

"What do *you* suggest?" Crystal asks, her eyes on me. I shift from side to side.

"I don't know." There are no stars to stare at. Since Josy left, I spend a lot of time pretending I'm interested in other things besides who stands in front of me. If I gaze in Crystal's eyes, she'll know I want her. She'll have power over me. I'm not sure I'm ready for that again.

Crystal takes a step closer, daring me to step up and talk to her like a man talks to a woman when he's not afraid. "You're a family man. What do you do with your kids?"

"You know...feed them, clothe them...mostly clean up after them."

"That's the basics," Crystal says. "What else?"

"I used to coach my son's soccer team."

"Cool!" Jack decrees, surprising me. "I coach soccer. How come it's 'used to' for you?"

"I don't know. I guess I just got swallowed up by everything after Josy left."

"How long ago was that?"

"About two years."

"Uh-huh," Jack says. "That's a lot of time lost. Are you going to let her get away with three years of your life? Four? The rest of it?"

"It's not like that." I'm just about to leave when Crystal pulls at my elbow. That's twice I've been touched by a woman on purpose tonight, although each touch was just elbow-related.

"What is it like for you?" she asks.

I can tell she is open to whatever I might say. "When I went to my doctor about the pounding in my ear, I was pretty strung out. He told me there was nothing I could do and, at the time, I had so much on my plate, I guess his advice was a relief. Now I'd like to think I could do something that could distract me. I mean, if the pulse in my ear is going to be wailing away until my heart stops, I'd like something to — "

"Hey, what?" Jerry says. "Look at that!" He points to the rear of the school parking lot. Three dark forms lurk in the darkness.

"Somebody probably just locked himself out of his car and they're trying to get in with a coat hanger."

Crystal goes white. "Nuh-uh! That's *my* fucking car!"

"Let's go in and call the police!" My voice shakes.

"They'll be driving it away long before the cops show," Jack says. "Relax, Hoss. This is just what the doctor ordered."

"Mm-hmm! Just what the doctor ordered," Jerry echoes.

Jack walks fast. Dr. Percy parked his car by the entrance to the school. It's a old, rusty sedan. I knew it was his because I'd seen him drive up in it, but the bumper sticker that read, "Tame your Id" was also a pretty good clue.

As he passes the car, Jack reaches out and grabs the antenna. With a short, swift blow with the side of his hand, he breaks it free from its base. Jack doesn't slow for an instant and stalks toward the figures. We are pulled in Jack's wake, as if he holds a rope that tugs us by our belts.

"Careful," I say, but he looks back with a disgusted sneer.

The three dark forms turn into two large teenage boys and one skinny, harsh-looking girl. "What do you want?" the girl says.

"I want you to get away from my fucking car," Crystal says. Her voice doesn't quaver but she doesn't yell, either.

The kid working the coat hanger doesn't even look up. "It's my car tonight. Why don't you old folks go fuck yourselves if you still can?"

"The police are on their way," I offer, wishing I had thought to bring my phone or gone inside to call the police.

The big kid by the hood of the car looks scared but he doesn't move. "Are you deaf? Get out of here before something bad happens."

"We're not deaf," I say, "but we do have a lot of ringing in our ears."

Jerry, hanging back, lets go with his wheezing laugh. I'm cheered by it but I don't have any more jokes or bravado to make this problem go away.

The big kid crosses his arms across his muscular chest, stiffens and gives us a look that says, *I'm a wall.* The girl looks back and forth from us to the kid breaking into the car. Clearly, if their leader won't run, they won't, either.

We hear the lock pop and the trio's leader looks at us happily from under his shaggy hair. Even in the dim evening light, I can see his teeth are black. If I ever see him again, say in a police line up, he'd be easy to spot as long as he's made to smile.

"Got it!" he announces. "Finders keepers!"

286

Jack surges forward, whipping the antenna up from his side. "Losers weepers!"

It looks like a magic trick, like a magician's cane appearing from nowhere. His first strike catches the big kid at the temple, ripping a line of bloody flesh down his cheek all the way to the jaw line in a vicious downward swoop. The kid winces and, when his hand comes away from his cheek, he howls and falls back. He stares at his hand as if that is the source of the blood.

The girl shrieks, "Jesse! Jesse! Oh my gawd! Are you alright?"

"He'll never be pretty!" Jerry announces brightly. "He'll never be pretty!" He sounds like a parrot.

I hadn't seen all this coming but I thought the kids' bravado would drain away with this show of force. Rather than run, however, the kid with bad teeth runs straight at Jack. Jack manages to whip him with the antenna, catching him at the shoulder. However, the kid comes in low with his tackle and falls on top of Jack. They wrestle in the dirt for a moment and I stand frozen.

The girl, who come to Jesse's side, flies at us. She comes at my face, her hands like claws. I grab her wrists and she kicks me hard in my left shin. Before I can push her away, she winds up for another vicious kick aimed at my groin. Crystal's bony little fist flashes across the girl's face and her nose erupts in blood. She steps back, the shock washing over her and, for a moment, she goes cross-eyed to try to look at her injury. Before the girl can run or attack again, Crystal steps close, reaches out and rips the chain hanging from her ear. The wailing reminds me of loons crying as she staggers back and falls over

Jesse's outstretched legs.

Jack wrestles with the leader and they are covered in dust. The kid has one hand on Jack's whipping arm, holding it down. He has Jack by the throat with his other hand. That's what got me moving. Without thinking, I take two short steps and the toe of my shoe catches the kid at the jaw, just below his left ear.

I thought of all the times I'd coached young kids to be goalies, showing them how to kick the soccer ball halfway up the field. The soccer kick always made a satisfying dull thump when it was done right. The same kick to the thug's jaw makes a sickening wet crack.

The would-be car thief lands in a jangled thump beside Jack. "'Bout time you showed up, Hoss," Jack says, but when he stands, he's smiling.

He sticks out his hand to shake. I am trembling. I bend to the still form in the dirt to take his pulse. It's strong, but he's unconscious. I roll him over enough to look at his face. His jaw is pushed to one side, pointing off to the right while his nose points straight ahead.

Jack looks over my shoulder. "Relax, Hoss. Nobody ever died of a broken jaw. He'll be thinking of you whenever he eats soup, which will be for at least the next eight weeks."

"Jesus!"

The girl bleeds down the side of her head. She tries to staunch the flow with her hand. The big kid by the hood, Jesse, finds his voice. "I'm calling my father! This was assault! We were just hanging out. We go to this school and you psychos attacked us for no good reason! My dad's a lawyer. You are going to regret this! My dad is going to ruin you!"

"Shut the fuck up," Crystal says.

"Look at us! We're scarred for fucking *life* here! You're going to jail, bitch!"

Jerry pushes forward and tips his baseball cap back. The light catches his face. Jesse and the girl gasp. Without a word, he steps close, bends, grabs Jess's head with both hands and kisses him on the lips before he can recoil.

"I'm the Boogie Man," Jerry says, his sharp white teeth illuminating his horrific lopsided grin. "You like my boogie?" With that he twanged the bulb of limp flesh hanging from the end of his nose. "I'm going to tell Daddy you like my boogie!"

Jesse leans against the car, scrubbing his lips with the back of his hand and smearing more blood across his face. "You think your daddy will like my boogie, too?" Jerry looks down at the girl. "Hey what? You want to kiss it, too? You badasses sure are getting freaky with the Boogie Man!"

The girl finds her feet and runs for the woods at the edge of the lot. She says nothing, though we hear retching noises a moment later.

"Kiss me again, Jesse! You're so passionate when you kiss the Boogie Man! You been kissin' me every night we come here. You been kissin' the ball on my face for months. We been kissin' each other's balls, hey what? Then your friends found out and they were going to beat me up. They were going to beat us up for our love. Good thing for us, my friends came along to stop all the hurtin'."

Jesse makes a guttural sound.

"It's okay now, Jesse. Now you and me can be together forever. Forever and always, whenever your friends think of you, they'll think of us and our eternal, unquenchable flame of love."

Jesse's jaw drops open and his eyes stream. He wipes his face with his t-shirt, looks down at the still form of his friend in the dirt, and backs away staring into Jerry's face. At the edge of the parking lot he turns and the darkness soon swallows the ebbing sound of his running feet.

"Hey, what?" Jerry says. We all high-five Jerry, even though I could see that the slap on her hand hurts Crystal. She winces and holds her fist like a broken bird.

I look at it, touching her gently. The knuckles are bloody but she's sure the blood isn't hers.

"It'll be alright, but I need some ice," she says. "I've seen guys punched out on TV all my life but nobody ever mentioned that it comes close to breaking your goddamn hand!"

Jack looks at her hand, pulling at it roughly. "Don't worry. You aren't shattered Crystal. You're surprisingly strong." He gives me a nod and a wink, his unspoken blessing.

Jerry giggles. "Shattered Crystal and the Boogie Man! Riding for justice!"

I look at the thug in the dirt. "That's two defeated villains. What should we do about him? He needs an ambulance."

"I have another idea," Crystal says. "How about you drive me home and get the ice cubes out of the fridge for me?"

She looks into my eyes and I don't look away. I flush red, thinking what else I could do with ice cubes before the end of the evening. I nod. "But what are we going to do for him?" The thug stirs and makes a low, throaty sound.

"What we'll do for him," Crystal says, as she pulls me toward the car, "is not run him over as we get out of here." I climb behind the wheel. She looks to Jack and Jerry. "You guys need a ride somewhere?"

"Nah," Jack says. "The Boogieman and me are going to find us a peeler bar. Hey what, Jerry?"

"You're damn right!" Jerry says.

As we pull out of the parking lot, the street lights pass over us, bathing Crystal in a bright, yellow glow which gives her color. She says nothing but she never takes her gaze off me. Whenever I glance her way, she is smiling.

When was the last time I felt so thrilled? I can't remember. I only feel my heart beating in my chest. I pay no attention to the pulse in my ear.

ANOTHER NARROW ESCAPE

I wrote this story in a rush in one evening: the night before Halloween, 2012. Sometimes, stories (and answers) come in a rush. I love the brain tickle and dopamine kick that writing yields. It's the juice of creativity, making connections from one step to the next until you discover where the story takes you. The first step was a woman passed out on a couch. After that? I had no idea where it would carry us.

Lt. Mathers makes an appearance in Higher Than Jesus and the dead lumber mill worker referenced below is the dead dad in The Dangerous Kind. I'm slowly populating (and depopulating) the town of Poeticule Bay, Maine (the place of the final battle in This Plague of Days). ~ Chazz

The warm whisper reached down to her, pulling her from sleep's cocoon. "Every woman has a secret.

I know your secret, Celeste. I want to know more."

She stirred but did not yet wake. Was that warm, oddly familiar, voice real? Celeste Mathers had been curled on her living room couch where she had collapsed, exhausted, at sunset. Darkness had gathered, but the heat pressed in unabated under the heavy white moon. The power outage had gone on for two days so far, a result of a summer storm that had battered the eastern seaboard. Tiny Poeticule Bay seemed to be Central Maine Power's last priority for repairs.

Celeste longed for her little electric fan to come to life, even if only to beat weakly at the sultry night. She was still woozy, her mouth dry from gin and tonic. She'd run out of ice to ease her drink's potency. Was that yesterday, or the day before? The gin first made her feel braver, then sleepy. This dark, old house, slouching and shambling on its foundations from generations of the Mathers family living here? Each summer night was a fever in a sweatbox.

Instead of a sweet goodbye and a frantic kiss, Chuck's final words before he left for Afghanistan for another tour were, "Get yourself to AA. Leastways, maybe you'll make some friends that way." Her husband packed such cruelty and punch into his soft, gentlemanly Georgian accent.

Contemplating the cold moon, Celeste had begun to think again of killing herself, more seriously this time. She knew she'd have to work her way up to it, but drinking harder was helping her get there.

It had been so long since that first attempt, she'd lost the business card for the therapist up in Orono the doctors made her visit. She guessed the card was in the kitchen drawer that held unfamiliar keys, outdated cell phones, loose screws, batteries and twine. She'd looked, but, when she couldn't find the therapist's card, she couldn't be bothered to find the therapist's number again. She just wanted to drink and sleep and wait for the courage to end things painlessly in one quick move.

The therapist in Orono had been a nice woman, but the truth was that Celeste was cured of her urge to kill herself, at least for a while, by her husband. She'd taken too many sleeping pills once, back in the bad early going of her marriage that preceded the progression through despair.

She'd awoken in the hospital, her mouth foul with bile and stomach acids, her shirt stained with a long black drool of charcoal from the stomach pump. She didn't know it when she took the pills, but she'd hoped for life and sympathy. She wanted to show she was fragile so her husband would treat her delicately. All she really wanted was gentleness.

Instead, when she woke, bleary and disoriented, all Chuck had for her was more venom. "Men kill themselves with firearms. Women play around with pills or stick their head in a stove or cut themselves and wait in a bloody bathtub for someone to find them. Women cry for help. Crying for help is weak, Cel. You want out? Then get out. You want to kill yourself? Do it. You're looking for me to go soft and cry all over you and treat you like a baby? Fuck that," he whispered in her ear. "And fuck you. Shit or get off the pot because I am not interested in being married to a mental midget. When you really decide to step up and kill yourself, just do it. I don't want to know anything about it until it's done. When you've done that, you'll have really done something. I'll want to know right away so I can start celebrating."

He walked out, smiling and tipping his hat at the nurses. They gazed after him, talking among themselves about the man in uniform who was so handsome, he was almost pretty. Chuck didn't want to know her anymore and Celeste had given up hope she could make her marriage better. He was away for long periods at a time and no one was hiring teachers. If not for that, they might have divorced long ago.

She wanted to sleep and not wake from inertia's rut. Depression, she was sure, sapped any energy she had to change, but a trigger didn't require a lot of energy. Second amendment remedies were, she reasoned, the easy way, if she could just suck enough courage out of another bottle of gin.

But *wait*. There *was* a man who wanted to know more...that wasn't a dream, *was it*? She began to swim back from sleep, slowly but with a destination in mind.

Her bleary vision was drawn to the yard sale reject, the too-soft seat of the low chair across the room. She felt the man's eyes on her before she spotted his silhouette. He was hunkered down, knees high amid pale moon shadows.

Sleep evaporated in adrenaline's heat. Celeste bolted up. Waking up like this was like falling on hot concrete. Her spine stiffened and her nerves jangled, readying her to run. The knife block sat by her kitchen sink. Beyond that, the back door. Twenty-five yards of a dead run after that, past the gray, clapboard woodshed and the well, the woods waited. There were no neighbors to flee to or to hear her screams for help, but she knew every tree and gopher hole on her property. Any man who came after her beyond the dark tree line would be easy to stick with the long bread knife.

Despite her nervousness, she summoned her teacher voice and it came out cool and strong. *"Who's there?"*

"Sorry, Mrs. Mathers. I called and you didn't answer. The windows were open. I saw you through the window and...I was worried."

She knew that voice. "I've got every window open to try to catch a hint of a cross breeze, but the door wasn't open."

"It wasn't locked."

"I'm unimpressed with that answer." That voice. It had to be one of her students. Who else called her Mrs. Mathers? The tension in her shoulders loosened, though if the lights worked, she would have reached for the lamp.

"I'm *really* sorry, Mrs. Mathers."

Ah. She'd heard those exact words before. "William Kendle."

"Yes, Mrs. Mathers."

The boy — well, a man now — had just graduated from Grade 12. Celeste had last seen him picking his way down Rocky Beach with that overdeveloped bottle blonde Bennett girl, hand in hand. They were headed into the sunset, beyond the sea wall at the lighthouse. Sandy dunes rose beyond the break that had proved popular among young lovers for generations.

Watching them walk away together, Celeste had felt a pang of recognition and regret. Her days of frantic hands in parked cars and urgent, dangerous moments amid the dunes were behind her. Time flows in one direction.

"Mrs. Mathers?"

She reached for her glass and refilled it, half gin, half warm 7Up. "The polite thing to do, would be for me to offer you a drink, William. But walking into a stranger's house is not friendly, so suppose you tell me what brings you all the way up the hill in this heat?"

"You."

"Oh? Do tell, though I should warn you that I've already told you everything I know about William Styron. I don't hold back in the last semester."

"I saw you through the window."

"You didn't expect to see me passed out drunk. I get it. Back when I taught elementary school, the little kids were always shocked to see me down at the General Store, as if they didn't expect me to eat. It took them a couple of years to get past the idea that I didn't actually live at the school."

"Passed out drunk surprises me, but it doesn't bother me."

"Nor should it. I fell asleep in my own house, William. It's not just a little bit creepy to wake up with you sitting there in the dark."

"I'm sorry, Mrs. Mathers."

"You said that. Tell me why you're here."

"I saw you through the window and I couldn't stop watching."

"Ah. Me all tousled and drooling and whatnot. Mm...no. Still creepy."

William Kendle leaned forward and the moonlight made his face a white lamp. "It's not creepy," he said. His face was earnest and, even in the dim light, she caught the pleading look in his eyes.

"You said you were worried about me?"

"The power's been out a while. I remembered you talking about the electric pump on your well. I got a big water bottle in the back of my pickup down at the bottom of your driveway."

The bottom of her driveway was blocked by her creaky iron gate. She'd gotten into the habit of locking it each night after Chuck went to war. "When the pump's out, a pail on a long rope will do. And most people take a locked gate as a sign nobody's home."

"I knew you were home. You complained you never leave the Bay."

Had she? Not in so many words, but yes, she supposed she had complained. In the closing week of the school year, she had delivered a barn burner of a lecture to her graduating students. She'd implored the boys to look for other options besides joining up. She'd told the girls to keep their options open and see more of the world before they settled down. At the time, Celeste kidded herself that she had couched her talk with enough of a flair for a valedictorian's generalities that they wouldn't hear her own frustrations seething through. She'd been drinking more lately, and maybe it had started with that speech. It was drink or boil over every day.

William stared at her, eyebrows raised.

"Should have knocked."

"Yes. I have no excuses. I have reasons, but no excuses. I saw you through the window and...I couldn't look away."

Celeste sighed. "I'm a little old for crushes from my students, William."

"I'm not your student anymore...*Celeste.*" He broke into a smile as he tested out the use of her first name on his tongue (and the equality that implied.)

"You," she said, "are a presumptuous young man."

"Really? I don't think I am. I saw how you looked at me when you thought no one was looking."

And there it was. All her frustrations hadn't been expressed in one speech about her concerns for her students' collective futures. She had other frustrations — "bedroom needs" her mother used to call them. William Kendle, a young man full of a young man's needs, had felt her lingering gaze. She hadn't looked away quickly enough as she watched him shoot hoops over the lunch hour, his muscular arms shining in the noon sun. There was something about his dark, deep set eyes and strong jawline that reminded her of another young man: her first boyfriend. Those roots grow deep and they stay in the marrow. No one forgets their first.

"You want a drink, William?"

"I was hoping, sure."

Celeste poured him the drink and held it out to him. When he stood, he towered over her and he took the glass slowly, his hand lingering over hers in the transfer.

"If I'm to start drinking again after passing out," she said, "we better toast something or you're going to suspect I have a problem."

"Let's toast goodbye," he said. "This is my last night in the Bay. I decided to take your advice and get out while the getting's good. I thought I had a job waiting for me at the mill. I was told there was an opening for me after that old guy, Mr. Kind, died. Turns out the foreman promised the job to his own son."

The mention of "that old guy, Mr. Kind" made Celeste feel...what was the word? Bleak. She was closer in age to the dead mill worker than this young man. She pushed the thought away. "The thing about small towns and family businesses is nepotism is expected and never publicly condemned."

"Guess so," William replied. "You give your stupid son a job, that's not called unfair around here. That's a legacy." He knocked back his glass and drank the gin in one go. "I'm taking it as a sign and heading west."

Celeste watched him, still towering over her and looking awkward now that his glass was empty. She picked up the bottle and waggled her eyebrows. He held out the tumbler for more.

"That's no way to drink gin. It's my gin, so take it slower this time and make it last. Plus, too much too fast and it'll do more than poison your brain. It'll make your stomach bleed."

"That's what it's for."

"If you're going to go out into the world and make your way, I should teach you about drinking. Most boys your age rush to get drunk. You'll stand out more if you don't hurry. Girls like a man who doesn't hurry."

"But if I hurry," his gaze lingered on her breasts now, "I can do it more often."

"I was talking about drinking."

"I wasn't," he said. He smiled and stepped closer, bolder by the minute. She didn't feel threatened. She felt annoyed with him that he thought bagging her would be so easy. She was annoyed with herself, too. He wasn't wrong.

Celeste stood. She barely came up to his shoulder, but she spoke with the same authority she wielded in her English class. "So what was the plan, William? Swing by with some water for your old teacher and give 'er a good one for the road?"

"Like I said, I was planning on hurrying, so I could give you more than one good one. And you're not old, Celeste." He stepped closer, so close that she could feel the heat of his body. Their bodies acted as a capacitor, the electricity building in the small space between them, all the hotter for *not* touching and completing the sexual circuit.

"I've already said goodbye to everyone else, Celeste. My folks think I'm already out of town and headed to California. I got a full tank of gas, chips and crackers and pop for days of driving and the road is calling my name, just like Kerouac in that book you suggested."

"*On the Road*'s too racy for the required curriculum in Maine. I'm surprised you read it. As I recall, your paper on *To Kill a Mockingbird* made me think you watched the movie but didn't bother with the book."

He shrugged and gave a lopsided smile. "It's a good movie."

"And so you broke in — "

"Walked in."

"Into my living room in the dark and waited for me to wake up."

"I couldn't go without...you know...testing a theory."

"And the Bennett girl? Does she know you're on your way or...?"

"Tragic case," William said. "We said we'd write,

but she didn't believe it, even as she said it. I could tell."

"How do you know?"

"There was no conviction in her voice. She might not even know it yet, but a month from now, maybe even give her two, one of the local guys will ask her out to a dance at the Legion. She'll take a while to come around and will put off the inevitable. Then she'll be back down in the dunes, going down on some dude. He'll get the honor of knocking her up. Years from now I'll see her and she'll be married with kids to the guy who runs the gas bar and she'll look at me and think, there goes the fella who got away."

"Did you practice that little speech?"

"In my head, I guess I worked it out."

"That's a shame because I'm sure you imagined it made you sound cool."

"Didn't?"

"Not by half. Makes you sound like an arrogant asshole."

"I had the idea arrogant asshole might be your type."

That made her laugh. "How many times have you met my husband? You're doing a worthy impression."

"Y'know..." For the first time, he broke his leering gaze. "It's a small town. We've run into each other plenty in the past."

"And the Mrs. part — me being married — that doesn't bother you?"

"If it don't bother you, why should it?" Slowly, he reached out as if putting his hand through the bars of a bear cage and brought his hot palm to her bare neck.

"What do you want?" she asked.

"I want to feel the weight of your breasts. I want to feel you moving under me."

"You're not shy."

"There's no time for shy. I'm out of town tonight, one way or t'other." He caressed her cheek with his palm. "You say no, I'm down the road, nothing ventured, nothing screwed."

"Don't say 'screwed.'"

"What do you want to call it? Making love?"

"Don't be stupid."

He brought his other palm up slowly, first to her face and then down her body, sliding languidly over her right breast and across her torso and back up to her face. "I'm not stupid. I'm about to get laid by the hottest teacher in school."

"It's a small school."

"Still."

Celeste closed the gap and raised her chin. He bent to meet her lips with his. He pressed hard at first, but she pulled back. "Slow," she said.

His mouth tasted like gin and she wanted more. The heat that had been pounding her night after night now invaded her body. She began to unbutton her blouse and he rushed to help her out of it. She took both his hands in hers and shook her head. "*Slow*, I said. You're in a rush to get to the part where you've already had me. You're still here because I want to enjoy the having. You're my first nineteen-year-old since I was nineteen."

He nodded his understanding, but his actions were more urgent and she had to remind him to take her, but slowly. He entered her on the couch and, the first time, left her wanting more. The first round went too fast, but under her tongue he was soon hard again and the second time he entered her, it was she who came too fast. It was disappointing, like a marathon that turns into an abandoned sprint.

Toward dawn, up in her bedroom on sweaty sheets, they had learned enough about each other's bodies that Celeste could make William match her expectations. Her orgasm reached enough height that she clutched him in a spasm that reminded her of younger days. When she came this time, an animal sound escaped her throat and she felt as young and as athletic as her partner. William caught up to her at the finish line and did some growling of his own.

She giggled girlishly as she rolled off of him.

"What?" he said. "You laughing at me?" Red-faced, he sat up and searched for his pants in dawn's weak light.

"No, no!" she said, sensing that despite his earlier confidence, he was still a boy whose ego could be easily bruised. "I was just thinking about a strange expression: 'Came first'."

She couldn't remember when she came first, as in: being anyone's first priority. She sacrificed her time for her students. With Chuck, the military was always first. She was giving up her health to gin so she could get up the nerve to give up her life.

William pulled on his pants. His naked torso looked strong and well-defined. The dim light from her bedroom window cut sharp shadows into the back of his upper arms. "You did, right?"

"Hm?"

"You came."

"Of course. Women only fake it with older men

when they want to get it over with and get some sleep. You? I rode you like a racehorse until it was real."

He smiled as he pulled his t-shirt down over his head.

"Good. I'm glad you had a good time. Your husband said you would."

She didn't ask him to repeat himself. As soon as he said it, it was as clear as a hammer to the head.

"'Roger her good,' is what Chuck told me. I'd never heard that expression. You should have heard him laugh when I had to ask him to explain it. Chuck's got a weird laugh."

She struggled for composure, and, sensing that facade would soon fail, Celeste rose from the bed and pulled on some clothes from the dirty laundry hamper.

"What else did my husband tell you to expect?"

William pulled something from his jeans pocket and it opened with a spring-loaded snap.

She stood frozen and barefoot, her eyes on the rusty switchblade.

"He told me that if I could get you into bed, then I could kill you."

She cleared her throat. "And if I didn't sleep with you?"

"Then I was just supposed to take the money he left for me and go on my way. He said you were a fine piece of tail back in the day and he thought I was...how'd he put it? He said I was inexperienced enough that I'd probably think so, too. Not for nothing, Mrs. Mathers, you did not disappoint. And I'm not that inexperienced."

"Great," she said weakly, her eyes still on the knife,

but her mind wasn't stuck in neutral anymore. "So if I let you fuck me, you kill me. If I hadn't fucked you, you're supposed to just leave?"

"I get paid either way, but more if you fuck me and I kill you. Chuck has the best alibi a husband could ask for. He's on the other side of the world fighting for democracy while you're here getting your ass dead."

"And you think you'll get paid? Really? No wonder I gave you a C, William. I was generous. It should have been a D. My husband is a Military Policeman. Where do you think he's getting money to pay you?"

William's smile faded. "It's only a few thousand dollars."

"Even so...you'd kill me for a few thousand dollars?"

"I got to get out West and start over. Times are tough. A few thousand dollars for a guy like me isn't a little bit of money, especially all at once."

She looked at the twisted sheets in disgust, but she noted the distance between them, too. The bed was a queen — a fairly wide expanse that kept them apart in the small room. But he was young, athletic and fast, with a basketballer's quick reflexes. She didn't know if she could do what she had to do. Could she do it fast enough?

"My husband never saw a few thousand dollars in his life. Never all at once."

William took one step toward her. If he came straight over the bed, she wouldn't have enough time before he started slashing and painting the walls with her blood. If he came around the bed? Maybe she'd have time.

Celeste had once sliced her thumb deep while cutting a bagel. She remembered the sharp intake of breath and she'd cried as she ran cold water over the little wound. It hadn't even required a stitch, but it had stung and burned. Getting stabbed to death would be like that, she supposed, times a million.

Would the blade puncture a lung first so she'd go down trying to gasp for air with one of those sucking chest wounds her husband had told her about? She'd thought of killing herself many times, and more lately, but she didn't want to go like that. She wanted to run away from pain, not toward it. Getting away from pain was the point.

"How are you supposed to get this money?"

"It's out by the well. Under a white stone," he said.

"William, you're an idiot."

"Don't call me that."

"Chuck's got the perfect alibi, but what have you got?"

"A knife and a full tank of gas. And he'll pay me more later, from the insurance."

"There is no insurance, you moron. Oh my god, I've fucked a moron!"

"Don't call me that! If he doesn't pay up, he'll be sorry."

"William, you blackmail someone over something they've done. It doesn't work to try to blackmail anyone for something you've done! Fucking moron!"

He raised the knife. "I told you not to — "

"What's the right word for a guy who threatens to kill me after he's stuffed all the DNA evidence up my box? You're a patsy and you're going to jail."

"Everybody thinks I left last night. Once I'm done, I'll toss your body down the well. By the time they get to you...they won't even come looking until September, I figure. Chuck says you have no friends. No neighbors for miles. Nobody's coming to check on you, Mrs. Mathers."

"Chuck will call the Sheriff on you himself. He'll tell the cops some sob story about his cheating wife."

William smirks. "Well...you are."

"It's plenty more complicated than that. I've been getting up the nerve to kill myself."

"Then I'm here to help you — "

"Die like a man," Celeste said.

The pistol was where Celeste left it, in the night table drawer. She'd only loaded one bullet. If one in the brain didn't work, she figured she wouldn't be in any kind of shape to try a second shot. That's what had stopped her from killing herself: The vision of a spray of blood and gray matter across the wall above the headboard and half her face and throat torn away, yet still somehow alive, a gasping zombie praying for death's release.

He came at her over the bed.

The safety was on and the trigger wouldn't pull.

When he saw the gun, she thought he'd back up. He only came at her faster.

There was no time to blow William's brains out of the back of his head.

Celeste stepped back and found herself trapped against the wall with nowhere to run.

William was over the bed and raised the knife above his head to swing it down on her, into the top of her skull.

She tried to kick him in the groin.

He twisted sideways so the blow only slowed him for a fraction of a second.

That fraction of a second was enough time for Celeste to summon up what she didn't know she had: A will to live that burned fierce and hot. It was also just time enough for her to swing the pistol up into his temple. The sight at the muzzle dug in and drew blood as the weapon flashed across his face.

He shrieked. His eyes wide, William clasped his free hand to his forehead and temple and gaped at the blood. "You *bitch!*"

If he hadn't taken the time to think about his wound, he would have stabbed her to death. However, the time it takes to scream and call a woman a bitch was just enough time for her to figure out the safety on her pistol and say, "Bad dog!"

"Oh," William said. He stared down the pistol's mouth. He dropped the knife. "I'm really sorry, Mrs. Mathers."

She'd never fired the pistol, not even at bottles and cans in the backyard. It kicked high, but she'd been wrong worrying so much. One bullet through the eye and into the brain did the job just fine.

She ended William in a quick move of her index finger. Point and pull. Win. She couldn't remember the last time she'd won anything.

Celeste scurried to grab the box of shells from the night table drawer and loaded the gun. She considered shooting William Kendle again, but that might seem excessive to the Sheriff...if she were, at some future point, to get caught. Still, she was ready if William went zombie.

She'd kept the secret of the pistol to herself. She'd planned to punish her husband with her body, letting it rot in the hottest Maine summer on record.

"Brains don't come out of walls, no matter how

many coats of paint you use." Chuck had told her that after serving in Germany at an Army base with a bunch of terminally unhappy Marines.

She'd planned for her corpse to suck the equity out of the house as she lay on the bed, an empty bottle of Jack and an empty bottle of gin at her decaying hips and the pistol on the bloodstained quilt his mother had given them as a wedding present. She'd thought revenge in her own death was better than beatings. Dead on the bed was better than feeling trapped in this coffin of a town. She would become a legend and this old house would be impossible to sell. She'd become the local myth in the haunted house up the hill that kids would use to scare each other on Halloween. As fuck yous went, it wasn't the best, her being dead and all, but it had made sense to her until William Kendle came at her, armed with a knife and dreams of his own escape.

Celeste went to the window and looked at the sun's slow rise from the Atlantic. She watched the ocean a long time. When she felt ready, she turned back to see the beautiful young man one more time. He wasn't beautiful anymore.

"You're a very bad dog."

A surprise waited in the backyard. On a whim and a hope she didn't even believe, she dug under the white rock. Just as she had kept the pistol a secret from her husband, Chuck had kept his stash behind the well to himself, too. No wonder he never had any money. How many years, she wondered, had he been saving to pay off someone to kill her?

Celeste looked up at her bedroom window. From the outside, no one can guess the horrors that wait inside an old house. No one knows the inside of anyone else's marriage, either.

Chuck wouldn't be back from his tour until at least Christmas...maybe longer. She could leave a message on the answering machine at the school telling the principal she wouldn't be back in September. Another ocean waited for her. She could go see where the sun buried itself each night. William's pickup waited for her down the hill by the gate. And the tank was full.

THE MIGRAINE TRAIN

Sex, Drugs & Romeo (the working title) is a coming-of-age thriller about Romeo Basilon, a young man who aspires to escape poverty through movie stardom. Before he can achieve fame and riches, he must star in a high school production of Romeo and Juliet to claim some acting experience. Complications ensue when the classmate who was to play Mercutio dies of a drug overdose and Romeo gets the blame. Worse, Romeo's mother disappears, the play's shut down and someone is hunting Romeo with a hammer. Here's an excerpt from the opening chapter. Enjoy.
I'll release the book in 2015. ~ Chazz

The headaches began when I was six. I don't remember anything before that. It's as if memories from ages zero to five are spiderwebs that break when I reach for them. Or maybe that's just God giving a rare free pass, helping me forget the time when I was most at everyone's mercy.

My earliest memory is Moms giggling and rolling on the floor. I had just asked her why she always had a glass of blood in her hand. "It's just wine, baby boy," she said. "I drink it because red goes with roast beef. And everything else." I can still see her looking down and saying, "Oh, shit. You made me pee myself a little."

We lie to ourselves so much we have no business thinking we can tell anybody the truth. For instance, when I'm a movie star, my biographers will get it all wrong. It's not true that all my problems at Truman Hall High School started with a 400-year-old blowjob joke. That myth will become legend thanks to William Shakespeare and the girl who played Juliet. Also, just so we're absolutely clear, Jerome was just the kid who played Mercutio. I did not murder him. I only killed what people thought he was.

Gossipers always mix it up. My hardcore fans will say that Bio-Dad abandoned me as soon as Moms admitted she was knocked up. That little is true. Then they'll say I was named after the escapee. False. Moms told me the truth about that nine years ago last April 20. I can be so specific because it was my eighth birthday. (My birthday's the same as Hitler's, but aside from dressing in black we don't share anything else astrologically.)

I wanted a black forest cake but Moms said it was too late to go out again. She had forgotten to pick up birthday candles so she lit a cigarette and stuck it in the top of a leftover cornbread muffin. I tried to blow it out. She cheered, "Harder! Blow harder!"

My cheeks hurt. The cigarette paper glowed and sank as the ash rose. Moms laughed and pushed me away. She popped the cigarette nub between her teeth, brushed gray flakes off the muffin and handed it back to me.

"Thanks, Moms. This must be what birthdays are like in prison."

Her eyes widened and her thick lips went to a thin line. "I already said I was sorry, smart-ass," she said. She drank wine from a water glass. "You know what time I think it is?"

Oh, no.

"Truth Time!" she announced. Her smile was back, but it wasn't her kind smile. I held my breath. For Moms, the cost of admission to Truth Time was a five-drink minimum. For me, the cover charge was death by embarrassment.

"I didn't name you after your father exactly. His name wasn't *really* Romeo. But he was *a* Romeo." After Moms explained what that meant, I saw a familiar aura around the red light on the hot plate we used for heat. Moms's voice boomed off the apartment walls, the sound too large for the small room. My eyes were slits. The Migraine Train came for me.

"Make a wish," she said. She handed me a lit match. "Here. Try again, Einstein."

I made a wish and blew out the match. She did not drop dead. Instead, she toasted me with red wine. My birthday migraine lasted two days.

The doctors drew blood and poked and prodded and X-rayed and scanned. Next they guessed and finally they surmised. By the time they were finished torturing me I was disappointed I didn't have a brain tumor. Give me a cold efficient New York City ER doc any time. Big city barbers who can't speak

English and doctors who are sick to death of humanity don't want to chat.

Our family doc back in Maine — we had one then — said red wine could cause migraines. "But you're a little young for that." He stopped chuckling when he noticed my frown.

"What if Moms drinks a lot of it?" I asked. I was only seven so I didn't know I should have asked to see the doctor alone. She was standing right next to me, of course. Her eyes turned from interested concern to death lasers.

Dr. Chuckles's eyes shifted from me to her cleavage. Me to her light mocha skin and dyed blonde highlights. Me to her full lips. Moms was a beautiful woman before the booze and the cigarette smoke cooled the hotness. Her jaw set to concrete, Moms crossed her arms in body language I could translate. "I am as embarrassed as all get out and you will pay, baby boy."

A beautiful woman capable of sudden, sharp anger is a striking sight, like pissing off a Greek goddess who is really intent on messing you up. I've talked to the children of alcoholics since and we all tell the same story. When you live with an alcoholic, living rooms aren't for living. All you can do is breathe and sometimes you can't even do that. Home is never home. Home is house. Home is where the useless pleading and empty promises of atonement happen. Home is where the threats and punches and beatings with hairbrushes occur. Home is where you don't want to go.

Chuckles caught Moms's look, but nerdy men don't want to believe hot women can be drunks so no intervention came. If I was a little younger or she was a little older or if Dr. Chuckles was someone completely different, he might have been my hero. Instead, he shook his head and stammered. "Red wine duh-duh-doesn't work that way, kiddo." He grinned at me with the widest mouth in Maine that wasn't smeared on a scarecrow.

"Migraines are a hormonal thing...though, stress can also kick off a migraine." He looked thoughtful for a moment — me to her cleavage, me to her cleavage. More nervous chuckling. "But you're a little young for stress, too, aye-uh?" Dr. Chuckles. Diagnosis: idiot. (And yes, people who say aye-uh in Maine are not confined to Stephen King novels.)

Other causes of migraines include cheese, ice cream, chocolate, caffeine and Moms impaling herself on any dick attached to a guy who's kind of a dick. Naturally I was screwed up. We were still living in Orono when Moms moved on to Lawyer Dad's luxurious, slippery-when-wet sheets.

"Highest thread count of the bunch," she told me about Lawyer Dad. "This one's a keeper!"

I lost the sight in my left eye for an afternoon over that factoid. "Blinding headache." Cliché, but too real.

Chuckles sent me to a therapist because when experts fail you, they blame you. They might even want to punish you. The tough cases always end with you trapped in a tiny IKEA-stuffed office with a Psycho Therapist. They doodle. You blame your mother. That's how therapy works. Or doesn't.

Dr. Moto, my voyeur-pedophile, was a vulture who'd found a way to make a living squeezing juice from bones and picking at brains. Moto said he could help with my "me-graines." (Decreasing them, I had assumed.) He was a Japanese-British transplant who was pretty smug about spreading mental health amongst us New England colonials. In the first minute of our first session he told me his treatment style was a mix of Freudian and proto-Jungian.

Uh-huh.

Keep in mind I was only ten by then, but I wasn't the naïve little kid I'd been at age seven. I got a heavy waft of shit of the bull right away. "Yeah, like whatever, dude." I was a sassy ten, face closing fast. I was almost sure he was a big fake, like maybe he was one of those guys who spends a layover at a British airport and keeps the plummy accent for life.

The first few sessions were the usual. I blamed Moms for everything which, in my case, was one of those clichés that happen to be Eternal Truths. He'd nod and ask me what my responsibility was. I repeated each time that I was ten so, "nada-colada manana, baba!"

Dr. Moto plucked his eyebrows so thin they could have been a faint pencil line. He talked much more than I did so staring at the empty space above his eyes passed some of the fifty-minute hour. Whenever I said anything about Moms he wrinkled his forehead really hard to yank those almost-eyebrows up toward where his hair used to be.

He asked if I thought it was significant that I used the plural, always Moms never Mom.

"Yes and no," I said. "No, because I've always called her Moms since forever. Maybe yes, I s'pose..." Then I shut up. "Actually, no and no."

I didn't want to explain Drunk Mom and Sober Mom but I'll lay it out here so my future biographers don't screw that up, too. Drunk Mom yelled a lot.

Sober Mom woke up and baked cookies made with peanut butter and the sweet honey of Regret. And always the promises to do better. For me, her, us. Eventually Moms proposed too many toasts so she blacked out. She couldn't remember all her yelling. No more cookies.

The Psycho's answer to my cookielessness was lists. To-do lists. To-dream lists. To-be lists. "I will Moto-vate you," he said.

(Yeah. I know. *Jesus!*)

He told me stress caused the chemical cascade that caused my headaches. "Chemical cascade" doesn't sound too bad, does it? Like a gentle pink and purple waterfall might be involved. I would have felt I was taken seriously if he'd described it the way it felt. Something like "You're tied to the tracks and the Hormone Train runs over your head with steel wheels and rips out your pumpkin brains. Then the whole train backs over what's left and grinds your brains away all over again."

Moto was probably all rah-rah, ziss-boom-bah on the list-making thing because it was the only thing he had in his pocket besides a raging boner. When all you have is a raging boner, everything looks like something you should nail.

Lists would get my world in order. I feel the need to point out one more time that I was only ten. I did not own a cape. Bullets did not bounce off my chest and I did not have a cave full of bats and cool but implausible weapons. Getting the world in order seemed like a job for somebody taller.

Still, I have to admit, it's one of the few homework assignments I've ever completed. (Life's full of firsts and lasts.) I still make lists even though it feels somewhat shitty, like I'm admitting Moto taught me something useful. Like I have to justify my little capitulation to you. Like I owe Dr. Moto for something despite him getting paid. Despite what he did.

Everybody was antsy about my progress toward pain-free mental perfection so I started making the goddamn lists in a goddamn little silver notebook. I had my reasons to follow through. I already had to keep a pain diary for the neurologist so this wasn't that different. I had a Whining Weiner Dad (I forget which one) paying the shrink's bill so one of them pushed Moms to push me. As if migraines are a choice.

More pathetic, Moms's toasts were beginning to sound like slurred prayers. "To my beloved son'sh recovery from migrainesh and shtresh!" Yeah. I know. Cartoony drunk.

Warming up, I made a list of movies I liked — *Star Wars* and anything with John Leguizamo in it. I was especially fond of *Executive Decision*. John helps save the day. Steven Seagal and his tough-guy ponytail gets blown out of a Stealth jet almost immediately. Give the people what they want.

Next, I itemized my pet peeves: School work (mostly irrelevant). Homework (as if any rational adult would tolerate working at home.) I squeezed bullies between the first two items. I scrawled Team Dad at the top of my list. Also at the bottom and somewhere in the upper middle. I was peevish. I wrote the word "therapy" several times but Moto zeroed in on the Dads.

Bio-Dad AKA Bad Dad, formerly Romeo Sr.

until I knew better. Last name: Basilon, so, a Jewish guy who thought, for awhile, that Moms's Hispanic ass was kosher. Location: The Wind (rumored to have fled West but that's all Moms would say.) Given all that happened later, he might have been the smartest of the bunch.

Rebound Dad. Self-appointed Lt. Colonel in the KISS Army. This was the one who let me stay up late to watch movies I was too young to see. Him, I liked. Last seen: On his doorstep, shirtless, waving goodbye to me with one hand. For Moms he used his other hand to wave, but with just one finger.

When Moms peeled out of his driveway she left a lot of black rubber tire on the white concrete. It was Rebound Dad's junky old car we lit out in. I didn't question that at the time, but looking back, it proves he was sure she'd return to him. It also shows that one vagina not only buys you more pathetic dicks than you need, but you can fill your pockets with balls, too.

I waved to him through the rear window's dirty glass. "Waving" sounds like it was to say goodbye. What do you call what you do with your arms when you're waving for help? Whatever you call it, I did that until Rebound Dad was just a dot. He never got his car back.

Slick Dad AKA "Schmuck." He and Moms made the driveway scene in Item #2 happen. According to my teachers I had "defiance issues" by then and I got the feeling Cheater Dad would have loved to cure me of said issues with the thick end of a pool cue.

However, Schmuck was under strict orders to leave the discipline to her. The Schmuck knew who buttered his dick so he did this passive aggressive thing where he shut up whenever I entered the room. It was like we were playing a game of Statue Tag with insane rules.

He smiled like a fish in a freezer, positive that I'd crack and beg him to speak to me. Dude was clueless. Passive aggressive is better than aggressive aggressive every time. Cheater Dad didn't last long. I miss the peace and quiet we had when Moms was out revenge-fucking his secretary.

Last seen: Who cares?

Lawyer Dad. He was the dude with the high thread count. His job was supposed to be digging alimony out of #3. He got distracted.

We lived at his house for almost a year. Moms yipped "Henry! Henry! Henry!" almost every night. Expensive sheets, maybe, but Lawyer Dad's house had criminally thin walls. Last seen? His driveway, pleading with Moms to be reasonable. He did not know her well.

Dr. Moto was the next man-freak in our lives, though our sessions were confined to twice a week for a month and a half. I hoped he was gay so he wouldn't get sucked into that horny vortex Moms called a mouth. They never hooked up.

At first I attributed his professional restraint to the fact that Moms was a drunken slut and possibly a carrier of numerous STDs. She was a hub in a network of cheating partners and their sluts. Wrong. He had his eyes on me.

When I showed Moto my Bad Dads list, he looked through his notes to compare Dad timelines with my headaches. "Have you noticed you get an increase in the frequency and severity of your me-graines each time your mother...er...has a new man in her life?"

"My" me-graines. As if I owned them instead of the other way around.

"Does it bother you, your mother going through a man once a year, bouncing from one to the next?"

Bouncing.

Must. Stare. At. Eyebrows.

"Romeo?"

Moto always asked me questions to which he already knew the answer. When I called him on it, he said his questions helped me "stay engaged." I remember he was very concerned about my "practiced disaffection" and, when I was really bored, "disassociation." I could only guess that the concept of Cool was not available in Japan or England when Dr. Moto was growing up.

"Romeo, you know I care about you, right?"

Bouncing. Bouncing.

"Romeo, you know I want to help you, correct?"

Henry! Henry! Henry!

"Romeo, you don't have to face this alone."

Eyebrows. Eyebrows!

I teared up. A hot baby tear escaped. My face wasn't slammed shut quite enough to make it stop. Not then. Not yet. I still had hope.

Then Psycho made his move. Maybe he told himself he was helping me. Maybe he was still pretending that we aren't all just looking out for ourselves.

"Do you want to know the real secret to the perfect

cure for me-graines, Romeo?"

I rolled my eyes. "No, Dr. Moto. I'd like the pain to keep pushing through my head like a rusty fucking spike." I said it as cheerfully as I could. It's kind of funny that way.

"Have you started masturbating yet?" He leaned forward in his chair. The walls sucked closer and the air got thin. My face heated up. My chair pressed hard into my back which didn't make any sense until I figured out it was me pushing into the chair. Even so, it felt like the chair was pushing me *toward* Moto.

"Nope," I lied. "No, uh..."

"Masturbation!" His face was like a light. "You should start now." Big used car salesman smile, so eager to rust-proof my undercarriage and hose my trunk.

"Now?" Wax the dolphin? Strip the gears on the stick shift? Jerk the wad? Churn the butter? "Here?"

"It's all about rerouting blood away from your brain. When the me-graine starts, there's less blood in your brain. That's when you see the haloes around lights and things seem brighter and louder and you feel nauseous."

I felt nauseous then, but it wasn't the Migraine Train steaming into the station.

"Then the body overcompensates," he said. "The body sends too much blood to the brain."

Stupid, *stupid* body!

"Blood vessels press on surrounding structures and the pain is...well, you know best what the pain is like." Again, the come-to-Jesus smile.

Oh, yes. I knew the pain. It was like he was saying, "Jerk off or die." He let his bare, smug face hang open. Way too many small, sharp white teeth to be human. "Masturbation is the secret cure for headaches and stress such as yours."

"Um. Uh-huh?"

He moved one hot, sweaty hand to my thigh, rubbing up and down. Mostly up. I thought his hand might burn through my jeans. His other hand covered his crotch.

I jumped up and ran out. Moms was in the waiting room when I burst through the office door. "Cured!"

A week later, fuelled by Lawyer Dad alimony, we ran away to New York. Together, as mother and son, we each ran a solitary race. She ran to. I ran from.

I've only got one picture of myself as a little kid. I'm all big cheeks and bright eyes and curly black hair. My face looks so...I don't know. Open? Living with Mom in New York closed me up. What happened later, with me and Juliet and Jerome? That's how I worked my way back to bright eyes.

ABOUT THE AUTHOR

Thank you for reading Murders Among
Dead Trees.
If you liked it, please leave a review
wherever you purchased this book.
If you enjoyed this trip on the crazy train,
my other collection, Self-help for Stoners, is
probably also for you.
You don't have to be a stoner to dig it,
man.

Robert Chazz Chute is a former journalist
and has won eight awards for his writing.
He lives in Other London.

For more on his blog and podcast network
or to
find out about new book releases, please
sign up for updates at
AllThatChazz.com.

The Crime Novels
Bigger Than Jesus
Higher Than Jesus
Hollywood Jesus
The Divine Assassin's Playbook, Omnibus Edition
Intense Violence, Bizarre Themes

The Dark Fantasy Novels
This Plague of Days, Season One
This Plague of Days, Season Two
This Plague of Days, Season Three
This Plague of Days, Omnibus Edition
The Haunting Lessons

Collections
Self-help for Stoners
Murders Among Dead Trees
The Little Book of Braingasms

Non-fiction
Crack the Indie Author Code
Write Your Book: Aspire to Inspire
Six Seconds

www.ingramcontent.com/pod-product-compliance
Lightning Source LLC
Chambersburg PA
CBHW020401260626
47156CB00007B/2193